Fontainebleau

OTHER BOOKS BY MADELINE SONIK

FICTION
Arms (novel)
Drying the Bones (short fiction)
Belinda and the Dustbunnys (a children's novel)

POETRY
Stone Sightings
The Book of Changes

CREATIVE NON-FICTION
Afflictions & Departures

DISCLAIMER:

Fontainebleau is a mythical city situated on the Detroit River. While some of the stories in this collection were inspired by events that took place in Windsor, Ontario, in the Fontainebleau subdivision of my childhood, none are factual and none of the characters portrayed in this collection exist, or ever have existed in reality. Windsor and the Fontainebleau subdivision are, in truth, quite lovely and far less sordid and seamy than the crime-ridden city of Fontainebleau that I've constructed in this volume.

Stories from this collection have appeared in different forms in the following magazines: *Grain Magazine*, "Air Time" and "The Boy Who Flew"; *subTerrain*, "Slick" and "Murder"; *Broken Pencil*, "No Kind of Man" and "Flight"; *PRISM international*, "Transactions"; *Pottersfield Portfolio*, "The Mermaid"; *Room*, "The Bone Game"; *Hard Boiled*, "Corrosion"; *The Dalhousie Review*, "The Ice Queen".

Fontainebleau

Stories by

MADELINE SONIK

Vancouver

Anvil Press Publishers Inc.
P.O. Box 3008, Main Post Office
Vancouver, B.C. V6B 3X5 Canada
www.anvilpress.com

Library and Archives Canada Cataloguing in Publication

Title: Fontainebleu / stories by Madeline Sonik.
Names: Sonik, Madeline, 1960- author.
Identifiers: Canadiana 20200185489 | ISBN 9781772141481 (softcover)
Classification: LCC PS8587.O558 F66 2020 | DDC C813/.6—dc23

Cover design by Derek von Essen
Interior by Rayola.com
Map by Martin Salvage
Author photo by Dyana Sonik-Henderson
Represented in Canada by Publishers Group Canada
Distributed by Raincoast Books

The publisher gratefully acknowledges the financial assistance of the Canada Council for the Arts, the Canada Book Fund, and the Province of British Columbia through the B.C. Arts Council and the Book Publishing Tax Credit.

We acknowledge the financial support of the Government of Canada through the National Translation Program for Book Publishing for our translation activities.

Printed and bound in Canada

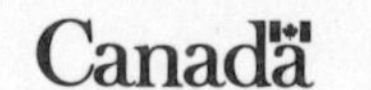

This book is dedicated to the memory of Carl Leggo, a great teacher, a great poet, and a great soul. His wisdom, compassion, and courage will continue to ripple through and beyond the many lives he touched.

Contents

Air Time

DARKNESS SATURATES the bar and amber light glints off bottles of bourbon and rye. Julia Wilson's thin face is only a shadow in the bartender's mirror. The man, Mike Riddel, orders her a draught; the other, Steve Finnegan, gets one for Audrey Slack. Neither of the men have thought to ask the girls' names. The music, without melody, pounds like a frenetic heart. Both girls swallow golden liquid.

The roller coaster at the fair with its smooth tubular rails, with its chilling dive drop and loop the loop, screeched to a halt over an hour ago. The operator left the ghostly park. Only a desert of animate trash remains, tumbleweeds, rushing out past the railroad tracks, out to the highway; only the disembodied smells of popcorn and sweat roam the ground. But there is a bar still open, and Mike and Steve push the girls to drink, they push them to chug. "Chug-a-lug, Chug-a-lug." They order a pitcher, and introduce another drinking game.

Julia smiles and Audrey giggles, they're like two little girls at a birthday party.

Runaways, the men think—thrill seekers bored with the safety of childhood.

Mike pulls a quarter from the pocket of his jeans. He's got a long thin scar on his wrist, a childhood wound, where a kid once cut him with a pair of pointy scissors. "So whatcha' do is this," he says, his mouth sloppy with beer, "player one, flips the coin. Player two calls it. If she's wrong, she's gotta take three swigs."

"Or alternately," Steve interjects, "take something off."

Audrey's laughter peals like the chime of hollow metal, like the sound of her inebriated mother's drinking cup, when it drops from her senseless hands. There's a rose tattoo on Audrey's shoulder and Steve touches it and asks if it's for real. Her dexterous fingers make "Ls" of each hand. "Loser!" she teases, and pushes the L's against his chest.

"What?" Steve smirks. "It could be one of those stick-on jobs."

Julia flips the coin. She's beautiful, but more serious than Audrey. Audrey's happy lips are thinner, she has a slight overbite. Julia's lips are fuller, she has perfect teeth. In fact, everything about Julia is pin-up perfect—which makes Steve and Mike think the family she's running from is more well-to-do. "Tails," she calls and her small pale hand unfurls. The silver disc shines like a moon from her palm—the lines on both almost nonexistent. "Heads," Mike announces. The men chuckle. Audrey picks up her glass.

Mike's hand steals under Julia's long black hair, under the back of her summer tank. Her soft flesh puckers. "Tails," she calls and wins, but Mike lifts her glass and makes her drink anyway. "Party-pooper," he says, when she's had enough and pushes the beer away.

Earlier that evening, on the roller coaster, she'd pressed into him, her body a feather sculpted by wind. She'd tried to pull free, but the centrifugal force flung her even closer. "Don't mind if I do," Mike said, opening towards her. She couldn't hear him. The din of the rattling car and the plummeting cries that rose from the first drop drowned him out. Then they were at the top of the hill looking down, feeling that sudden plunge that lifted them from their seats with exhilarating weightlessness. It was called "Air Time" and Mike would have liked to explain all of its gravitational intricacies to her, even though he knew she wouldn't understand any of them. She was still glued against him when she let loose with an ear-splitting scream. It reminded him of times gone by, things he'd forgotten and didn't want to remember, but he was glad she'd screamed, glad he'd heard exactly what her lungs could do.

Steve refills Audrey's glass and orders another pitcher. "I'm hungry," Audrey announces, and takes three small obligatory sips for guessing wrong, once again. Steve grinds his thigh against her bony hip and she strokes his arm. He'd rather not order food. He'd rather have nothing interfere with the alcohol, but Mike calls the waitress back.

The waitress has been drinking; it's on her breath, and in the tired inattention of her eyes. She's bleach blond, thickly made up, with black eyeliner, false lashes, and primrose orange lips.

If she noticed customers, which she doesn't anymore, when the police started asking questions, she would've been able to tell them all about these girls. She would've been able to tell them the girls were skinny, half dressed, and young enough to be her granddaughters... that is, of course, if she'd had children when she was their age—but she doesn't notice the girls, she doesn't notice the beer; she's trained herself to be sightless, to quell curiosity, to turn a blind eye to everything that attracts attention, and serving herself a shot or two throughout the evening helps make this possible. She produces her order book, nods towards Mike and says, "Shoot!"

Steve tries to get Mike's attention, but he's focused on the tattered cardboard menu. He orders two pounds of honey garlic chicken wings, potato skins, and a basket of nachos. Steve wishes there was some way to stop him, some way to remind him of the dangers of food. Not only will it delay intoxication, but they're going to be dealing with a real puking hazard, once they give the girls the drugs.

The waitress returns carrying plates, and groans because her shoulders ache from the size and weight of her massive, surgically enhanced breasts. Mike asks Steve for his wallet. "He's the man with the money," he explains, and it's true, Steve's billfold is cram-packed with cash. Once Mike has settled up, Steve retrieves his wallet and pushes it halfway down the front of his pants.

Audrey and Julia devour the food. "Been a long time since you ate, huh?" Mike asks.

"Drink up!" Steve says, tapping their glasses, pre-empting Mike's question. The last thing Steve wants to hear are their life stories.

Mike, on the other hand, would like to know how it happens, how two young kids like this wind up in a dump with a couple of unscrupulous sleazy pricks who ought to be in prison.

He's tried to piece it together before: overly strict parents, troubles at school, at that age, everything's a drama. But even while he can make all of the rest of it fit, what he'll never understand is their lack of street smarts, their inability to work things out, the ease with which they allow themselves to be taken.

Julia is less open than Audrey. Even when Mike rubs her back, even when she plays the drinking game, there's a stiffness about her that Mike would like to erase. Audrey, on the other hand, is all loosey-goosey, petting and stroking Steve, spreading herself all over him. Mike wishes he'd picked her instead of Julia. "Mine's low on lube," he would've told Steve privately if they'd had a chance to be alone and they both would've chuckled. Then he would've asked if Steve was sure he'd put everything in the hotel room: gauze and gags, the hypodermic needles. He might remind Steve about the last time and those Mexican twins who, in Náhuatl, screamed bloody murder before they'd even started. "No more immigrants for me, man," Mike had said matter-of-factly, and this had cracked Steve up at the time.

They'd first met at Tecumseh Auto, the shop where they worked. They started talking about films. Steve earned a little extra money filming "how-to's" for the local vocational school's automotive program and said he could use an assistant. Together they filmed "The Basic Parts and Function of an Engine," "Changing Brake Pads," and "What to do about a Faulty Compressor." It was fun and Mike liked it. He told Steve he was game for other projects.

"How do you feel about snuff films?" Steve had said, trying it out as a joke at first.

Later, he told Mike: "It's just gotta look real, we don't really snuff anyone," and Mike was glad, because it meant Steve only wanted the money; he didn't want to kill the girls. Sure, they both wanted their thrills—that heady, roller coaster rush of performing their most illicit fantasies—but they didn't want prison time. That's why, even though the girls would remember nothing, they always stuffed their purses and pockets with plenty of cash. It's pretty hard to go crying to the cops when you've got no clear memory, and money falling out of your wazoo.

Mike takes Julia's hand and kisses it. She doesn't pull away, but her flesh isn't receptive. Audrey smiles a slightly buck-toothed smile that makes her look attractively brainless, a prototypical dumb blonde, like she's got a full head of air, Mike thinks, and grins at his own word play. "You two related?" he calls across the table, knowing for sure that they're not.

Audrey giggles. "Jules is an old friend," she says. "She's with me because she escaped her old lady for the night!" Her agile hands are under the table, probably jacking off that bastard Steve. "You haven't lived long enough to have old friends," Mike says. Audrey doesn't contradict him, she doesn't tell him that sometimes she feels older than the earth.

Steve taps the girls' glasses again and thrusts his face close enough to Audrey to nuzzle her hair. He whispers something that makes her grin. "Sure," she giggles, and turns and whispers back to him. Then he leans across the table and whispers to Mike, who chuckles lightly. Julia is the only one who isn't smiling.

"Jules," Audrey calls across the table, "girl's room?"

Julia stumbles when she stands. Her walk is nervous.

When the girls are out of earshot, Steve quips, "Babe, I'm going to make you a star," and he and Mike go over details, how they'll get the girls into the hotel room, where they'll drop their unconscious bodies in the morning. Recently, Mike's been feeling pangs of conscience. He doesn't like the thought of young girls being dumped on the side of highway 402, dead to the world. Anything could happen to them.

In the bathroom, Audrey fixes her smudged makeup and removes Steve's wallet from the back of her pants. "A piece of cake!" she says.

"Don't mention cake, I'm so stuffed," Julia says, then plants a firm kiss on Audrey's full-lipped mouth.

The bathroom window is wide open; the balmy evening bleeds in over the wooden sash from the fairground, far away. The girls evaporate like alcohol into the night, and blow past the roller coaster's skeleton, across the city of Fontainebleau, wisps of honeysuckle and sulphur on the air.

Slick

THE BULLDOZERS gouged at the prostrate earth, wrestled with rocks and intractable roots, ladled banks of slippery clay from saffron holes, then drove away. The projects went up like red brick boxes and filled with dirt-poor families: two or three kids a unit, one single mom. The Thomas King Elementary school was built, a convenience store, Fontainebleau park and playground where people walked their dogs, where mounds of excrement killed off grass, hardened in the fierce heat of summer, crunched under children's running shoes.

There were twin hills between the projects and the school, breasts of the earth, padded with thick pastry snow in the winter. Toboggans tore from their peaks to their base, slid under the chain link fence, swerved out into traffic across the road. And as Jimmy Robinson ran past them now, he thought of his brother, Kevin. He saw his brother Kevin's face, pushed in like rubber. Saw his brother Kevin's head cracked like the shell of a nut under the wheel of a skidding car.

Jimmy Robinson was trouble at school. He picked fights at recess, chased girls and knocked them down, pinned their thrashing arms and legs with his strong skinny body and lifted their skirts. "Almost rape," is how Sally Jason's mother described it before she withdrew her daughter from the school. Old Bristle Top, the school's principal, beat Jimmy with a leather strap and sent him home. Jimmy's mother begged for Jimmy to be taken back. "He ain't been the same since Kevin got killed," she said, although she knew she wasn't being completely truthful.

Jimmy had always been Jimmy.

Every day for two years, with the exception of weekends and those days Jimmy had skipped, Old Bristle Top had hauled him into his office, made him drop his pants with his face to the corner and touch his toes. "You know the drill," he'd tell him, before he started hitting. His voice rose behind Jimmy. He'd pause after he spoke, while Jimmy waited, his bare ass thrust in the air. "I didn't do nothin'," Jimmy shouted. It was the only way he could stop anticipating the sting of that first strike. Jimmy braced himself even though he tried to relax. He knew relaxing was better. He knew the searing bite of the strap was a hundred times worse if he tensed. Today, because he was sure he was going to get thrown out anyway, he'd decided to skip the beating and go straight home.

The toboggan hills were desolate. Snow wrapped them, like the marzipan on Christmas cake. Jimmy recalled how one winter, his brother Kevin, Kevin the King, had come rushing down the first hill, a blizzard of white speed soaring through the sky on a sheet of steel. He was a streak, a shooting star, a blur of acceleration. All the kids screamed, mouths open, eyes jumping.

"Go Kev!" Jimmy shouted from the hill's peak. "That's THE man! Kevin Robinson!"

Kevin was always doing different things to increase his speed. Sometimes he'd wax the bottom of his makeshift sled, using paraffin instead of plain old waxed paper. Today, he did something super special, though he wouldn't tell Jimmy what it was. Then, he took a running start, threw himself forward onto the bumpy raft, shot into the air, then into another world. How many times had that sled gone down that hill? How many times had Jimmy watched Kevin moving faster than the speed of sound over the slick white glass, the snow and then everything suddenly slowing down. The old brown station wagon crawling up the street, the other kids tumbling from their sleds, shouting, pointing. "Kevin!" the name—the word—swelling from his mouth as if it were not sound at all but a pink chewing gum bubble that just kept growing bigger even without his breath.

There was a funeral after that. A boy's body in Kevin's casket dressed like a nerd. Steve Caputo and Peter Galka, kids who used to badmouth Kevin, crying like idiots. "It's not Kevin," Jimmy said. His mother grabbed him by the shoulder, pulled him away from the casket into an alcove outside of the ladies' room. "You shut up!" she told him, tears poised like knife blades in her eyes. "Have respect," her voice grew quaky. And then she said the only words she truly ever regretted saying in her life. Words, she thought about often, but never took back. "It's your fault he's dead."

Jimmy didn't believe Kevin was dead. He didn't believe the body in the casket was Kevin. "It's all bullshit," he shouted at his mother, ripping away from her. He knew it was bullshit because he'd seen what happened. He'd seen the station wagon. He'd seen how slowly it moved, how it twirled like a flower, how it bump, bumped, over Kevin's sled. Then Jimmy was at the bottom of the hill. He was standing over Kevin, looking at his dented face, his cracked skull, his open, awe-struck eyes. He knew Kevin wasn't dead because there was no blood—only a trickle of fluid, just like a thin grey vein in the snow. A police car came, an ambulance, hundreds of people gathered.

"THE man Kevin Robinson," Jimmy shouted over the din of sirens. "Astronaut Kevin Robinson." He grabbed the mangled sled, rushed to the top of the hill and threw himself on it. Steam rose from his bare hands, from his face. His breath burned him like the exhaust of a rocket. He soared into the pink sky. He knew the bottom of the sled wasn't even touching the snow.

A policeman, Sergeant Gilley, stopped him at the bottom of the hill. Stood in front of him, so he had to roll. Kevin rolled too, he thought. Gilley lifted him from the snow, brought him to his feet. "That boy in the ambulance... he your brother?"

"The amazing Kevin Robinson" was all that would come out, "daredevil Kevin Robinson."

"Come with me, son," Sergeant Gilley said.

Jimmy's mother worked at Franco's coffee shop on Ouellette Street. She wiped the Formica counters with neat bleach, polished the coffeepots with yellow shammies until they were blinding. Two nights a week she worked as a waitress at Club Venus, the topless bar. She worried about Jimmy more now that Kevin was gone. She worried about him shoplifting and having to go to court, about him vandalizing property and breaking into other people's units. She worried about him setting a bonfire in their living room. He'd tried it once before. Doused the old hide-a-bed with butane and tossed on a lit match. The flames vaulted and curled and left an indelible black shadow on the ceiling before they sputtered to nothing. The firefighters hauled the hide-a-bed out onto a patch of grass, hosed it down. For days smoke smouldered and rolled off the couch.

"Don't you go getting in trouble when I'm gone!" his mother told him every morning before she left for work. As an added precaution she grabbed the curve of his ear and pulled him so close to her face that he could feel the beads of spit and nicotine in her words. "You get in trouble one more time and there'll be hell to pay!"

Jimmy skidded over the opaque parking lot of the housing project. He fumbled to retrieve the key that hung from a grey shoelace around his neck, then blew on his fingers for warmth so he could unlock the bright orange door of the unit. He smoked half a dozen cigarettes and drank a quarter of a mickey of stolen whisky. He'd burn the expulsion notice when it came, but right now he called the school secretary with a put-on voice.

"I'm Jimmy Robinson's uncle Mike," he rasped. "The little bastard just told us what he did. Don't you worry, we're gonna fix him good this time." After he hung up, he found Kevin's old pocketknife, went outside and pried open the plastic box that housed the phone wires and slashed them.

"No calls tonight, ma," he said and tucked the knife into his fraying coat pocket. For a long time, he stood on Queen Elizabeth Street, hitchhiking, but when no one picked him up, he smashed the coin box of a pay phone at the convenience store, stole the quarters and got on a bus. He was thinking of going right down to the Detroit River, seeing if he could get rid of the rest of the money. He'd bought some gin there once for cheap. Picked up a carton of Marlboros and a six-pack of American beer from a guy fresh out of the Duty Free.

It had been a blistering hot summer's day and he lay between two columns, next to the abutment of the Ambassador Bridge drinking and smoking his brains out. He'd expected Kevin then. Thought Kevin would come. "I know you're there," he shouted at one of the columns. "I know you're somewhere!" His voice echoed, sounding loud and watery.

The bus lurched to a stop at an intersection, then began its slow curve down Quebec Street. The neighbourhood was dead, just a couple of garbage men and a postie, a girl in high-heeled boots and a fake fur jacket pushing a big blue baby buggy. And then, Kevin. It was Kevin walking into a McDonald's. Jimmy knew it was Kevin, even though he didn't see his face: long stringy hair, wiry body, loping walk. Jimmy hammered the bus cord ringer like a maniac. The bus driver kept driving. "Stop, you jerk!" Jimmy shouted, but the bus driver didn't even slow down until two stops later. When he finally did stop he told Jimmy, "If you ever call me jerk again, I'll rearrange your face." Jimmy ran back to Quebec Street, back to McDonald's. He yelled at the assistant manager: "Kevin Robinson. He was just in here. Where'd he go?"

The assistant manager was wiping up cola with a stringy white mop and looked confused. "Don't pretend you don't know what the fuck I'm talking about. Kevin Robinson! He was just in here! Houdini Robinson!"

"He owe you money?" the assistant manager asked.

"Forget it," Jimmy said finally, realizing the guy wasn't going to talk. Kevin had probably paid him to keep quiet. He'd always hated living in the projects. He hated living with their mother. He wouldn't want anyone making him go back. He probably had a room at the YMCA, or maybe a cheap bachelor apartment. "First chance I get, I'm gone," he used to say.

"Can I come?" Jimmy would ask.

"I'll think about it," Kevin said.

Jimmy expected Kevin to have made contact by now, to be waiting for him someplace.

He was getting pissed off that it was taking so long.

He ordered two cheeseburgers, fries and a coke, counted out four dollars in quarters.

"You rob someone's piggy bank?" the assistant manager asked.

"What if I did?" Jimmy answered. He sat at a table across from an old man in a dark coat and ate without tasting anything. Afterward, he walked the rest of the way downtown, past the funeral parlour, past the coffee shop, where his mother worked, past the River Park Hotel.

Although it was freezing cold, it stopped snowing. Sun rebounded off reefs of white. Jimmy extended the red fingers of his hands, stretched them to see if he could still feel, and trudged through the drifts, the ridges that cars had made, the half-shovelled sidewalks, coming at last to the dime store, the Metropol.

It used to be "the Metropolitan" until four letters fell off the sign. It smelled like plastic toys in the Metropol, like old wooden floors and soda pop, even though the soda fountain hadn't been functional for close to twenty years. It smelled like old penny candy, like jars of glass, like cough medicine. It smelled of cheap linen and rubber hot water bottles, slippers and sandals from China and India, lavender cologne.

There was a long oblong bin filled with acrylic gloves. Two pairs for the price of one. Jimmy picked up a black pair, broke the clear plastic thread that joined them, and pushed his cold hands into their tight warmth. He strolled down the aisles, lifting things from the shelves: a box of matches, a butane lighter. There was only one bored salesgirl at the till, a twist of brown hair twirling in her fingers as she looked out through the storefront window, and then down at her watch. There were only a few customers in the aisles and they all ignored Jimmy, an old couple and a fat woman and a man in white shiny shoes who looked like a gangster.

Jimmy went to the back of the store, past the cheap ladies' housecoats, the overly bright shirts. He went down a long narrow hallway and stopped at the men's room in front of the exit. There was a young man in there, a clean-cut American guy, nice suit, smelled like cloves and sunflowers. He told Jimmy he was married, that he was only in town for the day. He'd heard about this place, this washroom. He asked Jimmy if he needed some money.

"Queer!" Jimmy laughed as he pissed in the urinal. He kept laughing, even after the crestfallen man was gone. He kept laughing and smiled like a hyena back in the store where he tried on pairs of sunglasses and looked at himself in a skinny rectangular mirror. He thought of the queer driving over the border. Imagined him not being able to breathe until he got home. Imagined him crying, telling his glassy-eyed wife, "I love you so much." Then Jimmy pocketed a pair of silver sunglasses and moved to the next aisle.

A sharp blast of air struck Jimmy's cheek. The principal of his school, Old Bristle Top, stood at the door of the Metropol kicking snow off his galoshes.

Jimmy slid behind neon pink and green dresses and watched Old Bristle Top striding up an aisle. He wondered if he'd followed him here. His gloved fingers walked over the matches in his pocket, the lighter, the silver sunglasses. They walked over quarters and the blade of Kevin's sharp knife. He began to remember the thud of the chair that sailed from his hands that morning, that pirouetted and hung for a moment like a steel dancer before it hit his teacher, Mrs. Kennedy, and she crumpled in a heap on the floor.

If ever there was a time for Houdini Kevin Robinson to make an appearance it was now, Jimmy thought. Kevin could squirm out of anything, escape from anywhere. Even when he was shoulder deep in shit, shit worse than this, he could still pull himself free.

Bristle Top laced his fingers as he strode down an aisle. Jimmy crouched behind the bright dresses. He looked towards the door. His mind screaming for Kevin, half expecting Kevin to come stamping through, and then suddenly he heard Kevin's voice booming into his head just as if it were coming over the P.A. at school. "He ain't gonna take you to the cops, you moron. He's gonna take you back to his office for a whipping."

Jimmy's tense body relaxed. He stood and walked forward, smiled at Bristle Top, raised his gloved hand in a wave.

Bristle Top's face registered surprise. "Mr. Robinson," he said anxiously.

"You looking for me?" Jimmy asked.

Bristle Top looked awkward and embarrassed. He looked like he didn't know what to say. His hand, a small mallet, fell across Jimmy's shoulder. It sat there for a long time, reflecting the pink of the dresses. Finally Bristle Top spoke. "Come with me, boy," he said.

Jimmy followed Bristle Top past the ladies' housecoats and shirts to the back of the store. It was like he was trudging through snow, the entire world slowing. His mind replaying the chair that sailed from his hands that morning; that flew into the air becoming a makeshift sled, that glistened in the winter sky before it barrelled down its inevitable slope.

Transactions

IT ALL STARTS when Hal drops by and says he needs a car, and my brother Sam, acting like God, offers to rent the old man's antique Buick for fifty dollars. Hal slaps his thigh, and asks if fifty bucks is all Sam's gonna give him to take the heap away. I stick my elbow into Sam's ribs. I want the little twerp to shut his face, but then Hal slides his dirty hand into his pocket and pulls out half a bill.

Well, what can Sam do? He's gotta take it. He fishes the keys up, while Hal glides around the old boat, kicking tires. I'm hoping one falls off, but no such luck. Hal slides his commando knife out of his rucksack then tosses his pack into the back seat. "Okay, boys," he says, waving his knife around, "Let's see what this junk heap can do."

It's a hot day but me and Sam both break a cold sweat. Sam tells Hal we gotta be some place, but Hal ain't listening. Next thing you know, we're all cruising along highway 402, past the cows in the field, gold and green stripes of corn, away from

Fontainebleau, way, way out towards Essex just like we're going on a picnic.

Both Sam and me know Hal is crazy. He stuck a knife into some guy because he didn't like the way he talked, might have been the very knife he's strapped to himself for this joyride. It happened a couple of months ago down in Florida. He could have fried. They still use the electric chair down there, but his pappy's a judge and fixed it for him to come home. There was a whole big deal about it in the papers. Maple leaves forever and all that crap. Now Hal says if he's gonna do a murder, it'll be in his own backyard.

"Why'd ya go to Florida in the first place?" Sam asks like a retard. I could've kicked his ass.

"Old man sent me to Disney World. Some R&R after juvie, eh?"

"No kidding," Sam says, all excited, like he wants a blow by blow of the Magic Kingdom.

"Yeah," Hal says. He ain't offended at all. "It was real fun 'til this dip-stick got on my case for jumping the line at Space Mountain. 'Y'all know where the end of the line is?' he asked. 'Sure do,' I said and showed him."

Everyone knew Hal had a spur-of-the-moment temper. He never let on what he might do next. Even way back in grade school, he scared all the teachers. Mrs. Loomis was the only one who tried to get him any help. Instead of math, he got to go see the school counsellor. Just like Loomis, she was fresh outta college, bleeding heart, all hopped up on *making the world a better place*. "Get in touch with your feelings," she told him. "Don't bottle it up."

He comes back like a bomb about to explode. "My safety's off," he tells Mrs. Loomis and goes after Mike Riddell with a pair of pointy scissors. After that, there was no more counselling for Hal. His dad put him into "a special school" but they couldn't handle him there either. Finally, he winds up hauling water and chopping wood at good ole St. Jerome's. They call it wilderness therapy, but anyone who's been there knows it's just a cover to kick the shit out of troublemakers like Hal.

Sam knows enough to change the subject. He starts making small talk about UFOs. For a second, my heart starts beating normal again. Then the idiot twerp points at a corn field.

"There's supposed to be crop circles out there. I ain't never seen one, but I'd sure like to," he says. I would've smashed him in the face if he'd been sitting next to me, but instead I kicked the back of his seat and hoped he'd shut up. The last thing we wanted was to be in a cornfield with crazy Hal and his knife.

"All that UFO stuff is bullshit," Hal says. He's doing twenty clicks over the limit and swerves a little when he pops the lighter for his smoke.

"Oh yeah?" Sam says.

"Yeah," Hal says.

Before Sam can say another stupid thing, I butt in, "Maybe we can go for a drive another time, Hal. We really gotta be some place." I'm talking from the back seat, I'm sitting next to Hal's rucksack, I look into the rear-view and catch his eye twitch like a cricket. Hal slams the brakes so hard you can smell the rubber and the car skids. Sam's and my butt slide clear off our seats. Hal whips his head sideways like he's having convulsions.

"You mean you don't want to ride with me?" His eyes are bulging out of his shaved head like herniated balloons.

"He don't mean that," Sam says, his voice all wussy like he's begging for mercy. "We like driving with you, don't we, Charlie?" I nod. I'm watching Hal in the rear-view, trying to decide if we ought to jump and roll, but then everything settles. Hal touches the gas. We're cruising.

Hal drags on his cigarette like I've seen asthmatics pull on their puffers. Sam's trying to look like he's enjoying the ride. "Them UFO sightings are all complete bullshit," Hal continues. "There ain't no such thing as UFOs, there ain't no such thing as aliens, and there ain't no close encounters."

"Lots a people say different," Sam argues. "Lots a people say they've seen weird lights and junk."

"Lots a people is idiots," Hal says.

Yeah, I think, and Sam's one of the biggest.

"Before them crop circles appeared, people said they seen things in the sky. It was on the radio, a whole bunch a people, they seen fireballs and big round metal discs, and even feathery things that looked like wings, and some official guy said it wouldn't surprise him at all if there was aliens or UFOs or shit like that. You got a smoke?" my A-hole of a brother calls.

I'm watching Hal's face, looking to see if his expression changes, looking to see if he goes for his knife, and when he don't, I throw my two cents in to let him know I'm on his side.

"There ain't no such thing as UFOS," I say. "It's the Americans testing them nukes."

"No it ain't," Hal says.

"No it ain't," Sam says.

I notice Hal's eyebrow twitch again. I toss Sam a smoke and take one myself. "So what do you think, Hal?" I try to sound like whatever he thinks is right.

"It ain't what I think," Hal mutters. "It's what I know for sure."

While we're waiting for Hal to tell us what he knows for sure, it suddenly gets cooler.

The wind picks up and some mother of a black cloud rolls outta nowhere and starts pissing rain. We hit the city limits and Hal says, "How fast can this shell do?"

Me and Sam didn't have the guts to ask Hal where he's taking us. We're moving so fast, my cheeks stick to my molars. I'm keeping my fingers crossed that Sam don't rile him, 'cause if Hal hits those brakes now, we're out on the highway with road kill. I wonder for a split second if maybe I'm dreaming, maybe this is a nightmare, but then Hal twists the wheel, my head smashes the side window, and I know I'm not.

When Hal finally slows the car, he says, all gloomy-like, "I been to Hell and it ain't a ride I'd recommend."

Sam, being the moron he is, asks, "In Disney World?"

"No," Hal says, his voice all low and serious. "In the hole."

It's as dark as pitch outside now, and forks of lightning flash every which way. Rain thumps on the top of the old man's car, like he'll be thumping on us, if we ever make it home alive and he finds out about this little pleasure trip. I'm trying to think of some trick to get Hal to take us back, or at least jog him into a happy place so maybe he won't kill us, but before I can, Hal starts in with that glum tone again.

"They lock ya up in a little cage, mattress on the floor, bucket to crap in. Strip ya naked, call ya names, sometimes if ya give 'em lip, they spray ya with chemicals that stop ya breathing, but that ain't the worst of it. You wanna know what's the worst of it?"

Hal turns off the highway and drives up a muddy country road, lightning and thunder exploding everywhere, hail like headlights pummelling the old man's car. I wonder if it's a trick question. If we answer "yes" will he pull out his knife and shank us?

But Sam don't think. He just blurts: "Sure."

I look in the rear-view and hold my breath. If Hal is planning on killing Sam, he ain't gonna do it yet. "The worst," Hal says, "is having no one but bed bugs to talk to, no one to listen to but them horrible voices in your own head. Them voices tell you you ain't nothing but a worthless piece of crap and the world would be better if you just slit your throat, and the worst of it is, you start thinking they're right, you start thinking about all the things you done in your life, and the hard cold concrete floor opens like a trap door, and you fall down, straight into Hell."

"For real?" Sam asks.

Hal slows the tank. There's this rotten gate coming off its hinges, and a sign you can just barely read saying No Trespassing. Hal levels his foot, and the old man's car jumps at the gate. Broken wood and bent metal scatter in the wet brush.

Hal laughs like a lunatic. "Jesus said, 'I am the gate. If anyone enters through me, he will be saved'." He drives under a rusting arch. Hailstones shine like birds' eggs in the long messy grass. "That's how I know there ain't no such thing as UFOs," Hal says, "because I been to Hell, and I met Jesus there."

"Is that a fact?" Sam asks.

I can't make out where we are, and can feel myself start to panic, then a rod of light hits a tree and brightens up a tall flat stone, and I realize this crazy bastard has brought us into an abandoned boneyard.

"I met Jesus there," Hal says again, "and Jesus said to me 'I am the way and the truth and the life' and 'I am God the great and powerful'."

"I thought the Wizard of Oz said something like that," Sam says.

"Yeah, he said something like that too, but he really wasn't great and powerful and that was only a movie," Hal says. He slams the car into a gravestone and it topples. Then he parks on top of it. "Them lights in the sky ain't UFOs," Hal says, pointing at Sam, like suddenly he gets the fact that Sam disagrees with him. "There ain't never been a UFO. Them lights in the sky is rebel angels, just like the kind Ezekiel saw, coming down to earth, reminding us of our covenant with Jesus."

"Covenant?" Sam asks.

"Yeah," Hal says, "covenant. It means the deal we made with Christ."

"I ain't made no deal with no one," Sam says.

I boot the back of Sam's seat. "Cut it out, hard-on!" he whimpers.

"Let's go for a walk, boys," Hal says like he didn't hear Sam and like he don't remember it's pissing outside. He must think we're not gonna listen to him, 'cause he unstraps his commando knife, and uses it to signal us out of the car.

"We're coming," I tell him, trying not to sound scared.

Sam walks ahead of me, and all I can see is his straight, stupid skull, bobbing up and down as the rain hits it. Hal walks behind. The point of his knife touching my soaking wet T shirt. A thin vein of lightning crackles followed by an ear splitting kaboom. The air smells like sulphur. It ain't safe to be walking in this storm, I think, but then I feel the tip of Hal's knife, and don't mind the lightning so much.

I think about this past summer, how every day I forgot to notice the sun, and about my old girlfriend, Lizzie, who for sure was the best thing that ever happened to me. I'm trying not to act like it, but panic's got me by the balls. What if there ain't no more chances? What if this is it? I want to shout "Lizzie! Lizzie, I loved you!" even though I know she won't hear, but all the romance fades when Hal jabs me with his knife and screams: "Keep your ass moving, Bouchard."

There's this little tumble-down building, like a broken box, at the top of the muddy hill. Hal makes us go in and tells us to kneel down. Above is a bunch of old wooden trusses, pointing up, making a triangle, and the floor is cracked wood and broken stone. I'm looking for a window to dive through, but all of the windows are covered with boards. There's only a few glints of shadowy light poking in, making the big rickety cross at the front glow like a UFO.

Hal's waving his knife around and telling Sam to get down on his knees. I'm already down, and thinking to myself about that guy in Florida. "So this is the end of the line," I think and get sentimental and want to hug Sam, even though he's such an incredible jerk. But then Hal ruins the mood by booting me in the back. "Get you head lower," he shouts.

I'm waiting to feel the steel, wondering which of us he'll take out first, and where he'll dig first, and what he's gonna do with our bodies after, but the jab don't come. He's on again about being in the hole, and knowing you have no one in a place like that. No one to help you but Jesus. Outside, the rain stops. Inside, everything goes quiet. The glints of light through the boards get brighter and twinkly like stars. "I want you boys to pray for your souls, do you understand?" Hal asks.

I can't see Sam now, but I bend my head a little lower, hoping to God Hal makes a clean rip, and we don't have to lie on this cold stinking floor bleeding to death. It's driving me crazy waiting, and finally I turn around. Hal is kneeling in a dim twinkling halo. He's kneeling just like we are, except his hands are folded together. I can tell by the way his lips tremble, he's talking to someone and then I notice diamonds of light. Diamonds of light, like hailstones glistening and melting down his cheeks, falling from his shut and wrinkled up eyes like rebel angels falling from heaven.

Flight

LAURIE LAFRAMBOIS WAS PREGNANT and Jimmy Robinson stole a car. It was parked outside the Toronto Dominion on Ouellette Street, two blocks from the shop where Jimmy's mother was serving coffee. He didn't really want the car. It was a Ford sedan, with rusting fenders. A cardboard air freshener hung from its mirror and fuzzy plaid covers encased its seats. He drove past the hospital, the library, the funeral home, wondering how far he'd get before the police pulled him over. He wondered if he might make it to Toronto. He'd never been there before, but the starter's gun in his heart was telling him to go.

A guy from Essex he'd once done time with at St. Jerome's Wilderness Camp, Jack Goulet, told him Toronto was a good place to get lost in. "The buildings are so tall and the population so copious," said Jack, "that as soon as your feet touch pavement, you vanish completely away." Jack was older than Jimmy, knew things and talked funny. He had a synthetic plate in his skull. He'd been the victim of a farm accident in Essex and was at St.

Jerome's because he'd shot his parents. Jimmy wondered if he might meet up with Jack again. If he might melt into the very same Toronto pavement that Jack had headed for when he broke from camp so many years ago.

Jimmy stopped for a red light at the intersection at Quebec Street. He lit a cigarette and watched a bunch of schoolgirls from Queen Anne's in their ugly pleated skirts getting off a bus.

Some had hiked their skirts so high you could see the lace fringe on their bright little panties. The thought occurred he might lure one of these schoolgirls into his car, carry her off to Toronto, maybe take two, one for him, one for Jack, but then he remembered Laurie and the light turned green. "Green light Laurie," he thought and began feeling queasy.

He turned left on Tecumseh, and drove out past the shopping mall. The car thumped over uneven tarmac and into a legion of diminutive potholes that flecked the road like a rash. He heard something clunk, something fall from the car, a hubcap or fender, a rusty exhaust pipe. He didn't stop to find out what it was. He kept driving, past scraggy houses, past a boarded-up building that had once been a store, past telephone poles, past a motor inn. He could taste Toronto when he hit the deserted highway, feel his body fading away.

Sometimes when he was scared or lonely, he'd still hear his brother Kevin's voice.

"Those Queen Anne girls were really hot," the voice was saying now.

"I'm not going back. I'm going to Toronto," Jimmy shouted. He covered his ears with his hands. The car swerved. Kevin's voice stopped talking.

Laurie LaFrambois wasn't hot. She was a scag. A pregnant thirteen-year-old scag. She was younger than Jimmy and the only girl who didn't fight him when he pinned her to the ground in Fontainebleau Park and hiked up her skirt. He put his hand down her ragged underpants, he put his hand in her shirt and pinched her breasts.

"I guess that makes you my boyfriend now," she said when he'd finished with her and she heaved herself up from the mud and grass with dog shit on her back. "Aren't we gonna kiss?"

Her lips were thin and white, like scars. Jimmy had never been kissed before. She stuck her tongue into his mouth. He thought he might be sick.

"Don't you know anything about *making love?*" she asked.

"Love?" Jimmy echoed.

"Oh, never mind," she said.

Laurie's brother had taught her to kiss, her stepfather had taught her how to "make love." "I stick my thing in your thing," he'd said. "We don't tell your mother, O.K.?"

Laurie didn't tell her mother, but she told the kids at school, who told a teacher, Mrs. Loomis: "You know what her stepfather does?"

Mrs. Loomis had expected to hear something cute. He snores. He farts. He scratches his butt.

She didn't expect to hear: "He sticks his thing in her thing."

Laurie's stepfather was still in jail, the same place Jimmy was going to be if he didn't disappear into the Toronto pavement.

"I didn't do nothin'," he heard himself saying. He saw himself standing in a courtroom. Saw Laurie with her big round stomach, her huge swollen breasts saying she wanted to be a good mother. "I wanna raise my kid right."

"You can't have a kid," he'd said when she told him.

They'd just had sex under an old Chrysler truck in a Canadian Tire parking lot and she impatiently rolled free from him. "Who says?"

"You ain't old enough to have a kid."

"If I'm old enough to get pregnant with a kid, I'm old enough to have one." She yanked up her underwear.

At first he thought she was bluffing, thought she was trying to get him to marry her or something crazy like that. There was no way he could imagine her having a kid. But then she started getting fatter, wearing her sister, Lynette's, old maternity clothes, waddling instead of walking.

"My ma says she wouldn't let you marry me even if you wanted to. She says you raped me. She says you shoulda known better than messin' with a thirteen-year-old."

After that, she wouldn't let Jimmy touch her. Two policemen who cruised the projects had come looking for him this morning. He stood in the living room, peeking through a hole in the yellowed curtains. That's when he decided to leave.

The fields that flanked highway 402 were desolate. Churned up patches of mud and weed existed where rows of sturdy corn once grew. A cumbersome train rattled through the wasteland, running parallel to his car. Jimmy rode the gas pedal. He rolled down his window and shouted, "Woo-Woo!" The rev of the car growled "Torrronnnnto." And the train called out "Homefree!"

For a moment Jimmy was soaring through space. He was flying into the vast grey clouds shaking the world away. "Torrronnnto," the car purred, "Torrrrrrrronnnto," she sang. Jimmy laughed and punched the accelerator. It tore at a piece of green threadbare carpeting. It left a mark, a miniature horseshoe, embedded in the dusty vinyl mat. The car lurched, then started to groan. It started to thump like a steel bucket pounding down a hill.

"Fuck," Jimmy said.

Smoke poured into his window, poured through the cracks in the hood. The steering wheel seized. The car veered to the shoulder, pulling him down into a gully. Gravel and muck spewing like hail.

The absent world suddenly returned. It was suddenly spinning. Jimmy's head was smashing into the roof. When he woke, there were stars. The clear night sky shimmering above as if his broken head had released all its bright phantoms.

"You idiot," Kevin's voice bellowed into Jimmy's throbbing brain. "How could you be such a jerk?"

An eruption of stars burnt Jimmy's eyes. He tried to call for Kevin but his jaw was disconnected.

"You coulda been porkin' them Queen Anne girls right now," Kevin was shouting. "You coulda been in goddamned paradise." It hurt Jimmy to swallow. It hurt him to move his tongue, to moisten his lips. "Now you're all by yourself in this goddamned field with your guts fallin' out."

Jimmy fell asleep again. He dreamed he was at St. Jerome's. Jack Goulet twisted a plucked bobwhite over a spit. The smell of roast chicken permeated a cathedral of trees. Saliva rolled off Jimmy's chin, freezing in the dust. When the bobwhite vanished, there was frost on his naked hands, frost on his face. The icy ground beneath his back glued him to the spot and cracked when he tried to escape. He remembered the car flipping but could not recall how many years ago. He could not remember if he and Jack had made it to Toronto, if Kevin had ever come home.

The sun gradually rose behind a cloud of smoke. His hands gradually thawed. He reached into the fruitless earth and pulled from it the femur bone of some large dismembered animal. The bone was yellow and naked. A fine dirt vein ran over its curves.

Jimmy remembered hunting with Jack in the woods at St. Jerome's. He remembered killing a deer, gnawing the meat until its bones glistened.

He pulled himself up, gulped the morning air. The world swivelled and dipped. A mangle of ash and chrome and painted steel spun in his eyes. He couldn't remember how he'd crawled free. The highway seemed so far off. He couldn't remember where he was going or why and then he remembered Laurie and looked again at the mass of charred metal that once had been his car.

He headed away from the wreck, across the field, towards the railroad tracks. The police were probably searching for him already, and it wouldn't be long before someone discovered the ravaged car.

Sweat clung to his head like small clear pearls and mud attached itself to his feet. He walked like a drunken man, unsure of a teetering sky, his numb body finally collapsing a mile away against the wall of an old wooden tool shed that some farmer had constructed in more prosperous times.

Hints of sky-blue paint still clung to the decaying wood and an expanse of barren land relaxed before his misty vision. Houses that trimmed the land settled as his eyes adjusted, and patches of witch grass and wild rye emerged like shafts of gold from the tufted earth.

He crawled into the shed and thought he was with Kevin. "That car wreck shoulda killed you," Kevin said.

A smile tugged at his sore mouth. "Houdini Robinson," he muttered, recalling how Kevin saw a movie all about Harry Houdini once. "Houdini was the greatest magician that ever lived!" Kevin said. He got so excited when he talked about Houdini that sometimes it seemed he was trying to pick a fight. "He broke out of a Siberian prison, and jumped off a bridge into the Detroit River with handcuffs on his wrists. He died over there," Kevin said, nodding vaguely towards the border. "His appendix blew up after some idiot from a university in Quebec punched him. He died Halloween night."

After that movie, Kevin never stopped trying to escape. He got Jimmy to tie his hands together with rope and shut him into an abandoned freezer chest. "If I'm not out in twelve hours, come and get me," he'd say.

Jimmy would walk around the projects, pining for his company, worrying about the oxygen in that cramped tiny space.

But Kevin always broke free. He always showed up, right before Jimmy was supposed to go get him.

"Ta da!" he'd say, and Jimmy would badger him to know how he did it.

"Houdini never told, and I'm not gonna either."

Tony Deluca was a friend of Kevin's and he said he used to let Kevin out. He said he did it right after Jimmy put him in. "Twelve hours without my twerp brother," Kevin would say, and he and Tony would laugh and smoke and drink tequila. But Jimmy knew Tony Deluca was full of shit. Kevin could get out of anywhere: locked closets, steamer trunks, the juvenile holding tank. He bent coat hangers and bobby pins and paperclips. There wasn't a lock in the city he couldn't pick. He broke into buildings, just because he could. He was charming like Houdini too. Some people called him polite, said even in the worst families there's always one good one.

Jimmy tried to remember how he'd escaped from the crush of his car. He tried to remember so he could tell Kevin, but all he recalled was tumbling through space, stars and bright planets, then the absence of light.

"They'll think you're dead," Kevin told him. "They'll see the car, and think you burned to death. You're so goddamned lucky. You must have a rabbit's foot up your ass!"

Jimmy saw his mother weeping like she did when they told her Kevin was dead. He saw Laurie LaFrambois, her stomach like a huge shelf, her eyes like little piss holes in snow. "It's your fault he's dead," Jimmy's mother was saying to her.

"But I didn't mean for him to die," Laurie would sob. "I didn't mean for him to go away."

Jimmy fell asleep and dreamed he and Kevin were together again. They were jumping into the cattle car of a slow-moving train. When he woke, a train's whistle was sounding. The sky flared with bright electricity and rain began to batter the roof of the shed. He twisted his throbbing body, pushed his aching head out through the door and let the cold rain fill his dry, wounded mouth.

His stomach contorted with hunger, and he slept fitfully. He thought about Jack Goulet and St. Jerome's, thought about everything he'd learned there. He always carried a knife in his pocket. He ate insects while he waited until he was strong enough to hunt: longhorn beetle larvae that bored through the shed and left sawdust trails, lantern click bugs that glowed when they flew in the dark and squeaked when they crunched in his teeth.

In his fist, he clutched the femur bone he had found in the earth. It sang lullabies and when it spoke, it used Jack's voice. "Protein," it said, "an essential nutrient and a major constituent of the living cell."

It didn't make the bugs taste any better. It didn't make them feel any better when they squirmed in Jimmy's mouth. Still, he ate them, because he knew he had to.

He set traps in the field beyond the shed when he was stronger—the kind of traps they'd taught him how to make at St. Jerome's. He dug holes with stones and fashioned a spade from a dangling board. Thick brown grasses that scored his fingers he used as thatching. At night, chipmunks and field mice stumbled into the traps. He killed them with his knife, sliced off their pelts, cooked their pink bodies over an open flame.

"I doubt we'd find much better fare in New York," the bone joked. It wriggled in his palm. It chuckled. He gazed at its dry ragged socket. It was beginning to grow Jack's face.

"Go away, Jack." Jimmy said. "You ain't suppose to be here. You were years ago."

Jimmy dug deeper traps to accommodate larger game, rabbits and raccoons. Sometimes he worked an entire afternoon, hollowing out a site where he'd seen tracks, digging with his spade and sharp rocks, scooping dirt and clay. Sometimes he came across useful sticks, triangular rocks, arrowheads already formed. He carved a bow from a branch. Stripped a piece from his jacket for the bowstring and fashioned arrows out of the bits and pieces the earth provided.

He ate pheasant then and wild turkey. He thought of Christmas and Thanksgiving when he and Kevin were small. Their Gran had been alive then and used to fill their plates so high that they couldn't see anything in front of them but food. They ate until they thought they'd bust. "You don't feed these boys, Maureen," their gran would say, and their mother would smoke and pick at lumps of stuffing on her plate, "I feed 'em just fine."

"Why their little bodies are nothing but skin and bone," Gran persisted, "and their faces! Stone white!" She pinched Jimmy's bloated cheek for emphasis; when he hollered, his mother cuffed him. "Don't you never talk with your mouth full."

“Leave the poor boy alone, Maureen,” Gran said. “If you hadn’t run off with what’s his name you’d probably have had boys who knew some manners.”

Jimmy and Kevin had second and third helpings of everything at Gran’s. For dessert they each had half a pumpkin pie. Jimmy could imagine the pie. Its sweet, spicy softness. He could imagine Gran, patting the top of his head. “That mother of yours,” she whispered. “If she hadn’t gotten herself knocked up, she wouldn’t have had to run off and get married.”

For the first time in days, Jimmy thought of Laurie LaFrambois, her expanding chest and stomach, and began feeling sick. He wanted to take himself back to Gran’s place. He wanted to see him and Kevin stuffing their faces. He tried to get back there, but only got as far as Gran’s door, where his mother made him and Kevin wait, because something was stinking inside the apartment. His mother didn’t say what she’d found. “Go home,” was all she said, but Jimmy whined, “I wanna see Gran.” He was thinking of pie and cookies, of the cake Gran used to bake and keep in a painted metal tin. He pushed past his mother. Past a barricade of stench. He gagged and covered his face.

“When I say go home, I mean it!” his mother said, ripping the back of his jacket as she lifted and threw him into the corridor. He slammed into a wall. Everything turned bright violet, then black. The next thing he knew, he was at home in bed. His mother was standing over him, telling him Gran had been sick and unhappy, that it was lucky she finally died.

Tony Deluca said the newspaper ran a story about Gran that said she’d taken a bottle of sleeping pills, then put a plastic bag over her head. It said she was so neglected that she decomposed for three weeks before anyone found her, but Tony Deluca was a liar and Jimmy never knew what really happened to Gran. It was a cold afternoon. Earlier that morning, frost had painted the earth white, transformed dark mounds to charcoal, but the cool sun was unrelenting in its brightness and made pools of tears form in Jimmy’s eyes. He slung his bow and arrows over his shoulder. Held the bone a little firmer in his grasp. He’d had enough thinking. He was going to go into the field and hunt.

“When the going gets tough, the tough start killing,” the bone chuckled. “Wasn’t that our one-time motto at old St. Jerome’s?”

Jimmy didn't look at the bone. "Beat it," he said, loading his bow, as a kind of dizzy stillness fell across the field. "Heads up!" the bone said.

Above, the frigid sun began to tremble, and Jimmy witnessed as it sprouted a magnificent pair of wings. They were the largest wings Jimmy had ever encountered. The brightest wings he knew he would ever see in his life. He lifted his bow, took aim into the air, and let the arrow fly.

It rose toward the bright clouds, a shaft of naked wood before it twisted in flight, and sped back straight towards the earth, back towards Jimmy, blinded, by a flight he would never see again.

The Mermaid

CELESTE CAST OFF her steel walker and settled like a fallen leaf in the field's grass. Beginning where the gravel road grew vague at the end of Monica Street, the field spread lake-like. It opened past the dying maples, the reedy swamp, the abandoned and twisted mufflers of the car graveyard, past a grey shack, out in waves of swelling stink grass, to the sooty oil-soaked spines of the railroad ties. Beyond this, a farmer had built his house, and just beyond that the swelling city of Fontainebleau merged with a highway that extended all the way to Toronto, with a line running through its back, straight and white as a skunk.

Celeste had never been beyond the limits of this field's small world. She'd never gone to school, never made a friend. The heart of the earth beat restless through her. As a cinnamon-brown meadow locust sailed above her head it purred, and she considered her body, the part that extended below her waist, one long shapeless limb with feet as flat as fins at its base. Neighbours gawked when she tottered past, children called her names, sickos threatened to saw her apart, but in fifteen years she'd never felt sorry for herself.

She had three older sisters, all of them with magnificent legs, darker than chestnuts, waxed clean of hair, athletically contoured with lithe toes and pearly polish on each. They all wore jet black eyeliner that smelled of glue in the bottle, and stained their lips with fuchsia gloss. The eldest, Lizzie, had a tattoo of a monkey on her shoulder, while Audrey, the youngest, had a rose. Suzy, the second child, had no tattoo, but in each ear a string of twelve golden bubbles that grew increasingly diminutive, rising to a perfect arc.

All three sisters smoked cigarettes and drank beer, though Lizzie was the only one who didn't have to lie about her age to do so. The other two waited outside of liquor stores for friendly men to buy them six packs and offer them joints. All three sisters shared a love for the searing high of marijuana, while the faithful visions of peyote were new to Audrey, and quickly becoming her attachment.

It was Audrey, who with young old eyes at seven had first called Celeste "mermaid." Her mother had shouted and slapped her, though the name had not intended to hurt. It was just that Audrey's teacher, Mrs. Loomis, had read a story and shown a picture. It felt to Audrey as if the most startling secret had been disclosed, one that could change her sister's life. "You're not a freak! You're not a freak!" she screamed, all the way up Monica Street. "You're a mermaid!" It flew from her innocent lips, into the neighbours' shabby window screens, into the sky, into the field, and finally into her mother's hearing.

"Don't you ever call your sister names," she yelled, bringing her knuckles across Audrey's soft face. She slapped much harder than she thought she had. She didn't like to slap.

She'd been drinking, and left a bruise that made her heart ache. "Why would you call your sister names?" she asked later, but Audrey refused to speak, her puffy mouth tightening to a pout.

The others called Celeste "mermaid" then. They couldn't help themselves, the notion so guileless and ingenious. It accounted for their sister's alien beauty, for the nature of her large, mellifluous eyes. For the straight black hair that hung beyond the curve of her frail shoulders and shone cobalt blue under the sun's generous rays. No one in the family, as far as anyone knew, had ever had hair like that. It made sense to think of her as a misplaced being, a creature who by some terrible twist of fortune had struggled free from the wrong womb or landed on this patch of Fontainebleau from some distant watery planet. Celeste, herself, delighted in this possibility. For a few years she amused herself with solitary make-believe, lusty warm thoughts of a Prince, who would emerge for her from the sea or sky. But, her sisters told her, there was no watery planet and the ocean was hundreds of miles away. There was only the Detroit River and a couple of dying lakes, nothing at all suitable for a sea Prince.

There were arguments over what should happen to Celeste, although now it was Lizzie doing most of the fighting. Over the years, she'd assumed the role as the mermaid's protector, beating up neighbourhood kids who made fun of her and fielding calls from perverts who fantasized about "sex with a mutant" or performing operations to remove her lower half. "If thy hand or foot causes thee to stumble, cut it off," one Bible-mad caller regularly breathed down the phone, "If thy eye offends thee, gouge it out."

"I'll do more than just gouge your eye out if I find you," Lizzie screamed, knowing that if the mermaid were threatened in any way, she was easily capable of murder.

As she sat on her boyfriend's lap now, taking swigs of his neglected beer, she railed at her mother: "Take her to the States! Get her an operation!" There was nothing new in this idea, people had been saying the same thing for years. What was new, however, was the contempt in Lizzie's voice.

"There's no goddamned money," her mother responded, but Lizzie refused to let her mother's simulated toughness intimidate her. It was all puff and bluff with her; a bully's carapace constructed to frighten people and get her own way.

"You gonna pay for it? You think your damned old man's gonna pay?" she croaked as she fixed her weak, misty eyes on her daughter, and tried to look sober.

"For Christ's sake, you could call the newspaper or the radio or the fuckin' Sally Ann! They could get the money raised! If you'd unscrew your face from the bottle long enough to make a couple of phone calls..."

"Why you little bitch! Who in hell do you think you are?"

Lizzie's boyfriend almost couldn't keep up with the long, solid strides of her gorgeous legs. She swore at her mother, smashed the wooden door so splinters flew, then jumped into his truck and commanded him to drive.

Celeste watched her house from the field as her sister and the man she was dating sped from the driveway, gravel spitting all the way across the uneven lawn, swells of smoke and dust and hungry crows whirling to heaven. "You slut!" her mother screamed after Lizzie. "You make sure you're home by midnight! You make sure you bring her home, Charlie Bouchard! Do you hear me? Charlie? You bastard!"

It wasn't Charlie Bouchard anymore. Charlie was at least ten men ago and certainly hadn't been around for a year, but the men Lizzie took all looked the same: long oval faces framed with manes of gold, broad shoulders, strong bodies, tight jeans, black tee shirts, with green "Export A" packs poking from their sleeves. They wore work boots, instead of shoes, and smelled of gasoline. Lizzie loved the smell of gas, said if she knew she was going to die then for sure that's what she'd be drinking.

Their mother never noticed the sameness of Lizzie's men. She was blinded by misfortune, captive of her own despair. Celeste imagined her, slumped on the red kitchen chair. That chair was so old that white padding peeked from its wounds, and the vinyl seat was worn pink from her sitting. She didn't want to take Celeste to the States. Right from the beginning, when doctors first uttered the condition's name, Sirenomelia; even before there were questions of missing holes, and a misplaced anus, organs that appeared unconnected to their appropriate sites, and the prognosis for this newborn was death in a week without surgery, her mother was far too angry to be moved. She staggered home with the squirming bundle, fixed her in a piss-smelling crib, told her if she was going to die she better get it over with. There wasn't any coddling left in her. It had all been spent on rotten men.

If she'd been more social, she would have shared her story. After a few drinks, she'd say it to herself. There'd been a court order and accusations of neglect; newspaper reporters, social workers, public health nurses and right-to-die activists all swarming together on her mangy front lawn. "They even went lookin' for Gordy," she croaked out loud. "If you find that bastard, nail him to a cross. He owes me three years of child support!" They didn't find him, though. She didn't think they would. "He only ever showed up when he wanted a piece of ass," she muttered and took another desperate quaff from the tall metal tumbler she used. She swore this cup was the only thing that stood between her and skid row. Swore it was more than superstition her thinking so. She established a rhythm with her drinking: she worked it so she would feel a perpetual numbing, so that her mind and body would be painless and loose; she worked it so she would not forget where she was, not take her clothes off in public, not burn the house down. She spoke a little, drank a little, smoked in between. The metal cup had somehow become an intrinsic part of this ritual.

Celeste grew and thrived without an operation. Her strange body found its own way to live. Her mother thumbed her nose at all the meddling specialists who now invoked the uncertainty of a future. For them, the sheer ugliness of a girl with a fleshy tail was enough to intervene. They wanted to cut it, to graft skin to it, to make from it one reliable leg, then fit her with a prosthetic. She would be able to wear pants, to look normal. No one would ever know anything had been wrong. No one would guess, until she stood to walk away; then she would limp, and creak, and buckle.

It was true what the social workers said. Celeste's tail had interfered with her proper socialization. She'd grown-up shy, reticent, unable to demand. Lizzie had shown her how to bask in the field beyond her mother's house, and that is where she'd escape, a timid anchoress, whose only friends were the birds she fed, and whose only pleasures were the sweet and pungent smells of wildflowers, the simplicity of the sunlight in which she swam, and the detached and gentle caresses of earth and air. For fifteen years, this had been all she needed. The humming, pop-eyed dragon fly, the stilt-legged leatherjackets, the radiant moths. Her mind spun extraordinary stories peopled with these spirits of the field. In fifteen years she had not once felt cheated or yearned for something other than what she had, until this moment.

In the distance, a train's whistle sounded forlorn. The heaving train track groaned under the burden of its daily misery and Celeste rested her stinging eyes. The abrupt cold of isolation snagged her, as just above something large and feathered seemed to eclipse the sun. There were pheasants in this field, fat and tufted, speckled and skittish that would jump suddenly from their dens, filling the air with their trilling screams. She waited, listening, expecting this confirmation of unrest—yet did not receive it. She waited, feeling again the dark clouds' passage across the sun, a breeze on her face, in her hair. She waited, smelling the gamy odour of feathers, and then, at last she opened her eyes.

Whether she dreamed or whether this vision had broken from the dreaming world she could not say then, but for an instant it soared, glorious and golden above her, a creature formed, it seemed, part by fire and part by cloud. Its wings larger than any she had ever seen or imagined, cut the sky in a sleek, horizontal stripe before spiralling upwards and away, and she felt her heart, an angel, summoned, rising in her chest.

Later that evening when dusk softened the sky and Celeste tottered home, she wept. It was the first time she had experienced such grief, leaving the field, and being unaccustomed to tears, as her eyes were not made to shed them, the sobs convulsed from her throat, creating incomprehensible barbed warbles that filled the torpor of Monica Street.

Suzy was breathless and animated at home, telling a story. It was something that had happened that day, beneath the quivering porch steps, something about her digging through the earth, hunting for her new toe ring. It had slipped from her foot when she stumbled, flew in a glistening silver curve that her eyes couldn't follow. She knelt right there, under the porch, began rutting in the dust and bottle glass, chipping her nail polish, cracking her nails, sifting the grey clumps of dirt with hands like claws.

It stabbed her before she knew what it was. It stuck in the flesh of her palm like a thin, ivory talon, an arrowhead, made of rock, stained sepia, brazened, and beside it a clean brown bone. Amazed, she continued digging and sifting, forgetting the ring. It was as if her hands knew, as if her hands were possessed of an intuitive sapience. They uncovered a skull, cracked across the curving frontal bone, then another arrowhead, a jaw, a club, made from a strong stick and a rock still tied to fraying leather tongs. The earth gave way in a dusty exhalation, creating a gully of similar treasures: an ancient bow made from reeds, a drum covered in animal hide. Suzy was certain it would bring money. Certain it would pay for a car, a red Camaro, a pair of leather pants.

"They're Indian things, Ma." her voice wavered now. "Indian things! Don't you know what that means?"

Her mother perused her with a vague unfocussed stare. "Ain't no one digging nothin' up in my yard," she said, raising the silver tumbler to her lips, swallowing. "And don't you go sayin' anythin' about it either. I got enough to do without chasing assholes off my property, calling the goddamn cops..." She hiccupped and drew on her cigarette and rubbed her watery red-rimmed eyes. "Jesus Christ, you kids don't bring me nothing but trouble."

Audrey, who was lolling on the frayed couch, began to laugh. The television flickered a purple test pattern and hummed.

"Money," Suzy almost shouted. "That's what it means! We could get this place fixed up, maybe move to a better place, maybe get a dishwasher."

"I got four dishwashers," her mother muttered into her beer, "and I don't want no one doing nothing under my porch. You say there's a skull under there? How do you know that skull's an Indian's? How do you know we ain't gonna have cops out here asking questions and pressing charges? Maybe it's one of Lizzie's boyfriends under there. She's so goddamned messed up these days doing Jesus only knows what."

Audrey rolled off the couch, a grin floating like a soft light on her lips.

"I don't know what any of yas get up to anymore. None of yas tell me anything. You all just come and go like this was a goddamned hotel." An almost imperceptible fountain of smoke spilled from her nostrils. "My nerves are shot to hell."

Celeste wanted to say something. She felt a rush of words catch in her throat. If she could have set them free, she would have told them. She would have tried to recreate the vision she'd seen in the field. It was an omen, she was certain, of something good.

"For shit's sake," Suzy shouted, "you're always saying what you'd do with a little money."

"Don't you swear at me and don't you tell me what to do! You're just like Lizzie and the pair of you are just like your goddamned louse of a father. Why don't you go live with him? Why don't you go hunt him down, and ask him to put up with you?"

"Good-night," Audrey sang, drifting off towards her bedroom, drifting off to bed. Celeste struggled after her, leaving her mother and Suzy arguing, clunking down the wooden hall on her gleaming walker, propelling herself with the smoothness of the old parquet floor, sliding and shuffling and waddling until at last she reached the room.

The air was stale and somewhat rank. Upon a messy dressing table, Audrey had placed a potted hibiscus plant, a gift from a former lover. She squirted lemon cologne over the twisted sheets on her bed. She asked Celeste if she wanted some. The cool cologne tickled Celeste's bare arms, made her flesh pucker, her mouth water. Beads of fragrance filled her hair. She sat absorbed with her reflection in Suzy's large oval mirror. It was the only heirloom the house possessed, containing, or at least Celeste liked to think, all the people who'd ever gazed into it.

Their grandmother had bequeathed it to Suzy, though all the girls used it and often incorporated it into their make-believe fairytale games. "Mirror, mirror, on the wall, never let it crack and fall," Lizzie had declaimed. She always chose to be powerful rather than wicked and this spell, intended to ward off bad luck, she announced, was a testament to her strength and goodness. It never made sense to her that someone really powerful would want to do harm. Audrey, on the other hand, looked into the glass more passively. Even from a young age she'd found herself drawn to auras and images. Later, she'd discover the name for what she did: "skrying," like a shrill bird's cry, she thought, or the blade of a feather scraping the sky.

"You're in love, aren't you?" Audrey asked the mermaid now, her pupils reflecting large as coins. "He's a prince, isn't he?" she asked, and began to comb Celeste's shimmering hair.

"He came to you in the field today. He watched you while you were sleeping."

Celeste looked deeply into the mirror. She looked deeply into her own face. She tried to remember, to recover the moment. Panic rose in her reflection, a chalk cloud.

"Some people never feel love," Audrey told her. "I'll never feel it. I'm lucky." Her hands stroked her sister's hair, then caressed her straining throat, her cheeks. "Poor little mermaid," Audrey whispered. "Poor little soul." She kissed her sister's forehead with wax white lips.

Celeste rolled and floundered in her sheets all night long with her sister's voice—"He's a prince, isn't he?"—in her ears, her sister's caress on her hair. "Poor little mermaid." His warm wings spanned the world of her wonder, fluttered like pink petals on a flower.

As the sun rose, Celeste made her way through the newly bathed rye grass and meadow sweet of the field to the place she had fallen yesterday, threw herself into the damp weeds and called.

The sun filled the world with light. It drank cold dew from the grass, from the petals of flax that swayed and shook beyond her grasp. It woke the honeybees to map nectar. It warmed the sword-like mandibles of beetles, the bodies of goldenrod spiders; it directed the solitary scavenger ants, who were old and spent, to their treasures.

There were bones in the field where she lay. Hidden beneath the dowdy clay, the pelt of green. She'd frequented the field so often since she'd first seen her prince that she could now feel them move beneath her. Her scarlet face was a mark. When she arrived home, her sisters coated her peeling nose, her cheeks with aloe, but her lips, her mute lips, would not forget the taste of awe.

Lizzie argued with her mother. "What kind of life are you giving the mermaid? What kind of future?"

And her mother, secure with her metal cup, muttered, "I ain't God, I don't give futures!" Audrey stared into her red hibiscus, enthralled with the veins of its petal, protruding stamen and stigma, the blue of its aura, while Suzy saw her hands grope for treasure, considered how patiently she would turn small stones, how delicately she would remove the twigs and triangles of sorrel glass.

Celeste lay in the field day after day. She lay in the field waiting for the return while the world continued and the city glided beneath a numbing canvas of snow. Only the flaxen grass still rose, with its sharp seedless shaft; only this and the golden rod, crusting with ice at its font. She lay pressed like a specimen into the snow, her back into this moist ivory ossuary, and her indolent tongue called, as if it were a swallow flicking grief into the ponderous sky.

Lizzie, weeping with rage when her sister returned from the field, screamed at her mother.

"How could you let this happen! How can you let her spend her life alone!" She rushed to retrieve towels, to boil water, to make the shivering mermaid something hot to drink. "Jesus Christ, she's blue!" Lizzie shouted, removing the sheath that covered Celeste's lower half, massaging her flesh until it glowed.

"Don't you go telling me how to raise kids!" Her mother banged her metal cup on the kitchen table.

Celeste looked beyond the bent venetian blinds of the living room. The sky rolled over housetops, extended beyond the white field. It travelled with the train, away, over the turnpike, until night swallowed its swift flight.

Suzy smuggled bones and weapons into her bedroom. Behind her mother's back she flashed a quartz blade artefact she would sell. "I'm out of here," she called, looking at Lizzie.

"Where in hell are you going?" her mother demanded.

"Why don't you ever ask the mermaid that?" Lizzie said.

"Jesus Christ," her mother shouted.

"There are sickos out there!" Lizzie railed. "It's freezing cold. Anything could have happened to the mermaid. What's wrong with you?"

The front door slammed, Suzy was gone.

"Don't you judge me!" their mother warned Lizzie. "You've got no right judging me." Celeste fell asleep amidst the argument's din and dreamed of the field, how the sun had come again to the earth. How the sky had filled with gold, pushed off the winter, and opened to her call. A feather dropped from the sun. It sailed on spring's breath. On spring's currents it eddied, falling on her chest, her heart. And then the blistering shadow fell across her face.

Lizzie slapped a damp cloth on her sister's forehead. She held a glass of cool water to her peeling lips. "Drink," she told her. "Drink."

"God damn you," Lizzie shouted at her mother, "she needs a fuckin' antibiotic! How could you let her go this long without calling a doctor?"

"Where in hell have you been, anyway?" her mother slurred, unbalanced at the threshold of her daughters' room.

Celeste finished the water, extended the cup. "More?" Lizzie asked, pouring from an old tin vase she used as a pitcher.

"You answer me when I'm talking to you," her mother demanded. "What the hell right do you think you have anyway? What the hell right!" She swayed back and forth, her cigarette a firefly. "You and your goddamn sisters all taking off like that—leaving me like that." Lizzie raised the glass and placed it in Celeste's trembling hand. "You make me wanna puke!" she told her mother. "You make me wanna kill you!"

For a moment, her mother's mouth went slack. She threw her metal tumbler into the bedroom. It hit a wall, bounced on the floor, rolled. But she didn't follow through. She didn't grab Lizzie by the hair, shake her like a filthy rug. "You little bitch!" she muttered. Her voice cracking. "Go live with your goddamn old man then!"

Lizzie poured more water for Celeste. She swabbed her head with a fresh cloth. Her mother retrieved the rolling mug from the floor and struggled not to appear drunk as she stumbled away. Brown drops of beer rolled from her fingers. "Jesus Christ," she wheezed.

Celeste swallowed, her throat straining. Water dribbled from her mouth, falling, stinging on her chest. "Slowly," Lizzie told her. "Easy." She was afraid the water would come back up. Celeste drew the water in. She saw the sun above her, its molten wings. She extended her hands, her long fingers. "Wait," Lizzie told her. "Breathe."

For months, Celeste struggled with her breathing. She remained a prisoner of her bed, and Lizzie kept vigil. Even after the fever had gone, Lizzie and Suzy took turns nursing her until she was strong. All winter, Audrey had been missing. She'd hitchhiked to Arizona. The day the mermaid rose, she returned.

"You should have written," Lizzie scolded. "You should have at least let us know where you were."

Audrey put down her sweat-bleached pack, and held the mermaid's gaunt face in her hands. "I saw you in the desert," she whispered. "I saw you and I knew you'd be okay." Hail struck the window; it rattled the rotting wooden siding and lay on the creaking porch. "I have something for you," Audrey said, reaching into her pack, pulling from it a mound of crinkled tissue.

Celeste unwrapped the gift, peeling back layers of white, thinking of spring moths, of dandelion cotton and the spiked white heads of clover. She opened her gift, thinking of the field, how she would return now she was well, now it was spring.

It was a small milky green cactus she discovered. Patchwork seamed with an extravagant looping design, curved like the moon, and at its crest there was a minute pink flower, a daisy of sorts, but finer, with a fragile yellow calyx at its centre.

"It's an endangered species," Audrey told her. "I found it in the desert, and it said, 'take me to Celeste' so I dug it up. I smuggled it across the border for you."

"It's a goddamned Peyote cactus," Lizzie yelled. "Are you out of your mind?"

"The mermaid likes it," Audrey said. "She wants to keep it. Ask her." Celeste touched the flower.

"It was meant for her," Audrey said. "It told me!"

"Don't say things like that," Lizzie shouted. "You'll make her want to keep it." Even though she objected, Lizzie didn't take the cactus away.

Spring rain pelted down Monica Street, washing the sooty snow into the sewers, filling eavestroughs with rain. The pond in the field was replenished and new ponds extended, teaming with spiky mosquito larvae, long-legged water striders and springtail who gorged on milfoil. Celeste surged through mud and nubile shoots, through the strong straw mat of last year's meadow grass that had broken beneath the snow. Her feet slapped and splashed, the fluke of a happy whale, and she skidded, fell sometimes, lifted herself again on her chrome walker that gleamed with the spring light.

In the ponds she saw reflections. Clouds of twilight moving, breaking and rippling. The rain was not punishing, though its etchings were fixed and she stood, dripping, knowing the sun would find her before long.

And then, that day, Celeste had brought to the field a blanket, cheese and peanuts for the crows, and a loaf of white bread for herself. She had her clothing tied in a knapsack, collected the small ornaments her sisters had discarded as keepsakes, attached everything that she could to her walker and carried the cactus whose blossoms appeared to multiply like bright pink spores. She found her place and lay in the earth, surrounded by wet sounds and allowed her eyes to shut, for she knew it was wrong to gaze. The heat singed the lashes of her eyes, which opened, to behold the radiance, glowing, just before the sun was drawn behind a cloud.

Her cry was so pitiful, a caw that could not demand an embrace, but induced the wind to take pity and speak in her sister Audrey's voice, to offer the pink flowers of the cactus and a sea that would never stop.

The Boy Who Flew

WHEN THE TEACHERS at Thomas King Elementary were divvying up the grade sevens, Robert Dougal got put into a split class. This was because the city of Fontainebleau, with its sprawling blueprints and subsidized housing, was generating too many children, and this was also because Robert Dougal, or "Robbie" as his mother called him, was the kind of quiet and obedient boy who was useful in balancing out particularly disruptive classes.

While the school favoured larger class sizes over splits, in this instance a division seemed the only workable solution. The class was destined for one of the three new portables, and the students had all been as carefully selected as Robbie. The majority of the twenty students who would compose this small class were girls. Even the loudest and most demanding, Laurie LaFrambois, could be shamed into compliance. There would only be four other boys in the class besides Robbie, and these four, all with behavioural problems, were repeating grade eight. Each had also failed at least two times previously, though no teacher ever used that word—

the boys had been "held back" or "retained." This had been done to give them an opportunity to catch up. But they had not caught up; instead, they had fallen further and further behind. Now, they were no longer boys. Their legs would no longer fit beneath their desks; two of them had moustaches.

And so it was a priority that everything possible be done to get Dan Bouchard, Steve Caputo, Peter Galka, and Tony Deluca through.

Mr. Markovic, a broad-shouldered tall man who weighed two hundred and sixty pounds and walked with a thin wooden cane, would teach the class. He had once been a hopeful for professional football, but a car accident put an end to that. With the exception of his intimidating presence he had no particular gift for dealing with troubled or difficult students. Robbie had seen him pull boys from a line-up and whip them with his cane. But Mr. Markovic's violence wasn't the cause of Robbie's anxiety on this first day of school.

As he crossed Fontainebleau Park, Robbie's thoughts were on the terrible summer that had just passed. His mother had begun dating a man she'd met at Franco's, the coffee shop where she worked. Since the divorce, she'd not allowed herself to be involved with anyone, but she liked this man, who seemed gentle and considerate and fun. Most of the men she met at Franco's were coarse, they grabbed at her and the other waitress, Maureen, and made them both feel like meat on a hook, but Carl was a gentleman. When she finally brought him home, he shook Robbie's hand and gave him a large box wrapped in white paper with a red bow. Robbie never got presents if it wasn't Christmas or his birthday.

"Oh, you shouldn't have," Robbie's mother told the man.

Robbie ripped off the wrappings. It was a model kit. The picture on the box showed a see-through plastic man standing with his palms facing outward. You could see all his innards and the bones of his feet that seemed to float above the stand he was affixed to. Robbie opened the box and examined the pieces. There were tiny bones that assembled into a skeleton—lungs and kidneys, a liver, and a brain. Carl pulled a tube of model glue out of his jacket pocket.

"Better make sure you open a window when you build it," he said.

Robbie's mother gently touched her boy's head.

"Thank you," Robbie said.

The instructions were hard to follow, so the man said he'd help. He sat right up close to Robbie and showed him how the ribs fit into the sternum. "I would have killed for something like this when I was a kid," he told Robbie.

"It must have been very expensive," Robbie's mother said, her hands fluttering.

"Just money and fair words," the man replied. He winked at Robbie.

The following day he came to help Robbie with the model again, and the day after that as well. Robbie's mother took advantage of him being there and went shopping. She didn't like to leave Robbie alone. "I'm so glad you get along with Carl," she'd said.

As Robbie approached the schoolyard now, he thought of those days. Perhaps if he'd spoken up, told his mother how he'd felt, the entire summer would have been different. Perhaps she'd have stopped seeing that man and everything would have gone on just as it was. His feet would feel the way they used to—not like the see-through model man's feet that weren't really touching the ground; and his thoughts wouldn't always be going back there—trying to figure out what he did wrong and how he might have changed it.

The bell rang and Robbie found his place in line. He noticed the grass on the school's playing field was yellow and spiky and beaten down, but the bright sunshine gave it a strange otherworldly glow like something from outer space. There were crows that didn't really look like crows, purposefully hopping along the perimeter of the schoolyard. They could be aliens from another galaxy, Robbie thought. Lately, he'd been thinking a lot about worlds beyond this world, about space invaders and extra-terrestrial visitations. This too was something the man was responsible for.

The tarmac under Robbie's shoes was losing its stickiness. His feet felt as if they were beginning to float. Then, he was back there, on that awful day, driving in the man's car and hearing his mother's voice screaming and crying and begging God for something—but he couldn't make out her words.

The grade sevens moved into the portable, but he remained exactly where he was. A new line was forming behind him—a cluster of girls: Sara Fairchild, Melanie Jones, Margaret Smith, and the four difficult boys who were as tall as the teachers.

"Go, Dougal!" Mr. Markovic shouted.

"Ya Doo-gul!" Tony Deluca mocked and Mr. Markovic gave him a sharp swat with his cane. "Yowy!" he yelped, skipping away. His three friends laughed.

Robbie walked slowly up the stairs. He could smell Mr. Markovic's sweat. He was thankful to see that his desk was nowhere near the other boys, but panicked to see girls surrounded it.

"Hey, look at the fair-eee," Tony Deluca said.

Mr. Markovic began calling the roll.

The centre of gravity shifted in Robbie. In spite of himself, he thought of the tiny innards in the model. He saw his own small intestine being shoved into his oesophagus. It was difficult to breathe. "Hey Dooo-Gulll... you a fair-eee?" Dan Bouchard whispered loudly.

Mr. Markovic called Robbie's name twice, but Robbie couldn't hear it. He couldn't hear the students laughing. He couldn't hear Steve Caputo choking "queer." Finally, a girl tapped him with a plastic ruler. "You got a problem, Dougal?" Mr. Markovic asked.

"No sir," Robbie said, but as soon as the Lord's Prayer had been recited and Oh Canada sung, he slipped away again.

He considered the oddness of it—the sensation. It made him think of antigravity chambers and astronauts doing summersaults in the air. He fought to stay inside with his bones and blood and muscles, but it was as if some great magnet kept yanking him out—yanking him out and dragging him into space, and then he couldn't help thinking of aliens and wondering if they really did exist.

"You must never say anything to anyone," his mother had said. It was the first time he had felt that pull. She threw out the model while he slept, got rid of the man's photograph. Other physical reminders vanished—a baseball cap, a barbecue fork, a pen from the Holiday Inn.

Robbie's mother went to the beauty parlour and got her hair done, put on a perky dress and smiled. "It really did happen, didn't it mom?" Robbie asked.

"What really happened, Robbie?" Her eyes were wide, cornflower blue. "Darling, why don't you go outside and play before it gets too dark?"

Mr. Markovic had his back to the class. He was writing a poem on the board. All of the students were meant to copy it into their workbooks and memorize it. Dan Bouchard, Steve Caputo, Peter Galka, and Tony Deluca shot spitballs and gave Mr. Markovic the finger. They also made faces at the prim girls who attempted to alert him. The bell rang. Robbie snapped back into his body. He looked around to see if he could get a sense of what he'd missed. All of the girls were copying. He opened one of the workbooks that someone had placed in front of him, took the blue cap off a pen and wrote.

The girls closed their notebooks and stacked them in their desks. "When you're finished, you can leave in an orderly fashion," Mr. Markovic said. They filed out, row by row. The boys in the front had all earned detentions. Robbie wasn't sure when that happened, but Dan Bouchard was moaning, "I gotta have a smoke," and Steve Caputo was pretending to sneeze so he could say "hummer".

Robbie scribbled the poem into his notebook as quickly as he could and escaped the portable. His muscles were weak and his feet trembled. As he made his way across the school's amber playing field, he was unaware that he was being followed. He had not heard Peter Galka call him "faggot" or Tony Deluca shouting for him to wait. He was watching the crows who seemed to be all knowing, and feeling the pull of the magnet that was making him think of the day it had happened. He'd told his mother he was too sick to go with the man, but she'd insisted. "Carl doesn't have a son and you don't have a father, and boys without fathers need to do things with men."

Had the man heard her lecture? Had he come into the house and caught those final words—"do things!" Robbie wondered.

The man's car was a Ford sedan with a rusting fender. It smelled of gasoline, fast food French fries, pizza, and mould in spite of the pine tree air freshener that hung from the rearview mirror. In the back, the man carried a chainsaw. He'd been a logger once and still called the machine ole trusty. The car's original upholstery was encased in fuzzy plaid, and the passenger seat reclined much too far. Robbie struggled to see out the window, to watch the houses on his street passing. He felt an impulse to wave—to wave goodbye—even though there was no one in the street. They turned off Queen Elizabeth and onto

Rossini, but after that, Robbie couldn't say. Then, the city of Fontainebleau was far behind them and they were speeding along the 402 towards Essex.

"You wanna see something neat?" the man asked. Robbie remembered nodding. Great green oceans of corn swayed beside the highway and beyond the railroad tracks. Large black clusters of crows fanned above them. "You know anything about UFOs?" the man asked. "You ever heard of crop circles?" The man was talking too fast for Robbie to answer. "There's a great big design in the cornfield out there," the man said, extending his hand. "Some people say it's a joke, but some people think aliens made it. I'll show you if you want." He turned off the highway and onto a dirt road. "I know boys who'd kill to see something like that." Swells of grey dust rose like smog as clumps of dry earth hit the underside of his car. The man was driving slower now. "It's just a little ways down here," he said.

Robbie had walked out into the field with the man and saw how some of the corn had been bent straight down. The man had put one hand on Robbie's shoulder. He was saying something about aliens, how some people claimed to have been taken into outer space by them, stripped naked, tied up, and humiliatingly probed. He was talking on and on, but Robbie couldn't hear him. There was a ringing in his ears. "What had he expected to find in that field?" The police officer, Sergeant Gilley, would ask him that. "Did he really think there was anything out there?" In his mind, he saw the model with its transparent flesh and the way the man's fingers had probed it. "Why would he go with the man into the field?" There was no reason why he should go, yet he'd walked right out into that field with the man.

It was Robbie's thumping heart that brought him back to his body as he entered Fontainebleau Park. Tony Deluca and Peter Galka were only a yard behind him now. "Wait up, fag-boy," Tony Deluca shouted.

Maybe he should have stopped—shown them that he wasn't afraid—but the muscles in his legs began running, and the bones of his feet came away from the earth. There were corn tassels in front of his eyes as he ascended, bending and bobbing, flinging sticky pollen everywhere, and crows, which he suddenly realized, were intergalactic rovers spying on the earth. From his vantage, he could see the tops of their fanning wings before they dispersed, and beneath them, a boy, naked in a corn field.

He wondered if the boy would tell anyone what had happened, and then began thinking about aliens, and how when they let you go, if you tell people, no one believes you. He was aware of the peaceful clouds, astounded by the vibrancy and expanse of the empty sky. He looked down on himself one last time and gasped for air, dazzled by the transparency of his body.

Illusions

TONY DELUCA was his usual troublemaking, ball-breaking, smut-raking self. He went to bed late this particular night after leaving bags of flaming dog shit on porches, terrorizing resident felines, and tagging, with black spray paint, the windows of the portable classrooms at his former public school, Thomas King Elementary. He hadn't thought of Kevin Robinson since his death, and couldn't explain to himself now, as he switched off his light, why his old friend should appear, looming larger than life in the empty amphitheatre of his mind.

He didn't know if maybe the news he'd received about Julia Wilson that afternoon had triggered something, but every time he shut his eyes, Kevin was there. Kevin, not as he'd been in life, full of piss and vinegar and danger, always figuring out ways to do a bunk, always scheming, but as the corpse he'd become, that husk of Kevin that Sanderson's funeral parlour decorated with makeup and a black dorky suit, and laid out in a box like a big plastic doll.

They'd stuck balls of cotton in his mouth to puff up his cheeks and pasted a ratty hairpiece on his head to hide the tire tread on his skull. Tony had gone to pay his respects, as they say, and couldn't stop laughing. He'd laughed so hard, tears washed down his face, he couldn't breathe. Everyone thought he was blubbering. He went home that afternoon, and for some reason never thought of Kevin again until tonight.

Now, he blinked and noticed Kevin's eyes sunk back into their sockets; there were deep black circles underneath. "Tired," he thought, and wrapped his pillow over his head, but the image of Kevin wouldn't go away. It flared like an ember, startling him to wakefulness whenever he'd find himself dropping off to sleep.

Somehow he'd lost the thread of Kevin. All his memories of their times together had terminated as conclusively as the end of Kevin's life. He'd forgotten their friendship, their affiliation, the hours they'd spent together each and every day. He'd forgotten their conversations, their scams, their plans, but now, with Kevin in his mind, recollections surfaced like dead walleye on Lake Erie.

There was snow, an avalanche of snow, pelting down upon them like broken glass, and the metal sheets, destined for Chrysler's, that they'd hauled from a train and pulled all the way across the drifted fields, all the way across the roads, all the way up that perfect curve of a hill in Fontainebleau Park. Every winter, ever since he'd moved from the West End, he and Kevin had raced down that hill. Kevin had taught him some quick finger manoeuvres, and Tony had stolen his gym teacher's stopwatch right out of his pocket so they could train to go faster. "He doesn't need it," Kevin had convinced him. "Anyways, the school will buy him a new one." Tony always felt okay about lifting the stuff Kevin told him to take.

They tore down the hill, streaks of silver, on those metal sheets: fifteen, fourteen, thirteen seconds. With each return they'd skim off more time. Kevin added Crisco to the bottom of his sled, he hauled bricks and stones, and bags of sand, he stole his mother's spray bottle and filled it with water to ice a track. "I bet we can break the world's record," Kevin had said. He was always on about breaking records, always on about accomplishing impossible things, and this was why, Tony considered now, he'd wanted to hang around with Kevin, because Kevin never allowed things to get boring.

More than two years had passed since Kevin's last descent, and never once did Tony find himself reliving it. It had been absorbed by the snow and horror, sucked from him before he'd even acknowledged it: Kevin bisecting the road, and the car bisecting Kevin. Tony had looked beyond, past the brown hood of the station wagon. He'd expected to see Kevin there, on the other side. He was always playing tricks, pulling quarters out of his mouth, making ping pong balls appear.

"It's an illusion, you dink," he'd tell the astounded Tony, and Tony was sure that the station wagon was just another stunt. "Wow," he recalled thinking, "I wonder if he can teach me to do that?" He was sure the station wagon guy must have been in on it. There was no way you could pull off a stunt like that alone, but he couldn't see Kevin in the drifts across the street and the station wagon was spinning like it was out of control. Kevin's moronic little brother, Jimmy, was shouting something, and then the next thing Tony knew, some cop came and hauled Jimmy off and told everyone to go home.

He must have walked home that day, must have understood that it wasn't a trick, but there was a large, empty hole in his memory that refused to be filled. Kevin had once told him that nothing ever really disappears. This was after he'd made Steve Caputo's and Pete Galka's hot lunch money vanish inside of a cardboard box. "How many times do I have to tell you, jerkoff," he'd whispered, because Tony was always so ridiculously impressed, "none of this stuff is for real—I got the money in my pocket."

The two of them thumbed to Mac's Milk that day; the girl at the cash register sold Kevin cigarettes. He chatted with her like he'd known her all his life; meanwhile, his hands were invisibly cleaning out the candy counter, right under her nose. He backed up into the magazine rack, and a couple of porn mags disappeared. Tony watched it all in the big round mirrors at the back of the store. If the cashier had been watching those mirrors instead of being sidetracked by Kevin, she might have seen it all too, plus catch Tony stuffing bags of chips and hickory sticks into the lining of his jacket. "Things never really disappeared," Kevin had told Tony, and when Tony stole things, he knew this was true, but he always had a hard time believing it when he watched Kevin.

They'd gone to Kevin's room that day, as they usually did. His mom was always working, and his brother could be tricked into leaving them alone. Kevin fixed the door so no one could open it, then he unloaded his booty of candy and pulled the magazines out of his baggy jeans. Tony emptied the contents of his jacket lining onto Kevin's messy bunk. Kevin lit a smoke: "Paradise," he announced.

The two of them ate peanut butter cups, chocolate bars and smarties and looked at the bright pink snatches and tits of naked girls in various states of restraint. Tony had never seen anything like it. It made him feel sick, but he didn't want to tell Kevin. He wondered if girls really looked like that down there, all raw and slick, like the inside of a mouth.

One of the girls was hanging hogtied in the air. "A real swinger," Kevin pointed.

"Yeah," Tony said, his stomach lurching at the sight of the helpless girl's puckered asshole.

"I wouldn't mind getting inside of that," Kevin said.

"Yeah," Tony repeated, trying to feign enthusiasm, trying to stop the urge to gag.

Kevin got a boner. You could see the crotch of his baggy jeans poking out. "I'd like to tie Julia Wilson up, so she couldn't get away, then bang her to death, she's such a cock-tease."

"Yeah," Tony said, seeing pretty Julia Wilson in his mind's eye. It was impossible to imagine that she might possess the gaping pink slash or puckered asshole of these magazine scags.

Kevin unzipped his pants and let his boner pop out of his underwear. "Well, will you look at that?" he said, in mock amazement, like some dork might say at witnessing a lame magic trick.

"Let's see yours." He made a grab at Tony's pants.

"Cut it out, moron!" Tony said.

Kevin laughed. "No *hard* feelings?" He laughed again.

Tony knew that Kevin expected him to be hard, that guys were supposed to get that way when they looked at magazines like these, but for the life of him, the only thing being stirred was the contents of his stomach and his salivary glands.

"You ain't a faggot, are you?" Kevin asked.

"Screw off, shithead!" Tony said.

"Cause if you're a faggot," Kevin continued, "I don't want you in my house."

"For fuck sake, I ain't a faggot!" Tony shouted, trying to will himself into a state of sexual arousal. "I just feel a little sick."

Kevin put his thumb and forefinger on his penis and began rubbing. He dropped the magazine with the hogtied girl squarely in his line of vision. "You can go hang out with my fairy brother if you're a faggot," Kevin said.

The truth was, Tony was closer in age to Jimmy than Kevin, and when he'd originally moved here from the West End, Jimmy had been his best friend. They used to play with plastic soldiers and trade hockey cards and shit, but once Tony met Kevin, he pretended he'd always despised Jimmy, just like Kevin did.

"I ain't a faggot," Tony said again, touching the crotch of his pants, trying to make himself hard. He didn't look at either of the magazines, but the pictures of those slick twats and wrinkly assholes wouldn't leave his head. Now it was Kevin who was lodged there, larger than life, making him remember and intruding on his sleep.

"Nothing really disappears," Kevin said again, as he'd said long ago, and all the memories that had vanished with his death were crowding back, packing Tony's skull uncomfortably, like large black birds, giving him a headache and making him toss and turn.

He'd thought of Julia Wilson that day, imagined her long dark hair fanning over a white see-through dress that was as silky as the ribbon of a baby blanket he'd once loved. It was finally this memory of the blanket, the one that eventually he wore to a rag and had to throw out, that aroused him. It allowed him to join with Kevin in what the priest at his church called "self-abuse", and what Kevin called "choking the chicken".

When they finished and cleaned themselves up, Kevin made Tony promise that he'd never tell anyone what they did together. He produced a razor blade and pulled a drawstring from a pair of dirty sweatpants. "Cut my hand," he told Tony, who timidly took the blade, thinking of those scags' twats all over again, as blood flowered from the gash in Kevin's hand.

He looked away and barely felt Kevin slice his palm.

"Now, we're blood brothers," Kevin said, binding their wounded hands with the drawstring. "That means if you ever say anything, if you ever lie to me, or do anything I tell you not to do, you're cursed for the rest of your life."

"What about you?" Tony protested.

"I ain't going to tell anyone anything," Kevin said.

It might have been later that afternoon, or some other time, that they'd gone out to the railway tracks and tried to make a train derail. They'd found a switch, and Kevin kicked off its lock. "Misdirection," he'd said, as he fiddled with its position, "that's the key to all magic." Tony remembered how often Kevin fell into talk about magic, and how obsessed he'd been in figuring out the way certain illusions worked. He knew a lot about famous escape artists, all kinds of personal trivia, like the fact he told Tony that day about Bess Houdini dying on a train of a heart attack. Tony assumed the heart attack had been brought on by a derailment, but Kevin said, "Don't be such a dink-brain," so Tony shut up.

When they heard the train's whistle in the distance, they climbed to the top of a tree to watch the carnage. They speculated over all the possible ways it might crash. They imagined great explosions, people screaming, sirens wailing, but nothing could have surprised them more than when the train effortlessly barrelled past.

"What a gyp!" Kevin shouted.

"Yeah, what a rip-off," Tony said.

They shimmied down the tree and went back to inspect the switch. "I don't get what we done wrong," Kevin howled. "It shoulda worked." He got down on his hands and knees, the reek of creosote and hot steel enveloping him. "Well, will you look at that?" he said, just like he'd done when he unleashed his boner. "The train pushed this doohickey here," he pointed at a small metal gadget, "right to the place it's supposed to be. Some trick, huh?" He laughed. All the way through the muddy field, back towards Monica Street, he talked about illusions and a guy, Horace Goldin, who sawed girls in half.

"For real?" Tony had asked, feeling nausea sweep over him, as he thought of those porn magazines and the scags inside that may just as well have been cut apart; they were that gross.

"Smack yourself in the face, whenever you're gonna ask me, 'for real'," Kevin said.

"Why?" Tony asked.

"To save me from having to do it, you idiot. Ain't I talking about illusions?"

Kevin went on to explain how Goldin did all sorts of interesting stuff, like shooting girls out of cannons and making tigers disappear; then, in order to beat another magician out, Goldin started hacking girls apart. He put them in a box where their feet and head could stick through, only it wasn't really their feet in the bottom of the box, it just looked that way. Meanwhile, the girl wrapped her legs up near her shoulders. The audience watched while he sawed through the box. "Everyone was expecting to see blood and guts and shit like that," Kevin said, "just like we were with the train."

"Neat," Tony said.

"But there was no blood and guts," Kevin continued. "Goldin just slides the two sides of the box apart, and it looks like the girl's in two pieces, then he pushes it back together, and bingo, the girl gets out, not a mark on her."

As they headed back to the projects, Kevin proposed that they try to cut a girl in half.

"What girl?" Tony asked. He couldn't think of any who'd let him and Kevin touch them, let alone cut them apart.

"Maybe Julia Wilson," Kevin said, like he wasn't joking. "I think we ought to pay her a visit."

"She don't want to see us," Tony said.

"What makes you so sure?" Kevin replied.

Julia lived in a mansion on Riverside Drive and should have been going to Riverside Secondary, when she wasn't skipping, instead of M.F. Hepburn, the school Kevin attended occasionally. There were all kinds of rumours as to why Julia ended up in such a crappy school, rumours that her mother had put her into Hepburn because she knew the academic standards were low and that the teachers weren't beyond bribes, rumours that Julia was flinging with a math teacher at Riverside, that she'd been expelled her very first day for stealing money and cigarettes from her homeroom teacher and that she'd tried to seduce a hitman to knock off one of her classmate rivals. Kevin couldn't care less why she was at Hepburn. He just wanted to get into her pants, and although he knew the likelihood was extremely remote, and if it meant her consent, wholly impossible, he'd decided from the moment he'd seen her that this goal was something worth pursuing.

It was more than the fact she was beautiful that enticed Kevin and virtually every other male at Hepburn. She was desired because she was so obviously unattainable. Kevin had once told Tony that when he looked at her, he thought of this sugary, sparkly angel in a snow globe that his Gran had given him one Christmas. He couldn't have been any older than four, and it annoyed him that he couldn't open the globe and touch the delicate little angel inside. His Gran tried to quell his tantrum by showing him how to turn the sphere and make the snow fall, but he wouldn't be subdued. He hurled the gift at a wall. It cracked like an egg; a clear liquid, like albumen, suffused the floor. Gran had shouted at him and his mother had spanked him so hard that he couldn't sit down, but none of that mattered because he'd been able to pry the little angel from the wreckage, though she was far less impressive between his fingers than she had been in her magic sparkly world.

Julia's world also appeared sparkly and magical from the outside. She was a rich kid, aloof and solitary. She wore the best clothes, the best shoes. Her designer handbags were always stuffed with cash. She had the most expensive school supplies, a pack of sixty Laurentien pencil crayons, instead of the usual eight. Kevin realized that if he did get into her pants, she'd be just like the snow globe angel, that without a magic bubble intact, Julia would quickly lose her appeal. This knowledge, however, did nothing to squelch his desire.

Tony followed Kevin through the projects. He'd first seen Julia Wilson when he was repeating grade eight for the third time and waiting for Kevin at Hepburn. He knew that even when he got sprung from Thomas King, he'd never make it to Hepburn, and no one like Julia would ever be sent to Tecumseh Vocational, the place he was headed.

Julia reminded him of one of those long-necked, alabaster-flesh goddesses that Kevin had told him the Greeks used to worship. There'd been a picture of one, with really big knockers, on the outside wall of Athena's Bar and Grill before it became The Pizza Palace and was replaced by a lion dressed like a king. He'd had lots of fantasies about Julia, fantasies about holding her hand and walking with her in the moonlight by the Ambassador Bridge. He fantasized about meeting her one day at Hepburn and her inviting him on a picnic by the Detroit River. In his reveries, he would discover that she too was a lover of peanut butter and jelly sandwiches and Oreo cookies, that she too opened the cookies up and ate the creamy centres first, that she too shared his opinion that ketchup was a perfect food. "Wow, we have so much in common," she said in his daydream. "Would you like to go steady with me?" And this was always when his fantasy broke apart. "Me? You mean, me, Tony Deluca?" He saw and heard himself saying. "I can't believe it, she wants me? Do you hear that, world?" He shouted, hoisting himself onto one of the river's guard railings: "She wants ME . . . TONY DELUCA!!!"

"Well, I thought I did." Even though it was just in his imagination, the disdain in her voice was palpable, and every time he ran that fantasy, it made his heart break over and over again. "I had no idea you were such a loser," she said. "I'd never go out with you!"

"Wait, Julia," he pleaded. "I can be different. I can change."

"Loser," the girl of his dreams taunted. "Why don't you just get lost?"

He remembered that this was the fantasy replaying as he and Kevin got to Rivard Street and stuck out their thumbs. A truck stopped almost right away. The guy in the cab wanted to know if they knew where he could buy some weed. "Yeah," Kevin said, even though he didn't really. "There's a place on Riverside Drive. I'll show you, if you want."

"Thanks, man," the guy said.

"Don't mention it," Kevin said.

They travelled pretty much in silence, with just the radio station CKLW playing hits in the background. When they got to Riverside Drive, Kevin made the guy slow down and acted like he was searching for a house number, but he was really searching to see which house looked the most uninhabited.

"That's the house, right there," Kevin said, pointing to an impressive split level with an open, empty two-car garage and no lights. "Ask for Jcrry, and say Dcrck scnt you."

"Wow, thanks a lot man," the driver said, full of genuine gratitude.

Julia Wilson's house was in walking distance, and so Tony and Kevin started on their trek, but couldn't resist looking back at the man, every few minutes, standing at the door, ringing the bell, waiting.

They'd been to Julia's house once before on Halloween. Kevin had wanted to see where she lived. Even though it was October and frosty, he'd been able to find a couple of sheets on a clothes-line. He shook them to make them less stiff and carefully determined where he should cut the ghostly eye holes.

"But I don't want to be a ghost," Tony complained. "It's dorky."

"No one's gonna know it's us," Kevin said. He made Tony put the sheet on.

The house looked different now at dusk, shed of its Halloween decorations. The gates, which had been retracted, were now closed fast, and the house, looming beyond the curving stone path and topiary, had the appearance of a prison.

"So what do we do now?" Tony asked, surveying the gate's eight-foot pointed bars.

"Simple," Kevin said, typing a number into a keypad on a post. "Open sesame." The gates slowly rolled apart.

"How come you know the code?" Tony asked.

"They don't call me Houdini Robinson for nothing," he said.

He moved so swiftly up the path, Tony had to break into a run to keep up. "Where's the fire?" he whispered loudly.

"In my fucking pants, dink-brain," Kevin countered. "Move your ass."

Kevin knew the trees were rigged with security cameras, that the faster they moved, the less likely they'd be caught by a camera's sweeping lens, but, at the time, he didn't bother to explain this to Tony. As they got closer to the house and Tony could see the countless windows, he wondered how Kevin planned on finding Julia. She could have been anywhere in that beast of a house, or she could have been anywhere outside of it. For all they knew, she could have been in the Bahamas. It seemed crazy to be calling on her like this, but a lot of stuff Kevin did was crazy, and that was partly, at least, what made it worth doing.

When they'd come to the house in disguise at Halloween, there were orange lights in the bushes and a costume party in progress. Julia's mother hosted a masquerade ball every year as a fundraiser for the Heart and Stroke Foundation. Kevin and Tony slipped into the yard with the neighbourhood trick-or-treaters. They found Julia almost right away. She was on the front porch dressed like a princess, throwing chocolate bars at open bags.

"Trick-or-treat," Kevin yelled, in a high, put-on voice.

"Aren't you a little old to be trick-or-treating?" Julia asked.

"It's me, Kevin," Kevin whispered.

"Who?" Julia's pretty brow furrowed.

"Kevin Robinson," he whispered again.

"I have no idea who you are," Julia said.

Kevin explained that they went to the same school, that they were in the same grade, that they were even in some of the same classes. He explained that he was the guy in science who'd rescued her pearl earring from a laboratory beaker, that he was the guy in English who put love notes in her desk.

"Are you some kind of demented stalker?" she asked. "Do I need to call the police?"

Kevin and Tony left pronto. The last thing they wanted was to get pushed around by some cop. "It's all bluff," Kevin finally said when they reached the sidewalk. "She'd never call the cops."

"How can you be so sure?" Tony asked.

"'Cause she's crazy about me," Kevin said. "She's just pretending."

"Why?" Tony wanted to know.

"Because, dink-brain, she wants to keep it a secret."

Tony fought the impulse to ask "Why?" again. He fought the impulse to say, "You're so full of shit your eyes are brown!" He didn't like Kevin calling him names. He didn't like Kevin thinking he was stupid. They threw firecrackers into mail slots on the way home; they smashed jack-o-lanterns, and soaped windows with a big bar of lifebuoy that Kevin just happened to have under his ghost sheet in the pocket of his jacket. Kevin told Tony that Houdini died on Halloween, that he said if it were possible to return as a spirit, that's what he'd do, and that ever since he died, people have been having séances Halloween night to bring him back. "You're my blood brother," he told Tony. "If I die before you, you have to promise you'll try to get in touch with me, just like I was Houdini."

"You ain't gonna die," Tony said.

"But just say I do. You got to promise."

They didn't talk about Julia Wilson again for a long time, but Julia didn't disappear. "Nothing ever disappears," Kevin's voice rang out in Tony's aching, sleepless head. They were back there, at Julia's house, and Kevin was climbing a white trellis, whispering as loudly as he possibly dared, "What light through yonder window breaks?"

Kevin and Julia had been studying *Romeo and Juliet* in English class. Kevin thought it sucked, but Julia was crazy about it. Their teacher made them act out some of the scenes. Kevin memorized his lines. He wanted to impress Julia. A pane just above the trellis slid open.

"Shush!" Julia whispered.

"It's me, Kevin," Kevin announced.

"I know, dummy. Are you going to come in?"

Kevin hoisted himself up. He tiptoed on the very top of the trellis and shimmied into Julia's window. Tony wondered when he and Julia had gotten so chummy. He didn't know if he ought to wait, or climb up the trellis too. He wondered what Kevin and Julia were doing. He hated to think of Julia as a scag.

"She's such a fuckin' cock-tease," Kevin said when he jumped down.

"Is she gonna let us saw her in half?" Tony asked.

"Yeah," Kevin said dismissively.

They hitched back to Kevin's house. "Say someone you want to bang promises she'll consider it if you do something you don't want to do," Kevin said out of the blue.

"Like what?" Tony asked.

"Like something you don't get no fun from, and is probably gonna land you in jail for close to the rest of your life."

Tony knew Kevin was talking about Julia. "Beats me," he said. "Maybe once we make the magic box and slice her in half, it'll be such a great trick she'll let us both bang her for nothing."

"You're such a loser," Kevin said.

Tony couldn't remember if he went home that night or if he slept over at Kevin's. He couldn't remember if Kevin finally told him what Julia wanted or if he'd mentioned Julia again. All he recalled was his excitement at the prospects of building that magic box and watching Kevin cut Julia in half. If they made the box light enough, it was a trick they could do almost any place. He'd seen lots of magicians on TV, Ed Sullivan and *The Tonight*

Show. Maybe he and Kevin and Julia could go on some show, have lots of fans. Maybe they could do shows in New York and Vegas, places where all the big names went. "Tony Deluca and Friends"—he imagined potential show names for their act: "Tony Deluca's Magic Box."

It might have been the next day that Tony went rooting around in the new construction of one of the burgeoning subdivisions of Fontainebleau. There were dozens of houses in progress and no workmen in sight, which must have meant it was the weekend. He'd brought a kid's wagon and a few bungee cords, and walked off with four sheets of plywood and a tool belt. Later he visited the hardware store on Rivard Street and slid a handsaw into the lining of his jacket, and a bag of nails and six packages of hinges into his pockets. He'd always been good at building stuff, always been good at fitting things together. He drew up a plan for the magic box.

Kevin only added leg shackles. "If it looks like we've locked her legs down, the audience will never suspect when she moves them," Kevin said.

Tony measured and sawed and knocked the box together. He added the leg shackles inside and the fake feet that popped out with the press of a button. He painted the box midnight blue and stencilled on bright yellow stars. Even Kevin said it looked cool. Then Kevin up and got killed before they'd become famous, before they'd had a chance to be asked onto *The Tonight Show*, before they'd even got to cut Julia in half. "What a gyp!" Tony heard Kevin's voice saying in his mind, even though Kevin never could have said that because he would have been dead and not known what a gyp it was.

Tony forgot all about Kevin after he died, but he didn't forget about the magic box. For a long time, he kept it safe out by the railroad tracks in a broken-down holding shed. He visited it every day—every day he imagined himself in Vegas or New York, with a chauffeur driven limousine and crowds of people begging for his autograph. It was only recently that the fantasy changed—that people booed and laughed. "What kind of magician are you? Your *magic box* probably doesn't even work."

"Oh yeah?" he said, but that was all, because he didn't know what else to say. He didn't know for certain if the box did work.

Finally he got tired of feeling bad. He decided to find Julia Wilson. He didn't know if she was still at Hepburn, but figured he'd go and see. It was morning and snowing and the school grounds were desolate when he arrived. He didn't know exactly what he'd say if he found her, or why he'd brought his old sheet metal sled. The bell rang just as Julia's mother pulled up in her Lincoln and Julia hurried out. He watched as her mother drove away, and Julia, seeing she was free, turned and bolted from the school. He followed her as she headed down an empty alley.

"You promised," he confronted her, when he caught her up, "you said you'd let us cut you in half."

"I have no idea what you're talking about," she said, walking faster.

"I made the magic box so that you'd fit inside," Tony said, twisting in front of her, blocking her path.

"Are you some kind of crazy stalker?" she asked. "Do I need to call the police?"

"I know you're bluffing," Tony said. "I know you won't call the police."

"Are you out of your mind?" Julia pushed his shoulder. "I don't even know who you are."

That's when Tony grabbed her around the neck and covered her lips with his gloved hand. "I'm Tony Deluca," he said. "Tony Deluca, and don't you never forget that!" He knocked her down behind a dumpster and shoved one of his gloves into her mouth. He hogtied her with the strap of her designer purse, but he doesn't remember hauling her onto his sled, he doesn't remember dragging her to the holding shed or untying her and placing her in the magic box.

Tonight, the newspapers said she was missing, and Tony's head is splitting open with the effort of trying to recall. "Nothing ever disappears," Kevin's voice pounds in his brain, but whatever happened to Julia next has become so completely inaccessible that it may as well have vanished, for no matter what Tony does, he can't bring the memory back.

The Bone Game

TANUSHRI IS ADMITTED to Hotel Dieu Hospital at midnight and gives birth to a daughter, even though she should have given birth to a son. She obeyed her late mother's instructions and ate red, salty meat each day of her pregnancy, even though she hated the sinewy texture of animal flesh, even though the thought of any creature being killed for its carcass brought despair to her heart; but her mother wrote with such authority from her deathbed: "You must eat the meat as raw as you possibly can, remove any bones and place them in a cloth sack, then tie the sack and tuck it under the foot of your bed." It had worked for Tanushri's sisters as well as for all her aunts, but this time, obviously, it had failed.

When Tanushri's husband, Anil, arrived at the hospital, she had almost recovered from her tears, but when he expressed his grave disappointment, both in their child and in their marriage, her sobbing began again. Not only had Tanushri failed to bear a son, but since their wedding twelve months before, he pointed out, she had totally let her appearance go. She had become fat. Her face puffy, her eyes shrivelled and red from all the tears she'd shed.

"Would it hurt," Anil asked, "to comb your hair, to put on a bit of lipstick, to make yourself look presentable for your husband?"

Privately, and sometimes not so privately, Anil laments the fact he selected a bride solely on the strength of photographs his father had assembled. He values beauty greatly in women, he confides to Paul Markovic, one of his Friday night drinking companions, and Tanushri was, by far, the loveliest flower in the bouquet. But the flower went to seed and there was nothing other than beauty she possessed. She is not an educated woman and cannot speak intelligently about current events or literature. When he attempts to discuss his problems, Tanushri makes the most naïve remarks, demonstrating constantly her ignorance of worldly matters and her childish views on human nature. To all of this, Paul Markovic can relate. He too married a woman he'd outgrown, but Anil has it even worse. His wife, he says, spends her time pining for her family and grieving for her dead mother, and seems incapable of adjusting to life in Fontainebleau. She cannot keep house, nor can she grocery shop alone, and she sets fire to virtually every meal she cooks. There is nothing Paul, nor anyone, can do or say to ease Anil's burdens. Even the topless dancers at Club Venus fail to cheer him.

When Tanushri arrives home with the fretful baby, Anil's sorrows only multiply. The child, who Tanushri calls Tejas, is singularly without charm. Anil has never seen an infant like it. Most babies have some beguiling quality or other—some inherent appeal that nature furnishes as fortification against parental unkindness and neglect—but this child possesses none. It does not have the wide innocent eyes of an infant, its cheeks are not chubby and round, its nose is not a tiny jewel, and its lips are nothing like a rosebud. In fact, its features are startlingly sharp like a hawk's. But this alone is not to blame for the child's appearance—it is also the set of her eyes, the slant of her jaw, the distance between her nose and lip—all of these things conspire in bringing about an appearance that is more than simply unattractive. This baby, which Anil has fathered and which Tanushri has borne, is decidedly mean looking, and it pains Anil's heart to gaze at her, yet it fills him with guilt when he looks away.

"What kind of father am I?" he sobs, after drinking a glass of sweet grape wine. "What kind of husband?" he torments himself, falling further into wretchedness. It is as if his shame and misery are flames, and the wine the only substance that might quench them, and on the nights he has no one else to share his wretchedness with, he sits in his own living room, drinking and weeping, compulsively recounting his misfortunes, obsessively berating himself.

Over time Anil's dejection spills out into the kitchen, where he finds Tanushri and beats her for his woes. At first, it is nothing more than a series of shoves—but rapidly it becomes a smack, then a punch, then a kick—for which, afterwards, he feels even more desolate and embarrassed. But it is only when Anil breaks Tanushri's nose and the copious blood makes it necessary for her to be admitted to hospital that Anil realizes his personal disgrace must be shared with a much wider audience. The police arrest him and lock him in a small concrete cell. Never has he been so ashamed and remorseful. He is forced to call his father, who calls a lawyer. Within three hours, bail is set and paid and he is free to go, but the event lingers.

"These things happen, Ani," his father consoles. "You're still newly married. A marriage is like a shoe. It gives lots of blisters at first but in time becomes wearable. And your wife..." his father continues, "she's a traditional woman and knows how a good wife behaves. She'll say nothing and you'll be able to put all of this behind you."

But as good a traditional woman as Tanushri may be, and as ashamed as she is in having to relate even the most banal events of her personal life to a stranger, she is so deprived of warmth and so starved for the feminine voices of mother, aunts and sisters that she is completely engulfed by the compassionate words of the hospital counsellor, who encourages her only to return home long enough to collect her and Tejas' belongings and leave.

Tanushri's nostrils are packed with cotton and her nose is the size of a turnip. Her head throbs and she finds it difficult to think. If she could think, all that would be humming in her head would be the static line of a dead heart—like the one she saw on a hospital monitor when she was admitted to Emergency. She cannot consider what she is doing. She allows the hospital counsellor to take Tejas, and policewoman Edna Stares escorts her home.

"I need to speak to my wife alone," Anil demands, but Edna will not allow it. She summons a reinforcement, Police Officer Roger Foley, who appears within minutes, soft spoken, slightly vacant, but seemingly kind. "You are a man," Anil entreats him. "Let me speak with my wife!" But officer Foley, for all his appearance, will not intervene.

"Tanushri," Anil shouts, through officer Foley, and across the room. "We need to work our differences out together... not with outsiders interfering. Please..." he begs, his voice cracking like the hard shell of a nut.

What Tanushri is doing is disgraceful; it will lead to her censure. Her husband and his family will disown her, but she cannot stop herself. In her confused state, every woman's utterance evokes the authority of her mother, and Edna is telling her to ignore Anil, to pack her things, to move quickly, so she doesn't succumb to his words.

She throws her daughter's diapers, clothes and toys into a large green garbage bag, then begins to collect her own possessions. For the first time since Tejas' birth, she recalls the meat bones that still reside beneath the bed, and embarrassed for her forgetfulness as well as for her failure to bear a son, she tosses them quickly in among her belongings, promising herself to discard them as soon as possible.

The shelter she is taken to is situated on the corner of Tecumseh and Wyandotte and is a large, grey, characterless building with an elaborate security system that renders it as intimidating as a penitentiary. Tanushri cannot see inside. Bright sunlight ricochets off its windows. They are all made of mirrored, bulletproof glass, and later she discovers they are sealed shut and rigged with an alarm that will produce a deafening screech if tampered with.

Outside, under the awnings, two hidden cameras track passing movements. There is an armed security guard at the door and another in a booth full of screens who monitors every area of the building.

There are electronic doors that slide open and shut. From the inside, Tanushri can see everything that is happening in the street. She can see a man reading a newspaper as he waits for the lights to change, and a woman in a tight skirt and high-heeled shoes tottering out into the traffic, trying to hail a cab. The man unselfconsciously scratches his bottom. The woman keeps patting her windswept hair. This must be what it's like to be invisible, Tanushri thinks—to observe others without being observed—and she wonders if her mother might be watching her from some ethereal vantage, and if so, what she must be thinking.

Tanushri already regrets coming here. It is like the severing of a limb. It can never be undone. There will always be a hideous scar, a defect. Tanushri puts Tejas down. The baby toddles to the doors and hits them with her tiny fists. The floor is polished tile and Tejas is wearing her first pair of walking shoes. Everywhere she goes, the heels of her shoes leave thin black streaks. Tanushri apologizes to the security guard. She apologizes to the chatty woman who arrives to be her guide. "I will clean the floor," Tanushri offers, tears brimming.

The woman, Marjorie Loomis, tells Tanushri not to worry, and makes small talk, as she leads her to her room. It is carpeted and cozy. There's a flowered bedspread on the bed and at the window ruffled curtains. There's a dresser, a desk, a crib and a changing table. Beside the bed are a nightstand and a lamp. Although her guide calls it "basic," Tanushri thinks it's very nice.

"Everyone cooks together," Marjorie explains, taking her along to the communal kitchen, "but you'll find out more about that tonight," she adds. Tanushri can barely suppress her sudden joy—women preparing meals together—just like in her childhood home, with her aunts and mother and grandmother all talking together, and she and her sisters, each assigned a task, taking the world in through their words, but of course, this is not the situation at all. It is all very shameful and different now, she reminds herself, and the joy evaporates.

There is a common room in the shelter where the women and their children converge in the evenings to watch TV, listen to music, and play cards. On the floor above, there are classrooms where workshops on self-esteem, assertiveness, legal issues, and parenting are conducted, as well as high school diploma courses. "If you don't have a high school diploma, I highly recommend you work towards one," Marjorie says and explains that she herself teaches here. That she once worked for the public school system, but lost faith in it. "I'll never lose faith in learning, though," she chirps.

Tanushri would like to get a diploma. She would like the opportunity to learn, but surely this is not the appropriate place for it. "There are also lots of fun activities," Marjorie tells her, "like jewellery making and Latin dancing. Last week there was a fashion show—'dressing on a shoestring.' It's too bad you missed it."

Tanushri is curious about this woman, this former teacher. She wonders, though would feel it discourteous to ask, why she chose to place herself amid this shame. Tejas struggles from her arms and runs to a room she has spotted full of toys and children. It's a daycare, Marjorie tells her, and if she attends classes or a workshop or needs to go out for an appointment at any time, she can leave Tejas there for free. Tanushri has never left Tejas with anyone but the hospital counsellor, and doesn't know how she will cope with such freedom. She feels again a sudden rush of joy, as if her life were beginning, as if the prospects of a future were spilling out before her, like a litter of stars or the colourful toys that attract Tejas, but she quells the feeling, for she knows in fact there is no light and colour. There is only darkness. Her life is ending. She has made a choice with irrevocable consequences, and destroyed herself as certainly as if she had plunged a dagger into her heart.

Back in her room, she tries to absorb the full impact of her actions, but she is uncertain what the full impact will be. Thoughts burst into her mind like bubbles on a pot of soup. Even if Anil would take her back, could she ever overcome her shame? She begins to disperse the contents of her garbage bag, putting underwear in the dresser, hanging a blouse in the closet. She gives Tejas her favourite toy, a stuffed monkey, gnawed almost unrecognizable, but Tejas abandons it in favour of the sack of bones, which she finds on her mother's bed.

A tall lean woman, dressed in a tank top and cotton turquoise skirt, appears at the door.

Her name is Melanie and she has a room across the corridor. "I see you have the same designer luggage I have," she says lightly, pointing at the garbage bag.

There is such humiliation in what has happened—so much disgrace. Laughter cannot possibly be appropriate here, Tanushri thinks, and now, to make matters worse, Tejas has dragged the sack of bones under the desk, opened it, and dispersed the contents on the floor.

Drool is dripping from her chin, pooling like syrup on the carpet as she gnaws on one of them.

"Is that your ex?" Melanie asks, regarding the bones.

Tanushri doesn't like this woman who invades her solitude and makes light of her misery. She is lacking proper reserve and it's as if she's mocking her.

"Give me that bone!" Tanushri demands, and Tejas howls as Tanushri wrestles it free.

"Your baby looks forceful," Melanie offers. "Is it a boy or girl?"

"Girl," she murmurs. Even still, Tanushri feels degradation in announcing the gender of her child.

This is not the only time Melanie has been in this shelter. Her partner cracked three of her ribs, fractured her pelvis and broke her wrist the first time, but she went back. Six months later, she was in the shelter again—this time, with a punctured lung and a knife wound in her chest.

Tanushri, embarrassed by this intimate and unsolicited confession, doesn't know what to say.

"I was looking at my body from the ceiling," Melanie tells her, "seeing the blood, watching the doctors work on it, knowing I had to crawl back in there somehow, even though it hurt so much."

There are things that ought not to be spoken, things that one bears in isolation and anonymity, Tanushri thinks, collecting the bones strewn across the floor. She is relieved Melanie has finished her story—relieved her own story hasn't come bubbling out. The bones are like heavy blocks in her hands and she wants to be rid of them, but the presence of this shocking woman prevents their immediate disposal.

The bones are so white and clean; they fit so neatly into the cloth sack Tanushri made that it's not surprising Melanie assumes it's a game. That evening when Tanushri sits at the large dining table, self-conscious and remote, sharing only the rice and vegetables the women have prepared, Melanie describes Tanushri's game and suggests she might teach them all to play. She does it as a kindness, to help bring Tanushri out of herself, to offer her a way into this community of women, but the kindness is not appreciated. Heat rises in Tanushri's cheeks. She knows she can never tell these women the truth of it, and so she lies: "It was my mother's game. I never learned to play it myself."

A quiet voice at the end of the table emerges, and dumbfounds Tanushri. "I know the game. It's called the bone game. I can teach it." The woman who has spoken is Janet. She has a reputation for being both aloof and mysterious, a woman who does not often speak. Her room is a place of refuge for things of the natural world: the branch of a Yew tree, the pelt of a fox, the wing of a crow, stones and shells and seeds. Above her bed hangs a shield she's made from a disk of redwood, an eagle's claw, and an owl's feather. She also wears an owl feather around her neck.

Melanie is the first to express enthusiasm at the prospects of learning a new game.

"Is it anything like Mah-jong?" a woman inquires.

"Can you play it for money?" another asks.

Soon every woman at the table is talking about the game, while Tanushri just wants to shrink away.

"We've played bingo and bridge and gin rummy," Melanie says, "but The Bone Game!"

It's as if she's speaking directly to Tanushri, although she is addressing the entire table.

They ask her to deliver the bones, and Tanushri isn't strong enough to refuse. She feels there's nothing else she can do. If only she'd left them under the bed or disposed of them earlier.

If only she'd known beforehand that her mother's instructions wouldn't work. She lifts Tejas from her highchair and takes her to their room. Perhaps if she tells the women the bones are gone—that she's misplaced them. Perhaps they'll just forget. But before she has a chance to formulate a speech, Melanie is at her door, and Tejas has extricated the sack of bones from a drawer. "That kid of yours is brilliant," Melanie says.

The dishes have been cleared and washed, and the bones are set out on the dining room table for Janet to inspect. Her eyes are like light pools as they scan the bones. Tanushri holds her breath, wondering if Janet will announce her fraudulence—if she'll say, "these are just ordinary meat bones." But Janet begins to speak to the bones, then carefully divides the collection, putting the four small bones in one group and the eleven long bones in another. She removes a marking pen from her pocket and draws a circle around the circumference of two of the smaller bones.

"The one with the markings are the female bones and the ones without are the male bones," she explains.

Tanushri wants to stop her. To tell the gathering that Janet's lying. To explain. But she doesn't really want to explain—she can't explain, and so she stands mutely by as Janet proceeds.

The women line two rows of chairs facing each other and divide into teams, as Janet directs. Each team picks a leader, and each leader is given a pair of bones, which they will hide in their hands and pass to other players. "The object of the game," Janet explains, "is to intuit where the female bones are hidden."

"A guessing game?" one of the women asks.

"No. More than that," Janet says.

Tanushri is appalled by Janet's barefaced lies, affronted by the smoothness and inventiveness of her deceptions. It is as if the blood in Tanushri's veins is becoming hot, as if the pressure of holding her tongue, of not telling the truth, is causing a bodily fever. Tejas squirms in her arms, as if she too feels the uncomfortable heat and no longer can bear the proximity of her mother.

"Intuiting and guessing are not the same things," Janet tells the women, "but you'll see as we play."

A few of the women nod their heads, as if they find some kind of resonance in Janet's words, but Tanushri's head remains sullenly fixed. If only she could release her own tongue's trigger.

"There is something about the power of the voice, as well," Janet says, startling Tanushri, whose soundless voice is impaling her throat. "You need to sing in this game. A good song can help your team win."

The women want to know what kind of a song to sing, and Janet says that they ought to try an assortment—that they'll know when they've found the right one.

"That sounds like what my mother used to say about finding the right man!" a woman shouts.

"How about *row, row, row your boat*?" another offers.

"How about *find, find, find the bone*?" Melanie says.

A few women on Melanie's team begin to sing, and others scramble to the chairs and join them as the bones are passed. Tejas sways back and forth to the rhythm, free from her mother's arms. The other team quickly arranges itself and starts to sing "the foot bone's connected to the leg bone..."

Incoherent words explode from Tanushri's mouth, crackings and hissings, but no one can hear them above the din of the women's voices that grow louder under the inharmonious current of songs. Tanushri turns to Janet who is caught in the spirit of the music, her feet stamping the rhythm; the owl feather around her neck, ensnared by her voice, flaps as if it would fly off. Tanushri reaches for Tejas, who is dancing in rapturous abandon, but who slips from her hands as if they had no substance at all. And then it is as if Tanushri is surveying the room from a great distance, as if she has lost her body completely to the incessant pulse below, but can see with a piercing clarity everything that has ever evaded her.

Her life spreads out before her, disjointed, fractured, and in need of repair, but she sees how this might be done now. Her life with Anil seems to have existed a hundred years ago and, like the bones her mother insisted she collect, only as a means to this end—an ending, like all endings, that is fixed in the silent contracts of one's smaller life, and can never truly be anticipated.

It is her mother, speaking through Janet, who brings her back to her body: she is telling her to find the female bones. And as clearly as she sees her mother, sisters, aunts and daughter extending behind her in the past and before her into the future, she sees the hands that hold the female bones and shamelessly begins to laugh.

King Rat

"YOU'RE HIRED," Brian says and taps my head with a plastic sceptre that belongs to the Pizza Palace's mascot—a rickety seven-foot statue that's supposed to be a lion dressed like a king.

Before its base cracked and the yellow barricade tape went up, kids used to climb it. That's why it's missing its mane and ears. It's still got its eyes, though, bright and intact, polished and beady. It's the eyes, really, that make it look more like a rat than a lion, but far be it for me to say anything.

Brian, who I've known almost forever, gets to hire me because the owner, Frank Montanaro, made him manager. The guy who used to run the place took a hike to heaven—or somewhere—swinging from a beam in the restaurant's cellar. Brian showed "unique administrative initiative," Montanaro said, by phoning him in Italy. It was a lucky fluke Brian found his number. It was scribbled under the ledge of a pick-up window.

"I ain't averse to uplifting the lower ranks," Brian whispered in a scratchy voice. He was pretending to be Montanaro, "after all, I once was a penniless grub myself."

Montanaro lives eight months a year on a yacht; the other time he spends with his mother in Palermo. "I'm on my way up the ladder, Lynette," Brian says, "and nothing's going to stand in my way!" He's insanely thrilled he got upgraded, and sees it as corporate promotion, but there wasn't much else Montanaro could do. Everyone left when they didn't get paid. Brian stayed for the perks: free pizza, the delivery car, a crash site for when he and his lover Carl were fighting.

"I'm so happy!" he says and whacks my head again.

"You mean it about the job, right?"

"For sure, Lynette, if you're serious about taking it," he says.

"For sure!" I tell him, wondering why he thinks I might not be.

"Great! You can start right away as my serving wench!"

"And your apprentice pizza maker?" I'm probably being pushy, but I've never worked anywhere before and I've always wanted to learn how to make pizza, plus it's a good skill.

"Whatever you wish," Brian warbles, like that old blond chick who comes out of a soap bubble in his all-time favourite movie, *The Wizard of Oz*. He pretends King Rat's sceptre is his magic wand and waves it in the air. He's wearing his work clothes—a rustic grey tunic, a dirty pair of black tights, and a pair of pseudo-suede slippers that are so worn you can see a hole in his sock. Uniforms come with the job, and he takes my arm and skips me to the staff cubby so I can pick my own. There's a peasant top, slightly perspiration-stained, a skirt, slightly shabby, and a black vinyl corset missing only one of its loops. The outfit hangs off my none-too-thin frame like a medieval pavilion. Brian fixes it with a safety pin: "In a few months," he singsongs, "we'll be letting it out." He hooks my arm again, skips me to the kitchen, and spins me like we're waltzing. Out of the corner of my eye, I catch sight of a rat, the size of Brian's slipper. It darts from under a row of aluminium cupboards, leaps onto a shelf, and disappears behind the refrigerator.

"Ignore it," Brian says, "just close your eyes and look the other way. That's what I do." He extracts a fistful of mozzarella bullets from a tall white bucket and palms his brimming hand to his mouth. "Want some?" he offers.

While he's still chewing, the phone rings. "Pizza Palace, what's your pleasure?" he answers. A hail of cheese spatters the mouthpiece and that practiced syrupy voice of his does a 360 all the way to sour: "Didn't I tell you, 'Don't call me here'?" The volume control is set at loud, so I can hear Carl, a.k.a. Herr Hemorrhoid, begging Brian to be nice. I reach into the bucket for cheese, compare it to the lint balls on my skirt, and take a ringside seat on the prep table.

"What don't you understand?" Brian asks. "It's over!" He smashes the phone down and the rat scampers from behind the fridge and dives under the dishwasher. I know rats sense when bad things are about to happen, that's why they jump off of sinking ships, and I wonder if this one is trying to tell Brian something about Carl, but instead of getting him even more worked up, I just say: "For every one you see, there are fifty you don't... or something like that." It's the only other rat fact I know.

We pretend the phone call didn't happen. I taste the cheese. It reminds me of pencil eraser. Both of us have trouble with men. Brian once said, "If they weren't jerks, we wouldn't want them." But my Steve is nothing like Herr Hemorrhoid. It's true, he made excuses for why we couldn't get married, and then took a tree planting job out west: "It's only for a little while, babe, just till I save enough bread," but I don't hold that against him. He's a planner, that's all. He's saving for our future and a down payment on a house. He's nothing like Carl. For one thing, he's really smart and knows all kinds of stuff, like why you get water bugs in dirty swimming pools and how the Hostess Company puts cream inside those little Twinkie cakes. When I first started dating him, he told me all about the Lost City of Atlantis, and how once upon a time it was a really great place to live, but then an earthquake and tidal wave came and the whole thing shattered like sand into the ocean. It got me thinking about disasters, and how you think you're all safe and sound, and then suddenly, bam, out of nowhere, everything disappears. "Life is uncertain, babe," Steve said. "But one thing for sure—you'll always be my girl," and I know he meant it. That's why I stuck with him and that's why, whenever Brian asks about Steve, I make something up: "He's set our wedding date for the spring," or "He just sent me and baby Jess a cheque." Truth is he doesn't even know he has a daughter yet, because he's been moving from bush camp to bush camp, and I can't reach him. If Brian knew, he'd freak, but I'm not worried. I know I'll hear from Steve soon. Before he left he told me: "Babe. You're everything to me."

Brian lights a cigarette and inhales. He quit for three months, but now he's sucking back smoke like he's on a respirator and it's oxygen. Finally, out gushes what's on his mind: "I can't live with a liar," he says. It's like it's me he needs to convince. "Why is it so impossible to end this relationship?" It's not a question Brian wants answered. I'm glad, because I don't have a clue. Once he found a bathhouse membership in Carl's wallet. Carl said it didn't belong to him. Later, he said he only joined to use the sauna.

"Sauna my ass-ter-ic," Brian yelled. It wasn't the first time Carl lied. It wasn't the first time he swore he wouldn't do it again either. There'd been a whole bunch of men since he moved in with Brian. But after all the screaming and crying and threatening, Brian didn't leave.

You could have knocked me sideways. "He's got an addiction," Brian said. "He's going to get counselling, he promises."

Brian claims Carl did get counselling, but personally, unless his counsellor was Casanova or Mick Jagger, or someone like that, I find it hard to believe. He still cheats and lies, cruises the parks, visits "the sauna." Has "group therapy" with any twosome who'll suffer him.

"Sometimes I wish I were an ostrich," Brian says. "If I could bury my head in the ground, I wouldn't have to see the crabs in his underwear."

"Why not bury his head in the ground? If you want, I'll help you lop it off his body," I offered.

Generally, I'm pretty much a live and let live sort of person. I don't believe in making a whole bunch of judgments, but for some reason, where Carl is concerned, I can't help it. Maybe it's because Carl is so barefaced or maybe because Brian's so blind. But fortunately, or unfortunately, depending on how you look at it, the police are involved now and Brian's vision has been forced back to 20/20.

"He's a liar," Brian moans. "How can he expect me to believe him?"

I say nothing. I don't have to. But I'm busting to shout: "You can't believe him! You'll never be able to believe him! Bail now!"

I know it's not what Brian wants to hear. It's not what anyone, in his position, would want to hear. Sometimes the hard, cold truth helps—but more often it just wrecks friendships, and I don't want to risk that. I'm itching to make a pizza. I want to toss dough up in the air and spin it on my finger, like I saw a chef do on a cooking show. No heavy conversations, no arguments, no possibility of being fired before I've even started—I just want to work.

The phone rings and Brian picks up. Before he has a chance to recite the Pizza Palace spiel, Carl's crackly voice is begging for mercy. "I don't want to talk about it right now," Brian says. I can hear Carl's whinging and decide not to eavesdrop. I already know the details. A kid told the cops Carl diddled him in a cornfield next to Highway 402. Carl swore he didn't, but then other kids started calling the cops too. "It never happened," Carl kept saying. It was a conspiracy against him because he turned the lights off in the apartment Halloween night.

I go to the woman's throne room, the Pizza Palace's name for the public toilets. I look in the mirror and pinch my pale cheeks. Having a baby takes a lot out of you, but so do relationships. I feel lucky that at least Steve doesn't tie me in knots, like Carl does to Brian.

Sure, Steve's away, and I wish we were together and married, but he doesn't cause me grief on a daily basis. Still, Brian thinks Steve's a jerk. A few months back, he goes: "What kind of a guy deserts his pregnant girlfriend?"

"Fiancé," I go, "and he didn't desert me."

"Where is he, then?"

We argue. I cry. Then I tell Brian I never want to speak to him again. A week later, I start bleeding, and call him. He rushes over to the Y, wraps me in a blanket, and carries me to the pizza car. "Special delivery," he jokes. Blood seeps into the upholstery and I can't stop shivering. He activates the roof-top crown with its flashing jewel lights, and it throbs out a trumpet fanfare as we speed, like maniacs, to emergency. He tells the nurses he's my husband, so he can hold my hand through blood transfusions and a C-section. The next day he brings me a pizza with anchovies, because he knows that's what I'm craving. I wish I could tell him I don't know where Steve is, but I can't. Steve is a great guy. One day Brian will know that. In the meantime, I don't want him imagining anything different.

I wash my hands slowly without soap because there's none in the dispenser, dry them on my skirt because there are no towels. I meander back to the kitchen. Brian's voice quavers: "For God's sake, Carl!" He slams the phone down again.

Steve is older than me, but Carl is much older than Brian. They met in a coffee shop.

"Very fatherly," Brian told me when I'd asked about the guy he was seeing. "Very sweet." When I met him for the first time, he hugged me and kissed my cheek. I never told Brian how it made my flesh crawl. Instead I said, "Any lover of yours is a friend of mine." Things deteriorated pretty rapidly, let me tell you.

I'd seen Brian in love before, and over the years I've met at least a dozen of his worthless boyfriends. We could laugh about some now, like Raymond, who went ballistic because he came home after a business trip and Brian and I were fast asleep in his bed. "It isn't what it looks like," Brian tried explaining. I heard the commotion but could barely open my eyes. I was still so drunk from the tequila we'd knocked back the night before, waiting for Raymond's plane to arrive from Rome. The plane was delayed, and delayed again. "He's worth waiting for," Brian had said all excited. "I know you're both going to adore each other!" Those were the last words I was conscious of hearing before Raymond's howl, "Get her out of here!"

"She's my oldest friend," Brian shouted.

Raymond started hurling things: an antique candy dish, a bottle of dessert wine, a lamp. Brian grabbed my wrist, yanked me out of the bed, and whisked me down the fire escape. Pots and pans clanked after us, an aquarium full of tropical fish. Brian shouted "Run!" and we ran as fast as we could to the end of Quebec Street, beyond Raymond's line of fire.

"He begged me not to abandon him. How can I dump him? I feel like such a shit," Brian says. He's trembling.

Guilt-tripping is part of Carl's act. Their fights are as predictable as re-runs. Carl lies. Brian calls him on it. Carl says he's telling the truth, gets mad and makes Brian feel guilty for doubting him. Carl's lie resurfaces, but uglier. "It's all a mistake!" he whines, tells Brian he needs to trust and stand by him. That's where they are right now. The next stage is when Carl owns up. He wheedles and cries and promises not to do it again. He begs

Brian to give him another chance. If Brian says no, Carl makes him feel so bad that in the end, he changes his mind.

"What I don't understand," Brian says, "is why do I feel so guilty?"

Before I'm forced to speak, the phone rings again. Brian grabs another handful of cheese.

I grab one too. "I'm not going to answer that," he says.

I think that's a good idea, except for the fact it could be a customer wanting a pizza, or my sister Laurie, who's babysitting little Jess. It's the first time I've ever left her, and I'm feeling guilty too. Laurie doesn't have the greatest judgment; she's pregnant and she's only thirteen. Not that I'm really in any position to talk—but I am a few years older and my baby's father is a mature working man, who intends to marry me, not a scumbag dropout from the projects who's been in juvie. I asked Laurie to babysit because I figured she ought to learn something about babies, also because she's the only member of my family I'm still talking to.

Brian picks the phone up after four rings. "Pizza Palace, what's your pleasure?" he asks, trying to sound perky. It's Carl again, and as hard as I try not to listen, the volume control is cranked so loud that even when Carl's voice moves to a quieter, wheedling tone, I can hear him trying to convince Brian that nothing happened, that those kids are all in cahoots, that once the truth is known, his lawyer is going to go after them. "And then you can bet there'll be some big money coming down," he says. "And I'm going to spend it on you, 'cause you're the one who had to put up with this bullshit."

Bullshit is right, I think.

The rat makes scratching noises underneath the dishwasher and a few pieces of fluffy pink insulation come flying out. Brian doesn't notice, but I notice Brian. He's softening. His eyes are getting cloudy and his shoulders are slumping. I don't want to hear what he's going to say because if he says anything forgiving, I'm going to scream and probably lose my only chance of ever learning how to make pizzas. I go to leave the kitchen to spare him from seeing the expression on my face, but he stops me. "Wait! I need you to stay." I've known Brian since kindergarten, which is long enough to know that he's serious. He signals for me to come closer. He takes my hand and squeezes, just like I squeezed his when they were sticking me with needles in the hospital. "No, Carl," he says into the phone. "I'm not talking to you. I don't want *you* to stay. I want you to leave." He clasps my hand again. It's like the grip of a drowning man. "I want my witness to stay."

This time, Carl hangs up the phone. Brian knew he would. Carl can't stand the thought of another person listening—he can't stand the thought of not being able to revise his story when he feels like it. "A witness to Carl is like a cross to a vampire," Brian says and pauses and then he adds, "Carl is a vampire," like he's just made that discovery. "What do you do when you find out the person you love is a vampire?"

I don't say drive a stake through his heart, shoot him with a silver bullet, cut off his head and stuff his mouth with garlic cloves. As far as I'm concerned, all of these things are too good for the man who's been torturing my friend. Instead, I just try to imagine what it must be like for Brian to be attached to such a jerk, and how hard it must be for him to make the decision to end things. I remember how he told me once that love for him was like an electric shock. "Your hand reflexively closes. You can't let go." He was living with Matthew at the time, a bipolar alcoholic freeloader who maxed out his credit card before driving his red Camaro into the Detroit River.

When I consider most of the guys that Brian's been mixed up with, I can't stop myself from thinking how lucky I am. It's not like I didn't have my share of bad relationships, but Steve made up for every one of them. When he came along, I knew right away he was different. He was smart, had a wide honest face, and was far more mature than any of the guys I'd previously dated. He had a job at Chrysler, owned his own car, and had plans for his future. My mother detested him, said he was going to ruin my life. "You've got a brain, Lynnette," she said. "Your teachers say you could win scholarships." She wanted me to dump him, but he didn't get mad at her. He was very understanding. "Babe," he said, "your old lady just wants you to keep studying and not get sidetracked by too heavy a relationship. She just thinks you're too young to get serious with anyone right now, that's all." He made it so we only met a couple of times a week, secretly, at the River Park Hotel. My mom works there as head housekeeper, so we only went on her days off. Steve thought it was perfect because it's the last place she'd expect for us to go.

"What she don't know, won't hurt her," he said.

I had no idea the hotel was so swank. There was an indoor pool and hot tub. Lots of blue water and shiny silver chrome. There was even a golden statue of a mermaid in the centre of the pool that spewed warm water from a little metal hole in her lips. "Only the best for you, babe," he'd said, and he never wore his baseball cap there. Once he'd asked me to marry him, it was like we were on a nonstop honeymoon. He lived in a big house in the West end with a group of his buddies. They were all working at Chrysler, socking money away. "Not much of a place for a lady," he'd said, when I asked him to take me there. "Raunchy pictures on some of the walls, bad language, mold in the fridge, scummy toilets... you know what guys are like," he explained. He'd order room service in the hotel, and I worried he was spending too much money when we needed to be saving for our future, but he'd always say, "Remember Atlantis—here today, gone tomorrow," and "You need to make hay while the sun shines," so we made a lot of hay—we also made a baby.

My mother booted me out when I started getting fat and couldn't keep it a secret. "I expected better from you, Lynette," she sobbed. "I expected more." Apparently, she doesn't expect "more" from Laurie. Laurie, her dumb little angel, gets to live at home, scot-free.

Anyway, I called Steve at work and he took me to the Y. "It's only for a little while, babe," he promised. I couldn't move in with him, not even for the short term, because he wasn't getting along with his housemates. Great, I said, that means we can get a place together, but Steve had other ideas. They were laying guys off at Chrysler, and Steve said it was only a matter of time before they gave him a pink slip. Because I was pregnant and told him I wouldn't consider an abortion, he said the best thing he could do was go out west for the season and make some money.

I stayed at the Y until Jess was born; then a social worker got involved. Now we've got our own geared-to-income apartment in the Fontainebleau projects, and I'm getting a regular welfare cheque. Brian says that once the Pizza Palace is making money again, he's going to pay me under the table, so I should be able to save something for me and Steve and Jess. I imagine a little cottage-type house in Essex with a big fireplace inside and a cat on a rag rug and a wooden rocking chair where we'll read to Jess. Steve is going to be such a great father, and Brian will come visit us all the time, and when Jess is in grade school, I'll maybe finish high school, maybe go on to college for a teaching certificate or something. It would be fun to teach little kids.

Brian snaps his fingers in my face. He's done this ever since he learned how to snap. When I come out of my daydream, I feel so bad because I was feeling so happy. "Are you going to be okay?" I ask him.

"I think so," he says. He's been crying and he wipes his eyes and blows his nose into a serviette. Before he has a chance to throw it away, the phone rings. We both freeze.

"I'll answer this time," I offer. If it's Carl, I've already decided I'm going to tell him "Get a life!"—but it isn't Carl; it's a customer, a real live customer, so I say "Can you hang on a moment?" I cover the mouthpiece, and pass the phone to Brian. He asks for the order and uses a kind of shorthand to write the whole thing (medium pepperoni pizza with double cheese and pineapple) down. "Okay," he says, once he hangs up, "let's make a pizza!"

I'm so excited. These are the words I've been waiting to hear. But when Brian goes to unlock the cold pantry to get the pizza dough, he's missing his keys. "I'm completely discombobulated," he says, lifting boxes, looking under dishtowels. I offer to search the staff cubby and dining room, and when I leave the kitchen discover a customer in the entrance hall lifting her little girl towards King Rat. The girl is cute: dark curly hair, brown eyes, just like Jess, but maybe a couple years older.

"My husband's parking the car. He should be here in a few minutes," the woman says. She's attractive but looks harassed and a little angry. I wonder how long she's been waiting and make a mental note to ask Brian if there's supposed to be some kind of bell on the door.

"Can you seat us now?" she asks. I collect two menus and a King Rat colouring placemat.

I lead the woman and her daughter into the dining room. Even though Brian hasn't had time to show me what to do, I've seen enough waitresses to know. I find a booster seat for the baby. She scribbles on the placemat. I wonder if she really looks as much like Jess as I think—Steve's broad face and dark eyes—or if it's just my imagination because I'm suddenly missing my baby so much. I try to think of her and Steve but the lost city of Atlantis pops into my mind like an unwelcome bubble. I try to imagine the little cottage in Essex, with the cat and rag rug and all of us living happily ever after, but I'm getting all choked up. Tears, I can't stop, roll down my cheeks.

"What's wrong?" the woman asks, and her question uncorks something I've been trying not to say. Words gush from my mouth like a tidal wave. I tell her all about Jess, and how much I love her, and how this is my first day ever working. I tell her that I'm not married, that my mother kicked me out when she found out I was pregnant and won't even talk to me anymore; that my fiancé went tree planting and I haven't heard from him and can't contact him, and that he doesn't even know he has a daughter yet. I don't know how long I blather, or exactly what I say, but the lady gets me a stack of napkins and a glass of water from the sideboard. When I finally go quiet, she puts her hand on my shoulder and says, "You poor thing," which starts me gushing all over again.

Murder

THE CROWS SOARED over the field, circling in long looping spheres, cawing with high raspy voices. The noise, as they gathered, was deafening: a discordant alarm bell tolling some great unearthing, an urgent broadcast sent out to the cosmos.

It wasn't the sleek ears of corn that excited them: a memory of its sweetness, the toughness of its husk or the downy waxiness of its silk. Corn, though copious in these parts, didn't spring from this particular field, and even if it had, harvest time was months away. The flapping cacophony could not be blamed on the sighting of an enemy owl. There were none in the vicinity today, only pheasants and sparrows and meadowlarks.

Lizzie saw the crows gather from the end of Monica Street. She saw them twist and dive and dip in the sky, and covered her ears against their shattering cries. Her feet hurt from pacing the pulpy field in search of her sister, pacing and pacing to the point of blisters. She'd walked in straight lines from the edge of the street out to the railroad tracks, back and forth, calling "Celeste," her sister's name. Now she stopped to study the crows and discern what lay beneath their raucous canopy.

On a knoll of soil, half a dozen converged, hopping forward, pecking, and exposing a substance, sticky-red. The substance was blood and belonged to a body. The torso was completely encrusted in clay. It had fallen, face skyward, amidst damp flixweed. The knuckles on the hands were knotty and the tips of the fingers square, and the legs, yes, for Lizzie could see them now, were long and whole and belonged to a stranger, not to Celeste.

The face was gaunt, overlaid by a turbid mask of dirt, with an expression of acute bewilderment. One of the eyes, feral blue, glassy and hard as marble, gaped while the nose, sharp and curved as a beak, pointed uneasily toward the crows. In the place where the other eye should have been, blood congealed like creosote around a straight wooden spar.

As Lizzie knelt beside the body, the crows dispersed in a feathered cyclone. The spar may have been a remnant from a felled tree or a branch severed by lightning from the scattered outlying oaks. It may have been a piece of weathered doweling or the segment of a thin walking stick. It may have been the shaft of an arrow.

Lizzie laid her head against the victim's chest. Her ear could not perceive a heartbeat. Her palm could not feel breath. The police would have to come now, she thought. The police would have to come at last.

They had not come, years before, when her sister was still an infant, when their mother was neglectful, and the law should have intervened. Celeste had never been made a ward of the court, in spite of her birth defect, Sirenomelia, which fused her legs and deformed her organs. She was susceptible to illness, susceptible to thugs and sadists. She never should have been allowed outside alone, but the police refused to come again—even when Lizzie explained. There were missing person protocols, they'd said, and Celeste was not a child.

The crows fluttered and hopped and cawed. They found their way back to the body and cocked their heads as Lizzie retreated from the field. They pecked and ripped at the fissures in the body's flesh, collecting what they could in their ebony beaks; afterwards, they flew off in all directions to dine in solitary repose.

Mud the colour of coffee broke from Lizzie's boots onto her mother's living room carpet; it splattered on her mother's kitchen wall. Mud that once had been rock and plant and animal, eaten and expelled by earthworms, composed thousands of years before. Lizzie's mother didn't see the mud. She was drunk and apneatic, exhausted from sickness and belly pain, unconscious on the floral couch. Lizzie reached the old black phone perched on the kitchen wall and dialled.

Her mother's eye blinked open at the click. "Put it down." Her voice was low and gravelly.

Lizzie reached the emergency operator.

"Put the phone down," her mother croaked, reeling from the couch, "or I'll put it down for you."

In the field beyond the house where the corpse lay, the sentinel crows listened to Lizzie and her mother fighting. They listened to the whiz and buzz of sound travelling through wires on the wooden utility poles where they often stopped to preen. They knew the noise of humans and could identify trouble, even though they didn't know exactly what was said. There was only an airborne palpitation of words as the phone flew towards the ceiling then cracked on the floor like a hard, black egg.

Lizzie's mother despised other humans as much as crows despised birds of prey; she'd become a recluse, long ago, not as a defence against people, but as a defence against the malevolence they generated in her thinking. She didn't want people coming anywhere near her house and she didn't go anywhere near people. She even refused to see a doctor, in spite of her failing health and had forbidden Lizzie to tell anyone about Celeste's disappearance. She wasn't surprised, however, when Lizzie, the most wilful of her children, disobeyed. Now, they were at each other's throats, and the crows were wary. They knew the sounds of human turmoil frequently produced shotguns and that shotguns, especially in these fields, frequently produced dead crows.

Lizzie pushed through the creaking aluminium door, full of resentment, wishing to flee. It flared in the sun, a bright god, flickering, at last, to nothing. The sentinel crows observed this waning, they, who had fled so often and who suffered the most enduring and resentful of grudges.

There were particular cats in the neighbourhood, who harassed them and whom they regularly mobbed. There was a human with a head as pink and bare as a newborn nestling that hurled stones and shouted whenever they gathered in a nearby pasture, and just this morning, as the sun was rising, they declared war on another, who had screeched at the now lifeless one, before staggering back through the field.

They'd approached cautiously, not realizing the arc of wood was deadly. A pointed rod hurtled from the arc, hitting and killing one of their sentinels. In that moment, as the remaining crows scattered, and the nictitating membranes of their eyes closed shut, they captured the image of the aggressor, transmitting the terms of combat. As long as there were crows on earth, that human would know no peace.

Because Lizzie was not that human, the crows allowed her to pass into the ocean of field. The dark features of her baby sister, the wispy blue-black hair, the large, deep blue eyes that eventually turned the blackest shade of brown were the images that arose in Lizzie's flustered mind. She recalled their expression, their intelligent knowing, the strength of their will. How could anyone emotionally abandon such an expression? It pitted her against her mother, yet she was incapable of moving from her mother's house until she could bring her sister, "the little mermaid," as she called her.

How she longed to tell someone about Celeste, how resilient she was, how doctors had given her up for dead, how she'd defied them. She would have liked to tell someone that she'd almost got Celeste out of this goddamned city; she'd almost raised enough money to take her across the border far from prying eyes and neighbours who labelled her "freak"—far from the obscene telephone calls of sick bastards, far from their mother. Lizzie wrote and sent photographs to every hospital in North America. Only one in Memphis, Tennessee, offered help.

In her sister's younger days, when it seemed she would die, Lizzie brought her to this field in the hopes that the natural world would heal her. She bundled her in a blanket and carried her lovingly in her arms. She set her down in a nest of long grass and then knelt beside her, pitting the earth with a prayer of tears.

Some of the neighbours talked about Lizzie's mother. They said she was negligent, though none of them ever made a move to help. None tried to stop her from panelling over windows, from disconnecting doorbells, from shutting the house up so tight that no one could enter or leave. She sank deeper into the solace of alcohol. She lived a drunkard's seclusion, detesting all people and their judgments, loathing and pitying the little monster she'd brought into the world, threatening to do away with anyone who trespassed on her solitude.

When Lizzie grew old enough to rebel, she ripped down the boards at the windows, and came and went as she pleased. The field adjacent to her mother's property rolled eternally away, the earth responding with its strength. It could hold both the mermaid and her sister's grief. It could calm their weary hearts with its solid bearing. Every day, for an entire summer, she brought Celeste to the field. They'd lie on their backs and coax the hard primordial soil to surrender its mysteries. There were bones in the field shaped like keys, wise bones they called them, and pretended they had the power to set them free. The sun bathed their ashen flesh until it gleamed pink and their dry eyes apprehended luminous doors that opened into secret realms.

Now Lizzie wondered if Celeste had crawled through one of those doors, if the mermaid had found her appropriate habitat.

The sentinel crows were the first to hear the siren as a police car hastened like an arrow up Monica Street. They shouted to their comrades, warning of this new chaos, but their comrades remained, for a while, unperturbed. Some almost as large as newborn babes and glossy black, feasted on the corpse and it was only the appearance of two human strangers, emerging from the shrieking car, who stopped them. The sentinel crows flapped from poles to trees, redoubling their dissonance and amplifying their alarm, cawing and cawing for caution. The interlopers' faces couldn't be discerned, but the buttons on their jackets twinkled and the badges pinned on their chests gleamed.

They were police officers: Roger Foley and Bill Green. An emergency operator had dispatched them after tracking Lizzie's call. Both expected a domestic dispute and weren't prepared for what they found. The body could have been anyone's, Lizzie told them. Strangers were forever tramping through the field. Kids came here to play hooky, couples to make love, hunters to illegally shoot pheasant, junkies to make deals and do drugs, but Lizzie had seen nothing suspicious, nor had she heard anything out of the ordinary, she said. She cared only about finding her sister—only about finding Celeste.

The sibilation of the word rose to the sky and was familiar to the attentive birds who innocuously loitered awaiting the "all clear." Lizzie had never bothered them and Celeste had frequently fed them peanuts and chunks of bright yellow cheese.

If the birds had known how to speak and been inclined to say, they could have told Lizzie that Celeste had visited the field with her shiny walker just the other day. As it was, however, they clacked and rattled and cawed. It was the strangers they observed the most, the strangers, whose peaked hats shadowed their faces, making identification impossible. They didn't appear to be ill-wishers, however; but humans were capricious and so the birds remained remote.

The stranger named Bill Green had a notepad and was jotting down everything that Lizzie said. The other, Roger Foley, was struggling to remain within his body, as a dark weight settled on his chest. He had knowledge of something gruesome, which he wasn't at liberty to share. Yesterday, the partial remains of a woman, with dark eyes and long black hair, were pulled from the Detroit River. The body had been sawed in half. Only the upper part had been recovered.

Two crows hovered over the corpse, others bounced on telephone wires or the twisted branches of the dying maple that marked the end of Monica Street. Another police car arrived and neighbours gathered, wondering at the commotion of sirens. One of the new officers knocked on Lizzie's mother's door. It was aluminium and sparkled and when at last it opened, the sun reflected off its grille making a sudden brilliant flare. The door didn't open wide enough for the crows to see inside. If it had, they would have beheld Lizzie's mother, groggy and dishevelled, and carrying a defoliating broom. She was hidden in the shadows of her vestibule, observing the flock of neighbours on her lawn. "Where's the circus? Don't none of these people got other places to be?" The crows heard her smoky voice croak like a raven's, but didn't understand the words she said.

The officer attempted to disperse the neighbours, but more arrived. "Get off my property," the voice from the vestibule croaked again. "You got no right to be standing anyplace near my house!"

The sentinels flew from poles to trees as onlookers tentatively shifted from the lip of the ragged lawn and Lizzie, standing close to Foley, cupped her mouth with her hands and shouted:

"What you gonna do Ma, call the cops?"

"Don't you get smart with me! Just 'cause you got yourself an audience," her mother rasped in reply.

Even Lizzie, who well knew her mother's misanthropic rages, couldn't have suspected the depths of her hatred or the bloodthirsty broodings that filled her ailing mind. She transferred her weight from one leg to another. She pressed against Roger, who finally, after tenaciously struggling to remain grounded, allowed his consciousness to take flight. Above, with the vigilant crows, he observed Lizzie's beauty. He also observed this remote and disregarded land which seemed both unknown to him yet familiar. How easy it would be to commit murder here, he thought.

His physicality made Lizzie feel safe. He smelled of sweat and something young and wild, a wolf cub or the pup of a fox. The wind caught twists of her hair and flung them like silk cords over his chest. She touched his broad callused hand with her delicate, manicured fingers, bringing him back to the discomfort of his body.

Crows fluttered and cawed and a painful stinging arose in his throat. He hated taking these departures, hated coming back again. He'd been making excursions like these since childhood. Out of body experiences, they were called. Lots of people had them. As a boy, it had been his way of coping. Now, they were reflexive and difficult to stop. As hard as he tried to remain anchored, whenever discomposure struck, he found himself sailing upwards, witnessing his movements, though it wasn't impossible for him to tune out and completely lose sight of himself.

He'd once asked a visiting police psychologist if he ought to be worried. "Probably not," the guy had said, "unless it's affecting the quality of your life." Roger wasn't sure what that meant.

"You ever get migraines?" the psychologist inquired. Roger sometimes got headaches, though he didn't know if they were migraines. He didn't know if this inability to stay anchored in his body was related. The psychologist gave him the name of a neurologist, but Roger hadn't followed up, and things had gotten worse.

He appeared composed, however, as he cordoned off the area with a bright plastic containment ribbon. His ability to be deadpan was a talent. All the while he was asking himself:

Why do so many bad things have to happen? Why do people have to suffer? He'd been asking himself these heartbreaking questions for years and never came any closer to answers, only to the conclusion that he probably should be in some other line of work. He felt so close to Lizzie's sorrow—so close, that it may as well have been his own—and he wanted nothing more than to magically erase the tragedy that he was certain awaited her.

A frightened pheasant concealed in the sedge took flight, its wings like oars in a river of sky and its brown feathered body like an ascending angel's. Lizzie imagined Celeste's dark sapient eyes. For a moment, she imagined her diving into the field, which turned to ocean with every blast of wind and each wave of long rumpled grass. The air grew colder and a crow swooped down from a dead maple. Its wings clicked and creaked as it swept above the wooden turret that jutted from the corpse's bloodless face. It veered towards Lizzie's mother's house. In all her memory since Celeste's birth, Lizzie couldn't recall her mother walking out the front door when the sun was high in the sky. She couldn't recall her ever venturing onto the front porch, or down those porch steps, if the possibility existed that another person might be nearby. Instead, her mother crept outdoors in the evening or in the wee hours of the morning when most human creatures were still asleep.

A train's desolate whistle bled into the sky, it bled into the dark voices of vigilant crows and into the abrasive pitch of Lizzie's mother shouting: "Get away from my goddamned house." Some spectators made a feeble show of compliance, straddling the lawn and the gravel road, but none could fully sacrifice being on the front lines of misfortune.

It was the crows who first observed Lizzie's mother pass beyond the sparkling aluminium door, wheeling her broom like an archer, and the crows who first saw officer Roger Foley adjust his cap, as he moved protectively towards Lizzie.

"Don't think I don't see you!" Lizzie's mother's hoarse voice cracked. She trailed down the porch stairs undeterred by the crowd, which broke apart to avoid her assault and reconfigured whispering spiteful assessments. Her breath shook her wiry frame as she headed past the horde of onlookers, past the bright plastic containment ribbon, and past the dead forlorn unknown, making a beeline for her daughter. "Now we'll see how smart you are!" she shouted, trudging to where Lizzie stood in the field. Her broom, like a skittish bird, flew up into the air, knocking the cap from Roger's head as he attempted to shield Lizzie.

The crows were scrutinizing faces, both the man's and the woman's, searching for enemies, for they could see everyone clearly now. Before Roger was able to wrestle the broom free, positive identification was made. Throngs of birds whirled above, dark eyes flashing, wings pounding; the squawking reverberation of vengeance rising louder than the boundless clatter of bones twisting, and Lizzie, with no thought of her saviour, diving, just as she imagined Celeste had done, into the fierce rippling breakers of the yawning field.

Homecoming

AT THE MORGUE, the coroner takes fingerprints and identifies the corpse as the presumed dead fugitive, Jimmy Robinson. His body is laid out on a cold steel gurney and a forensic pathologist takes samples of earth that are collected from under his nails and strands of hair.

"Do you think there's any connection between this one and the girl they hauled up from the river?" officer Roger Foley asks, knowing at this stage the question is absurd. It's not that he expects an answer, but he wants to ponder it himself. He carries it with him into the waiting room, where a hysterical woman sobs: "We already buried him, don't you remember?"

She clutches Foley's blue sleeve. "You let me take a jar of ashes from that car wreck! You said it was all finished, that you was satisfied my boy Jimmy burned."

"I didn't say anything, m'am," Foley answers, feeling heartsick with the realization this must be the victim's mother. "It was another officer who was on that case." He tries jiggling his arm free.

“My Jimmy!” she shrieks. “My Jimmy!” A woman officer, Edna Stares, arrives and leads Jimmy’s mother through a curtained door.

“We need you to look at the body,” officer Stares says gravely, calming Jimmy’s mother with her quiet voice.

The gurney is wheeled into a cubicle as Jimmy’s mother weeps. “His eye,” she whispers, seeing a gauze patch.

Forensic technicians removed a curious stick before packing the eye socket, but officer Stares doesn’t explain. “The body was injured,” she says.

“It’s my boy,” Jimmy’s mother sobs. “It’s my Jimmy.”

“Why do you think your son would steal a car and run, Mrs. Robinson?” the officer asks.

“I don’t know,” Jimmy’s mother weeps.

“Did anyone want to kill your son, Mrs. Robinson?”

Jimmy’s mother drops her sodden face into her hands. “Who’d wanna kill my boy? Who’d wanna kill my Jimmy?”

“We’re not sure, Mrs. Robinson,” officer Stares’ well-modulated voice says. “He may not have been murdered, but we’re not ruling it out.”

“You think I killed him?” Jimmy’s mother asks. “Is that what you think?”

“No, Mrs. Robinson, we just need you to identify your son.”

Jimmy’s mother wipes her eyes and blows her nose on a wad of tissue. “Jimmy had his problems, he got himself into trouble. I’m sure you got all of that written down someplace, but he wasn’t the kind of bad to get killed over.”

“Thank you, Mrs. Robinson,” Edna Stares says before leading her away.

Outside, traffic blurs Quebec Street: people move too quickly on pavement and melt suddenly into cars. Everything behaves as if connected, as if it were orchestrated by an unseen network. Jimmy’s mother thinks how Kevin and Jimmy both are dead now and how alone she is. She thinks about how little money she earns and how hard her jobs are, how much she hates them and how tired she is. She thinks of her own dead mother, and of the suicide note she’d written: *Since I ain’t got no family and no one comes to see me no more, I may as well be dead.*

Jimmy’s mother sobs again.

She doesn't go back to work at the diner that afternoon; nor does she go to her second job, at Club Venus, that night. She sits in the still, unlit living room of her geared-to-income unit, watching darkness spread over the walls and furniture as if it were a stain of coffee spreading through the fibres of her dress.

She smokes one cigarette after another, downs shot after shot of whisky. When the police first told her Jimmy was gone and gave her the ashes from the car wreck, she'd grieved, but didn't truly believe them. How could he be gone? She half expected him to turn up any day. Now, she'd seen his body with her very own eyes. She'd seen her poor Jimmy, who must have been wandering out in that field for days, hurt and hungry and friendless.

Darkness pastes its way through the blinds, along the banister that leads to the upper floor, to Jimmy's bedroom, to the place, she decides, she'll die, if she can find the courage to end her life tonight.

She takes the bottle of whisky into her son's small grey room, so sorrowfully in need of paint. A scratchy green army blanket rests bundled in a hollow at the centre of the old, collapsed wooden bed. There's a broken baseball bat in the corner, a heap of gum and candy wrappers, hockey cards, a broken model airplane, a tangle of string. There's a pair of jeans, shirts, underwear and socks all squashed together, a moldy bowl of Cheerios. Jimmy's mother left everything untouched. But now, she's compelled to lift the clothing, to fold it, to put it neatly away.

In the closet, a colourful old headdress lies buried beneath stained bed sheets.

Jimmy's gran, Maureen's mother, had given Jimmy the headdress along with a toy bow and arrow many years ago. That same Christmas, Gran had given Kevin a cowboy hat and a cap gun. Maureen recalls how Kevin and some of his friends had tied Jimmy to a telephone pole and tried setting it on fire. Maureen knew Kevin wasn't really bad. He was just easily influenced by others. He was as good as gold on his own. Nothing at all like Jimmy.

There are empty cigarette boxes in the closet, and the small squares of gold and silver foil that Jimmy removed from the packages and set alight. Even in darkness she can see streaks of ash from their paper backings and burn holes in the thin brown rug.

For a moment, her face flares with blood. She hears the echo of her own raging voice screaming at Jimmy. "You little bastard!" Tears fill her eyes. Beneath a cigarette box, the name Laurie LaFrambois and a phone number appears on a scrap of lined paper. On the back of the scrap, Jimmy has written in his almost indecipherable script: "For a good time!"

Maureen crumples the paper in her fist and mutters. "I don't want to know." She drinks from her bottle. Whisky singes her tongue like a yellow fuse. It steals her breath. It makes her recall how she laboured giving Jimmy life—how the contractions came so suddenly, warm water spilling over her legs. Her mother said labour was like being swallowed into the bowels of hell.

"Yeah, yeah, ma, you always exaggerate." But when it happened, it turned out she was right.

When Maureen was in labour with Jimmy, she couldn't breathe at all and she couldn't speak. It was like a nightmare where you're calling for help, but nothing comes out of your mouth. If she could have called for anything, she would have shouted for painkillers, an epidural, gas, twilight sleep. "As soon as I feel anything, I want to be knocked out, you understand?" she'd told her doctor. She didn't realize that he'd be away in Florida playing golf, that she'd be yo-yoing back and forth between the hospital and the bowels of hell, waiting for a damned intern to play God.

She pushed. Shit-head, the father, was there. He said she moaned like a cow. He stayed while she gasped, while the bowels of hell sucked her down and spit her back. "Know what you sound like?" he asked, and as soon as there was a break in contractions, she made a fist and smashed him as hard as she could in the balls. For her, that marked the beginning of the end. Jimmy had always been trouble, right from the very first. Morning sickness and migraines from the moment she conceived. Six months along, she started bleeding and had to stay in bed for two months. Her labour was long and the birth difficult. Shit-head said Jimmy was ugly. He'd asked the intern: "Can't we just leave it here until it starts looking human?" The intern laughed but Shit-head was serious. She told him "Don't bother coming home," and he didn't. For an entire year, Jimmy screamed with colic, and with Shit-head gone, there was no one but her. When Jimmy finally shut up and started crawling, he found and drank half a bottle of Liquid Plumber. She prayed for the day when he would understand her—when she could tell him what he could and couldn't do, but he never acted like he understood what she was saying. Even when he started talking, all he ever did was give her lip.

She sobs into the feathers of the headdress as she transfers it from the closet rubble. He'd wanted so much to be a cowboy, like his brother. He said Indians just got beaten up by everyone and massacred, they got their land stolen from them, and no one gave them any respect, but Maureen refused to buy him a different hat. The memory pierces her heart like a sharp fixed point. More than anything, she just wants another chance. Tears blind her as she stumbles into the bathroom. In the medicine cabinet there's a bottle of Valium, and she thinks maybe she'll take the whole thing and just keep drinking. She takes another swig from the bottle and closes her eyes. But what if she doesn't die, what if she only ends up brain dead and on life support? She needs to think up something better, something guaranteed.

"Haven't I ever told you, there are no guarantees, Maureen?" It's her dead mother talking, as clear as if she's walked into the room. A prickle rises at the back of her neck. The phone rings and she quickly heads to the kitchen. It's such a long journey, down the dark hallway, down the stairs. Her mother's voice remains, an echo in her ear. There's a story she'd heard when she was young, a story about a phone line broken in a graveyard that allowed the dead to communicate with the living.

"Who is this?" she slurs when she picks the phone up. She half expects her mother.

"If you'd listened to me, Maureen, and not got involved with what's his name, none of this would have happened. You wouldn't be wanting to kill yourself and you wouldn't be hearing voices."

It isn't her mother on the phone though. It's a thin, childish voice, a quaking, uncertain voice. "Mrs. Robinson?" it squeaks. "I knew your son Jimmy. The police came by my house today and my ma said I got to phone you."

"Who is this?" Maureen repeats, feeling now that it should be her mother.

"Tell her!" a gravelly voice shouts in the background, emphasizing each word.

"I'm Laurie LaFrambois," the thin voice warbles. "You could kind of say I was Jimmy's girlfriend."

Maureen squeezes the paper, still clutched in her fist, but the name, Laurie LaFrambois, doesn't ring a bell. "If you're sellin' something, I don't want any," she slurs and kisses the whisky bottle with numb lips.

"I'm not selling anything," the voice says.

"Give me the friggin phone," the gravelly voice demands. "Is this Mrs. Robinson?"

"Who in hell's this?" Maureen asks. The dark world around her spins, and she grows more confused.

"I'm Jean LaFrambois, the mother of the girl your son knocked up, and I want to know what you plan to do about it?"

"Mother?" she asks.

"My daughter's a baby. She's only thirteen. Your boy is almost an adult and should have known better."

Maureen's legs turn rubbery. It's impossible, she thinks. "My boy's dead, and my mother's dead. Go away!" She slams the phone at the metal hook, but it slaps the wall instead.

"You're making a fool of yourself, Maureen!" her mother's voice twangs. She stumbles through darkness towards the kitchen sink. No way she could find the bathroom. In the sink, there are dishes—a pan, a plate, a greasy spoon. She throws up. "Now you've made yourself sick, Maureen!" It's her mother's loud voice, the voice that disapproves of everything.

"You never told me what was right!" Maureen sobs. "You only ever told me what was wrong!" She takes a long swig of whisky and squeezes the crumpled scrap of paper. Moonlight filters through the tattered kitchen sheers and the dark telephone receiver swings like a clock's pendulum. Maureen wipes her mouth and hunts through the open kitchen drawer for the sharpest knife she can find. This is the way she'll do it, she decides. Drink more whisky, take Valium, slash both wrists.

"Pull yourself together. You're acting crazy," her mother's voice rebukes.

"You always said I was!" Maureen shouts, taking another long swig before setting the bottle down and lifting a knife.

"For goodness sakes, Maureen, it's not sharp enough to cut butter. I was always saying you needed to get those knives sharpened."

"Just tell me what's right!" Maureen sobs, the knife poised over her wrist. Whisky backs up in her throat. The whole world grows silent. "You can't say anything, can you? You don't know what to say, do you?"

Maureen stops shouting. She hears footsteps. She holds her breath and bites her lower lip.

"Who's there?" she calls. "Ma?" The sound of aching feet drags through the living room. She can hear the rhythm and thump of their limping. "Ma?" she asks again, shaking, electric with dread. Darkness pervades the kitchen, until a dazzle of moonlight shimmers through the window. She puts her knife down, lifts the whisky, crushes the scrap of paper in her hand.

"Who's there?" she shouts again. "If you're here to kill me, I'm not gonna stop you." Her hands tremble with such intensity that the whisky fizzes in its bottle.

"You're making an ass of yourself, Maureen... carrying on like this," her mother whispers.

Maureen shuts her eyes and sees him, covered in knots of mud, the flesh of his fingers stained brown, hair glued into sharp dirty spikes.

"You're not Jimmy, are you?" she chokes. Whisky pools and burns in the back of her throat. "You can't be my Jimmy?"

"That's what I've been trying to tell you. Of course he is, Maureen, our little Jimmy, come home after his scrape with death... now mind you're good to him... none of your 'you little bastard this' and 'you little bastard that'."

The bottle drops, falls onto the linoleum and rolls. Rivulets of yellow travel the floor.

"They told me you was dead. I saw you with my own eyes. Tell me it ain't true." She hiccups.

Her vision's impaired, everything appears doubled. She covers one eye and squints. His face, empty, like a sleepwalker or a drug addict, materializes. "I died and been reborn," he says, slowly, laconically.

"You ain't making sense, Jimmy." She hiccups again. "Dead is dead!" Her hand attempts an emphatic thigh smack, but only hits a cupboard. "Are you drunk?" she asks.

"No, I ain't," says the spectre, "and from now on you got to call me Tenskwatawa."

"Who?" She closes her eyes. The lids are too heavy to keep open.

"The Prophet," he thunders. "Tenskwatawa."

The name sounds somehow familiar, a North American indigenous name, something she'd once heard on TV or learned at school, or something Kevin and Jimmy once told her. Maybe it had something to do with Jimmy's play headdress? She forces her eyes open and reaches towards her bottle.

"No more of that shit! The Great Spirit says 'no'!" The voice booms and her aching head feels as if it might split open.

"What do you mean 'The Great Spirit'?" she mutters. "Who do you think you're talking to?" The spectre of Jimmy spins. She'd like to give him a good dressing down, but her eyelids are so heavy she has to shut them and she can't always find Jimmy in the darkness. "You come back here after playing dead, after giving me the fright of my life, after making me feel so bad about myself I wanted to die and you take my only comfort?" She claws in the general direction of the bottle. It shatters. Whisky and glass chips wash over the floor.

"Why, you little bastard!" She tries to shout, she tries to swear, she tries to tell Jimmy if he doesn't get off his John Henry high horse, she'll knock him off, but her voice won't come. Just like when she was in labour. She feels only frustration and fury as she always has with Jimmy. She lurches in the darkness towards the place she thinks he's hiding but finds herself in the living room, where she's sure she sees him, taking a position in her good wing-backed chair.

It's the best piece of furniture she owns, and Jimmy knows he's not allowed to sit there. Now, she can do nothing to prevent him, and to make matters worse, he's covering the tweedy-gold upholstery in mud.

Maureen locates a garbage pail and throws up. Her throat relaxes. "You should be on the couch," she mumbles, wiping her lips. The couch, threadbare, with deep pockets of wear visible in its cushions, has remained vacant since the day Jimmy went missing. Now, his face materializes above; there's nothing of its former adolescent softness or uncertainty.

"No!" he states unequivocally. His voice is so loud, it makes Maureen's head feel as if it's being blown apart.

"Go into the kitchen where I can see you. Phone that number you got crinkled up in your hand."

Maureen had forgotten the scrap. She'd forgotten the loopy handwriting and the girl's name.

"Call that number. Tell the girl you got money for her."

"I don't got money for no one." Maureen swallows. She tries not to puke again.

"Do what I say. The Great Spirit says you gotta," Jimmy commands.

Maureen's eyes flutter shut. She sits down on the couch, but finds herself in the kitchen, beside the silent swinging receiver. Her hands release the damp paper. Her eyes work to make sense of it. Her shaking finger dials the number. It rings three times before it's answered with a thin, perplexed "Lo?"

"This is Jimmy Robinson's mother. I got some money for you."

"Get-out!" Laurie whines. "Is this for real?"

Maureen finds it difficult to make her lips work properly. "Yes," she lies.

"So like... you want me to come over, or something?"

The room slants. Maureen needs to lie down on the floor. "Yeah, yeah, come over."

"I'm real sorry about Jimmy," Laurie squeaks. "If I have a boy," she offers, "I'm gonna name him Jimmy."

Maureen has forgotten, but now remembers the apparition. It's sitting in her good chair, impatiently beating the arms. "Don't be long," she belches, and hangs up.

Maureen lies on the floor of the spinning room and thinks of the girl. She sees her hoist herself from a vinyl La-Z-Boy rocker where she'd been watching TV and imagines a sudden rise in her abdomen, as the baby kicks and her maternity jumper does a little dance. The image makes Maureen feel even sicker.

She's never seen the girl, to her knowledge, but visualizes her as small, and imagines she must walk slowly, as if she's balancing a medicine ball on her belly. Maureen follows Laurie in her mind's eye. This helps her stop feeling so queasy. She imagines the girl skirting the school's parking lot, stopping at the new crosswalk beside the old toboggan hill, exactly in the place where Kevin was killed. The projects are on the other side of the street, and she imagines the girl rehearsing what she'll say. "Nice to meet you... Jimmy told me lots about you." She's the type of girl, Maureen thinks, who for etiquette's sake will lie. She'll approach the unit breathing heavily, because like Maureen she'll be unable to walk a block pregnant without huffing and puffing. Her hair will be pushed behind her ears and when she rings the doorbell she'll listen for the chime inside. The dark and cold of the house will surprise her. She'll be surprised Maureen smells of vomit and whisky and looks both drunk and slightly crazed.

Maureen knows her eyes are bugging wildly, that beneath them are circles so dark they could have been drawn with charcoal. And she knows that the girl will smell Jimmy, permeating from the living room, reminding her of a couple of weeks ago when all of the sewers in Fontainebleau backed up.

"Why you always have to be so melodramatic is beyond me," Maureen's mother's throbbing voice intrudes. "I don't know why you need to punish yourself like this. You never were satisfied with happy things."

Maureen finds herself in the living room again. The apparition, Jimmy, rises from his chair. Brown mud at his feet and clay embedded at the ends of his fingers. He extends his arms. One blue eye glistens like wet turquoise. The girl suddenly appears; the child in her belly squirming and twisting like an eel, reaching right up into her throat as Jimmy takes her into his mud-encrusted arms and kisses her.

Maureen's mouth opens and she gags. "Didn't I teach you no better than that?" she forces the words through her mouth. "That kind of public display! And in *my* house, you little bastard."

"Leave the boy alone, Maureen. Haven't you already done enough damage?" her mother's voice admonishes.

Jimmy's head turns with a squish. "Quiet," he commands. "Get the hell out of here, Gran, you're dead... and you," he fixes his turquoise eye on Maureen, "stop your droning! Go make food. The Great Spirit says you gotta."

Everything goes black. Maureen feels the room spin round and round. She needs the cool kitchen floor beneath her back. Her throat pinches and the lips of her mouth pucker and stick together, just as if she's been sucking on a tube of lemon-flavoured epoxy glue. She staggers into the kitchen and finds a loaf of bread in her hands.

"Jeez! Are you magic or something, Jimmy? Do you know hypnotism? Maybe you can make my ma give me her bedroom when the baby comes. It's way bigger than the closet I gotta sleep in." She hears the girl speaking and sees her son's blue tinged lips stretch, like elastic bands, over his crooked teeth.

"You don't gotta worry about any of that anymore," he gushes. To Maureen, he sounds just like Shit-head. "I'm gonna take care of you now." Shit-head used this exact line on her.

Don't believe him! Maureen thinks. She'd shout it, but her mouth won't open. Even if she still had her whisky bottle, she couldn't poke the top through. She imagines the girl's washed-out blue eyes, round as a child's on Christmas morning, just like hers were once, and Jimmy—Shit-head—reaching for the girl, his fingers staining her blouse with mud.

"She ain't you, Maureen," her mother's voice says. "Just 'cause you was stupid, don't mean Jimmy's girl is. And Jimmy ain't Shit-head. What you need to do is mind your own business, join AA, get yourself some help."

"My ma's gonna have a cow!" Maureen sees Jimmy's girl say as he presses his blue lips against her face.

"You stink real bad, Jimmy, but I can get used to it."

"No!" Maureen's mouth struggles, she spits, but the room spins so violently and her throat closes so tightly, she can't say it. She can't warn the girl, tell her what happens when you accept what so obviously is rotten. Somewhere an urgent bell rings.

Jimmy's mouth gnaws the girl's neck. "Call me Tenskwatawa, OK?" He bites the small round indentation of her throat. "That's my new name. It means The Prophet, and that means I get to tell everyone what to do. Including you!"

The girl wheezes, a hiccup catches in her breath. The bell rings again and again and Maureen watches as he begins to undress her.

"Stop!" the girl whispers, "Your ma!"

"I don't give a care," the dead prophet spits. "What kind of a mother is that?" he asks, and his words reverberate like a dense boom through Maureen's spinning brain.

It's the doorbell ringing, but Maureen doesn't know it. Her world continues to reel. "Such disrespectful behaviour," the slurring words become a froth escaping from her tangled lips, "and such a pregnant fool."

The image of a knife, compulsively spreading butter and mustard over slices of bread, trembles in her mind. Her filthy son. That poor friendless girl. “It ain’t right!” she thinks, and would say so if only she could unstick her lips. If only she could get everything to keep still long enough. “It ain’t right, you filthy bastard.” She knows she would have gone after him, would have done him in, if only she’d been in control of herself, or at least that knife, which curved like a silver bow in her mind.

Makeover

"IF YOU WANT to drag your feet, go do it in the unemployment line" is the pep talk Jean LaFrambois, the head housekeeper, gives the chambermaids of the River Park Hotel each morning; and by the end of every day, there are several she's "let go". The euphemism sounds liberating, and some maids, when they see what's expected, leave happily, but Margaret Markovic wants to be fixed to something solid. She craves a stable mooring, a permanent anchor.

It's more important to her than money, although money is certainly the reason she took the job—money and, of course, the fact that cleaning is something she can do.

She knows how to wash a wall, disinfect a toilet, scour a filthy floor spotless. She knows how to tuck the edge of a pillow slip like a pleat and make a streaky mirror gleam—all of these things she learned in childhood, and all of these things she's practiced over the years, first as a helpmeet to her ailing mother, then as a wife to Paul.

Jean said she'd like to see if Margaret was up to the job, and put her on probation. They both knew, though neither said, that Jean's daughter, Laurie, had once been put on probation. She'd been a student of Paul's at Thomas King Elementary and had been found in *flagrante dilecto* in the boy's washroom with the juvenile delinquent, Peter Galka. But probation at Thomas King was different from work probation at the River Park. There were no expulsions here, only firings, the word itself evoking for Margaret frightening military sharpshooters and steely riflemen.

The rooms at the hotel are all spacious, with separate areas for sitting and sleeping. They contain white oak furnishings, leather couches and La-Z-Boy chairs. The bathrooms are grand affairs with orchid tiles and Jacuzzi bathtubs, and whenever Margaret enters one, she's struck with a nostalgic longing so great she can barely breathe.

It's the orchids that arouse the past—that make her see a prom corsage, a Cattleya orchid, with the fragrance of fruit punch. Paul had pinned it to her dress-strap, with young trembling hands. The dress was cream-coloured, darker only by a shade than her satin, cap-sleeved wedding gown, which she married in a year later. Paul's parents insisted on a traditional Serbian ceremony, where bride and groom are crowned and then marched around the altar as king and queen of the new union. Before the children came, they'd kept those crowns intact, and as newlyweds, they'd worn them to Niagara Falls, their honeymoon destination.

She hated to admit it, but the Niagara Falls hotel was the first she'd ever stayed at, and the Jacuzzi tub, not quite as elegant as the River Park's, the first she'd ever beheld. It was the first time she'd ever bathed with another person, the first time she'd seen a naked man and the first time she'd ever felt overcome by the certainty of her life's unfurling destiny.

She hadn't always loved Paul. In fact, when they first met in Mr. Delcort's grade nine science class, she'd found him impudent. He sat beside her, writing silly notes and drawing rude pictures, full of his own importance as Hepburn's rising football star. She prayed he'd stop distracting her. She lived in dread of Mr. Delcort and the riding crop he carried, which he called the Scorpion because it could inflict a sudden biting sting.

When the crop eventually struck Paul and his tough linebacker's expression contorted to shock, she found herself reflexively shouting "Stop!" Delcort, so taken aback, halted the beating. Afterwards, it was generally reported that Margaret wrestled the Scorpion from her teacher's hand because she was in love with Paul. While the entire story was a fabrication, its circulation fostered their relationship, preparing the ground for love's blossoming.

Paul stopped drawing obscene pictures and passing juvenile notes. He expressed his gratitude to Margaret in behaving properly and Margaret, in turn, found herself opening to the possibility of his adoration. Paul soon became her high school sweetheart, the only one she'd ever had.

Margaret knows she's a dreamer, that these dreams of the past help her negotiate her days, but she also knows that indulging in them here, when she should be working, will lead to her ruin, and so she shuts her inner eye and hauls her bulky metal cleaning trolley out into the hotel's corridor. She slides and twists her master key into a new room's lock and enters as swiftly as her trolley allows. Searing exhaust from the bitumen of Ouellette Street assaults her. Heat permeates every molecule of air. On the vanity, before her, dazzling sunlight illuminates the tresses of an oddly animate wig. The hair, abundant and black, frames a long-necked stand, and quivers like an alert animal when Margaret turns the air conditioning on.

She's never seen a wig close up before, and can't imagine what kind of real woman might wear one, though, as a child, she endlessly revamped her Barbie doll's artificial coiffures in a miniature beauty shop which featured four distinctive wigs. She'd match the hair with a variety of outfits and then evolve adventures for her doll in which she could project an array of future selves.

There was the flaming orange-haired nightclub singer who donned a beautiful sparkling black dress and the brilliant lemon-blond dancer, who in a silver tutu, tiara, and slippers was a prima ballerina. By day, her Barbie, with a nut-brown bubble cut, might wear the midnight blue cape of a registered nurse or the sheath skirt of an airline stewardess. Inevitably, her doll's activities would involve some form of heroism: singing or dancing in war ravaged countries in spite of impending coups, saving lives in hospitals or handling dangerous crises in the sky. In one of the storylines she especially liked, stewardess Barbie had to take over for a sick pilot and bring a jumbo jet full of passengers through a hurricane. Once on terra firma, with a change of wig and outfit, Barbie would become a kimonoed tourist-spy in Japan or a foreign correspondent in Nairobi, reporting on all of her exciting escapades. Margaret never tired of changing Barbie's look or storyline, as if one's life could be inevitably shaped by the outer frills and accoutrements one dressed in.

She thought of this as her fingers instinctively moved towards the wig; however, she refused to touch it. Most of the chambermaids at the River Park wouldn't have been able to resist. Most couldn't refrain from sneaking squirts of expensive perfume or trying on the guests' furs. Margaret was rare in her self-restraint. She hankered after something else, far less tactile, far more ill-defined, far more time-consuming.

In the bathroom, she plunges her hand to the bottom of the toilet, swishes a stringy rag around the bowl, and thinks of Paul. He'd been changing, all along, but she'd failed to notice.

She'd failed to notice the strangeness of his purchases: the power tools, the electric guitar, the Firebird convertible—which was the same aquamarine blue as her toilet cleaner. She failed to notice when his enthusiasm for shopping eventually waned, when he started gaining weight and took to staring blankly at the television screen. It was only when he got into his housecoat and slippers and called in sick to work that she finally noticed, and by that time it was too late.

She shoves the rag down deep into the toilet's closet bend, and twists. "Is it me?" she'd asked him, not wanting an answer.

"No," he'd responded, kindly, politely.

Small flecks of shit float to the water's surface and she flushes. He hadn't been happy with his job, said he was scared of the crazy kids he had to teach and the junior psychopaths he had to babysit. Once, a grade-four boy, wearing a pair of homemade wings, jumped from the top of the school at recess and knocked him to the tarmac. Paul was certain it had been premeditated, certain that the boy had wished him real harm. Margaret nodded sympathetically, but reminded him that not all kids were bad, that he used to love teaching.

"Did I?" he asked morosely.

"I thought you did," she said.

After twenty-five years of marriage and two children, he left. He'd taken nothing with him, save the Firebird and a chainsaw, and the clothes he was wearing. He vanished as completely as a footprint in the sand. There was a note, a final communication. "Gone out" was all it said, and when Margaret read it, all she could see in her mind's eye were the two long taper candles she and Paul had held aloft at their wedding as the priest spoke of godly light illuminating their shared path.

Two long strands of hair remain clinging to the bathtub wall like passengers on a capsizing ship, despite Margaret's efforts to wipe them away. What would drive a person to abandon a life, she wonders. Was it fair to resent Paul? He'd left money in their joint account, bonds she cashed, stocks she'd sold. Even his guitar, which she'd given to a neighbour's boy in exchange for roof repairs. For a while she'd been able to live just as she'd been living. She continued keeping their house, mothering their two daughters in spite of the fact they loathed her and were old enough to be living alone. She postponed getting a paying job. She continued hoping he'd return.

She squirts the tub with heady disinfectant and swipes at the hairs again. The scent evokes memories of Hotel Dieu, the hospital where she'd had Marcia and then Tammy, with Paul arriving too late, both times, to witness the births, and also, of course, that frightening time, after Paul had been injured in a car accident.

She thinks about the relationship Paul had with the girls. How he gave them things: clothes, spending money, and then she thinks of the exorbitant orthodontic bill sitting on the kitchen table, and the fight that erupted with Marcia last night. "I couldn't *liiiive* if my friends knew you cleaned toilets in a hotel," she'd said, and Margaret had snapped, telling her how much it cost to feed her, let alone put braces on her teeth.

She wonders what happened to the babies Marcia and Tammy once were. Time devoured them, it seems, and left in their stead, although she didn't like to think this way, two strangers who would just as soon she vanish from the face of the earth.

The two strands of dark lusty hair finally stick to Margaret's soapy cloth. She presumes the hair came from the wig. She touches a strand. It's soft and curls naturally and makes her think of Paul's receding hairline and his pink shiny scalp which he was convinced grew more noticeably hairless each day. "I'd still love you if you were bald," she'd told him, but it was no consolation. Why would she assume it would be? Wisps of his hair collected everywhere. It made her wonder what the world might look like if everyone lost their hair at the same time. It wasn't a thought she liked having. It wasn't one she'd felt she could share with him, and obviously there were many thoughts he'd had that he didn't want to share with her. But she didn't like thinking this way. She didn't want to resent him. Their years together had not been altogether bad ones. She'd loved him. She still loves him.

The police searched his desk drawers at school, and in neat tight handwriting, Paul had put down on paper all of the pros and cons of remaining with Margaret. On the pros list there were only three things: "don't have to cook, don't have to clean, don't have to do my own laundry." The cons list, which filled both front and back sides of a foolscap sheet, consisted of things Margaret chose to forget.

She wipes soap and toothpaste residue off the vanity mirror, comparing her dull brown-grey hair, pulled back in one of Marcia's old ponytail holders, with the vibrant black mane of the quivering wig in the other room. Once she'd asked Paul if he thought she should colour her hair.

He was reading a newspaper. "What for?" he'd absently inquired.

"To make me more attractive?" she'd responded, not meaning for it to come out as a question, but perhaps the question had been appropriate. Why had she contemplated dyeing her hair? Paul had mumbled and rustled the newspaper, signalling the conclusion of the conversation. She decided against the change. Now she wonders what possible difference dyeing her hair might have made.

She rinses and wipes a drinking glass, wraps it in a little bag that says "sanitized for your protection," and pushes her trolley out into the bedroom. Her memories are quicksand she struggles against; they retard movement, impede progress. She works faster now, trying to outrun them. Perspiration beads her forehead as she hoists a heavy floral bedspread and removes an elegant red dress from its folds. She sets the dress on a chair, makes the bed, tidies objects on a night table, but even with this burst of concentrated speed, she doesn't seem able to recover lost time, nor stop the rising tide of memories, which are increasingly difficult to quell.

She'd like to let the dusting go, but knows Jean will be checking every surface with her white cotton gloves. She slides her shammy over skirting boards and base heaters, banks it over picture frames and window ledges. On tabletops, her hand works in circles, as if slathering suntan lotion on the kids when they were small, or mineral oil on the knee Paul shattered when he slammed his car into a lamppost on his eighteenth birthday. He was drunk and speeding and could have been killed. Throughout their married life, whenever she massaged his aching leg, she'd never neglected to silently thank whatever forces had preserved him.

The accident had changed his life and hers by association. He'd won, then had to forfeit, a football scholarship to Michigan State. He had to abandon professional football as his life's enduring dream. Slowly, he began to walk again, though never without the aid of a cane. At the time, Margaret hadn't considered the cost—he was alive, after all, and eager for her to be his bride. "I can't imagine a future alone," he'd spoken in an eerily melancholy voice from his hospital bed. "I have no life if you refuse me." Of course, she told him, she'd never refuse him.

She'd never abandon him, even if the rest of the world did.

A long, waxy smudge on the dresser mirror draws an equator through her reflection, bisecting her face and her greying hair. She applies her shammy and accidentally strikes the wig stand. Strands of black hair stir and rise. She steadies it with her hands. A wave of heat streams through her fingertips like fire on a cannon's fuse. She wants to touch the wig again, but removes herself from temptation and dusts the skirting boards at the other end of the room.

She won't waste time checking her wristwatch, nor think about her parents, who gave it to her on graduation day. Her mother said the watch was "dull but durable," and her father added "Like a good wife, eh?" and winked at Paul. She wonders why time passes so quickly, why, after all these years, she still has this watch.

Paul had been her "lovable dreamboat" when she graduated, like Barbie's Ken. Such a strange, dated word, "dreamboat," she thinks, and for the first time comprehends its meaning and sees Paul, a pirate, sailing off with all her dreams in his cargo hold. She doesn't want to resent him or think unkind thoughts. If only she'd been more attentive, more sensitive, perhaps he wouldn't have left. Her dreams of connubial happiness were so numerous and desperate and blinding, they obscured her dreamboat: she couldn't spot him heel, or see when his mast hit the waves, or feel when his cabin filled with water. Now he's gone, as is everything he'd held for her, and she is bereft of "happily ever after" dreams.

She wipes around a window's apron and sill, remembering Barbie's aqua green speed boat and how she played with it in the shadow of the Ambassador Bridge. It wasn't a "Dream Boat," but a boat, she'd imagined, of Barbie's dreams. Even though the Detroit River was polluted, Margaret waded out from the grainy shore and set the boat afloat. The water was sticky and opaque with effluent, and although Margaret attempted to scrutinize its depths, her feet inevitably scraped against sharp metal and other vestiges of life's wreckage, deposited in the river's bed.

Barbie, oblivious to Margaret's suffering, negotiated the grey lapping waters of the river solo, even though there were two orange seats in her boat, and a Ken doll whose proper place was beside her, according to all the television advertisements. Ken had never been all that connected to Barbie in the storylines Margaret manufactured. He was more like a large fashion accessory, a giant clutch purse or umbrella with legs that Barbie occasionally toted along.

Margaret's mother, frail and sickly for as long as Margaret could recall, saw Ken as one might an outcast child, and because of his gender, encouraged her daughter to always give him a starring role in her games. "Men need to be at the centre of things," she'd instructed from her pink invalid's chair. "They need to know they're not dispensable." Yet Ken *was* dispensable to

Margaret. If he happened to disappear into the murky currents of the Detroit River, she had long decided, she wasn't going to go searching for him.

She begged and wheedled and harassed her mother about buying an astronaut's uniform for Barbie, but her mother deemed such a purchase "completely inappropriate" and bought, instead, the matching uniform for Ken.

"He doesn't need it," Margaret tried explaining desperately. "He's not going anywhere." She looked into her mother's implacably sweet face, and saw no glimmer of comprehension. She realized her mother would never understand her games.

At home, she put Barbie into the shining silver space suit, white helmet, and gloves. "It's a little big," she had Barbie lament, "but we don't have time to fix it." She placed the doll in a shoebox and started the countdown. After blast-off, she flew Barbie all over the house, and later, on Barbie's return to earth, dressed her in a full-skirted party frock decorated with tiny pink rosebuds and polka dots for her grand homecoming celebration. It was Barbie's long, black, sultry wig she'd chosen to match with the airy feminine outfit. The combination was unusual, and she couldn't recall the rationale for her selection, but remembered she'd been extremely pleased with her choice in spite of her mother's disapproval.

"Completely inappropriate," her voice delivers her mother's words. The hands of her dull and durable wristwatch relentlessly advance. She's not sure how long she's been fondling the black wig.

The hair is real, not synthetic, she considers. It's hair that once grew on another woman's head. Perhaps a gallant woman, who sold it to help her family, or a strong and resolute woman, who sold it to help herself. Perhaps the woman sold it, with certainty, without regret, without considering, even for a moment, how long she and that hair had been together.

Margaret's hands tremble as she lifts it. Never has she tampered with a guest's belongings, never has she tried a wig on. What would she do if the guest arrived, or if Jean came, checking up? What would she say? She decides to put the wig back on the stand, but finds herself pulling her hair into a knot instead. She bends forward, and slides the wig on in one tidy motion. At once she feels the weight of the hair as it tumbles heavily over her shoulders. It feels substantial and centring, and as she gazes into the mirror she laughs at the shock of it. She wonders what Paul might think if he were still around—wonders what Marcia and Tammy might say if she went home like this. Would they recognize her? She lifts her hands to remove the wig, but can't bring herself to take it off. Instead, she turns and glances over her shoulder at the mirror. The hair swings back and forth. It accentuates her strong hips and straight spine. There's a sturdiness about her, a charismatic amplitude, a power she possesses, but one she's never been aware of. Had she always walked with such confidence? Had she always been that tall?

Without fully realizing what she's doing, she unbuttons her smock and skirt and kicks both under the bed. She lifts the sleek red dress she carefully laid on the chair. In a million years, she'd never wear a dress like that, she thinks. It would be "completely inappropriate."

She puts the dress on. It's smooth and perfect. She laughs. Her reflection in the full-length closet mirror captivates her. She never noticed herself before, never noticed the dark beauty of her eyes or her happy spontaneity. When was the last time she'd laughed?

She knows this woman in the mirror is her, but who is she? She turns around and around, absorbing her image. "Who am I?" she laughs. "Where did I come from?"

She brushes at the long black strands with her fingers, a blinding ray of sun glances off her watch. Quick heavy footsteps echo from the hall. How long has she been parading in front of the mirror? Her heart gallops. A key clatters in the door's lock, and Jean's fuming face appears. Margaret will throw herself on Jean's mercy. She'll say she lost her mind. But before she's able to speak, Jean's expression softens.

"Excuse me, Miss." Jean clears her throat and her mouth contorts into an obsequious expression. "I didn't mean to barge in. I'm looking for a maid."

"Maid?" Margaret hears her voice say, "There's no maid here."

"I'm so sorry," Jean apologizes, then quickly shuts the door.

Margaret fluffs the long black hair and straightens the sleek red dress. Who is she? Her laughing eyes gaze deeply into the mirror as if it were the murky waters of the Detroit River she was wishing to pierce, but no memory, whatsoever, surfaces. It's as if her entire history has suddenly been washed away, as if in donning this unthinkable costume she's cast away even the most imperceptible constraint, unmoored herself completely from the harbour of past hopes, and cast off on a new uncharted course.

Corrosion

ELISE COMBED her fingers through her hair. “My daughter’s been missing for over twenty-four hours,” she told police officer Roger Foley. “Julia Wilson,” she said, “that’s my daughter’s name. She’s five foot two. She turned sixteen in July.” Elise knew she sounded business-like, curt—almost as if she’d been rehearsing these details. She watched the gangly officer collect a form from a drawer and scribble down information, then she reached into her handbag and pulled out a picture. It was a recent school photo in which Julia appeared clean, well-cared for and happy. The picture was encased in a delicate antique frame.

“She’s pretty,” Roger commented, feeling his heart skip.

“Yes,” Elise’s voice was impatient.

“Was there trouble at home?” he asked.

Elise pointed at Julia’s face in the photo: laughing brown eyes, thick black hair that swept over one shoulder, a perfect smile. “Does that look like a troubled child?”

The officer glanced at the photograph. "No hard words pass between you?"

"We quarrelled now and again," Elise confessed, "but Julia would never run off. She wasn't like that. She was an angel."

Roger shook his head. "Kids can do crazy things sometimes."

"My daughter was extremely sensible," Elise said firmly. "She'd never allow an impulsive heart to rule her head. She'd never run away."

"Was there anyone who she was particularly close to? Any friends?" He tapped the picture's frame.

"Julia had many acquaintances, but no one she'd consider a real friend, except for me. We were very close. Most of the girls she went to school with, understandably, were jealous."

"Any boyfriends?" the officer proceeded.

"There were no boys," Elise said. "Julia was shy with the opposite sex."

"How did she get on with Mr. Wilson?" he asked.

"There is no Mr. Wilson," Elise said.

"I don't mean to offend, Ma'am, but sometimes an estranged husband..."

"I'm a widow, sir." Elise's eyes met Roger's.

"I'm sorry," Roger said, and he sincerely meant it. There was so much pain and suffering in the world, so much misery. He felt the familiar disconnect, which sent his observing consciousness to the upper corner of the room and turned his body into nothing more than a functional husk.

"Believe me, I've thought of everyone. I've phoned everyone. No one knows where she is."

"I'd better have a list of names, anyway, Ma'am," he said mechanically, witnessing his own exquisite composure. "Just for the record...of people you've phoned, and teachers at her school, and anyone else she's had contact with. We'll do our best. In the meantime, go home and wait. She'll come home on her own, that's my bet."

"I wish I shared your confidence," Elise said. "I just have the feeling she won't be found alive."

Roger was having another out-of-body experience. He watched himself set a ham and lettuce sandwich on a desk. "She stood there and said she knew we wouldn't recover her daughter alive. It's creepy." He was up by the top shelves in Detective Sergeant Gary Gilley's office, listening to his own tough voice rant.

"After you've been around a while, nothing's creepy," Gilley said.

"But she was so certain." Roger marvelled at his performance, his ability to keep his weighty tearful grief in check. "I was sure it was just a little battle, you know, the kid asserting some independence. 'She'll come home,' I told her. You could have knocked me down with a feather this morning when we got news she was the Detroit River corpse. Who in hell would do a thing like that to a pretty, well-brought up kid like her?"

"There are some real sick bastards out there," Gilley said. "You want a root beer?"

"I mean this kid came from a good home. She was an honour roll student. Her mother doted on her," Roger's voice mechanically continued. "I was sure she'd show up in a day or two, say she'd been hiding out at a friend's place, even maybe a boyfriend's place."

"But not a very pretty cadaver, eh?" Gilley said, popping the tab on his root beer. "Well, at least it caught your attention. Maybe now you can stop all of your OCDing over that missing deformed kid, what's her name, 'Starfreak?' and get your real work done."

"The name's Celeste and I wasn't OCDing," Roger's voice was belligerent. He'd been sure the remains dredged from the Detroit River had belonged to her. He was only waiting for confirmation—only waiting, to tell Celeste's sister, Lizzie, and end what he imagined must be unbearable suffering. Now, Lizzie's ordeal would continue and pretty Julia Wilson was gone, instead of a kid with fused legs and missing organs—a kid, though he'd never say this to Lizzie, who'd probably be better off dead.

"The worst is that the guy who did it is probably long gone," Gilley said, ignoring Roger's tone and demeanour. "He's probably celebrating in some crack house in Detroit. He'll probably practice his little hemicor... hemicorporectomy," Gilley stumbled over the word, "on a few more pretty girls before someone figures out who he is."

"You're too cynical," Roger said.

"You're just new," Gilley leaned back in his chair. "Once you've been here a while, you'll see. Sickos like that don't live in communities where everyone knows everyone else's business. It's too risky. Just draw your blinds too often and people start talking."

"So this place is okay to murder in, but he wouldn't want to live here?" Roger noticed his tone growing more confrontational. He didn't like it, but sometimes his voice had a will of its own. "Are you saying we don't even try to find this guy?"

"I'm not saying we don't try." Gilley rolled his brown paper lunch bag into a ball and aimed at the garbage. "I'm just saying we shouldn't be hard on ourselves if we fail."

The bell rang and the rush of noise in the stark school halls sounded like an explosion.

Roger Foley, in plain clothes and sunglasses, was having a good day—a day in which he hadn't once slipped beyond the bounds of his body or experienced that weird helpless disconnect that he'd come to loathe.

He followed a group of boys from Julia's former homeroom class out into the smoking area. "What are you, a narc?" Larry Grant, a thin, stroppy boy asked. "And don't give me you're a student here, 'cause you'll make me laugh so hard I'll piss myself."

"Neither," Roger said. "I just want to know what you can tell me about Julia Wilson."

"Stacked," rasped Chuck Evans, a boy with spiky blond hair and black leather boots.

"You her boyfriend or something?" He lit his cigarette.

"No, I thought you might be," Roger said.

"Ha, I wish." The boy leered. Smoke streamed through a gap in his teeth.

"She wouldn't have you?" Roger asked.

"Let's just say, she liked older men... old enough to own their own wheels... their own companies preferred." He took another drag of his shabby cigarette. "Why do you care? You a cop?"

"Does it make a difference?" Roger asked.

"Talk to my lawyer," Evans said.

"Why? You guilty of something?"

"I ain't done nothin'," Evans said, "I just try to stay away from cops, that's all. I have a kind of allergic reaction." The other boys snickered.

"Then, it's probably more comfortable for you to talk to me here than down at the station," Roger said.

"Oh Jeez, a cop! What is it, Friday the thirteenth?"

These boys reminded Roger of the teenager he'd been: adrift, angry, a prison term waiting to happen. "Tell me," Roger said more patiently, "a lot of people seem to think Julia stayed away from boys, do you know why?"

"Duh...you ever met her old lady? Mrs. Tight Ass Wilson? She wouldn't let her perfect daughter crap alone. Used to bring her to school every day in that Lincoln and pick her up every afternoon. Julia used to sneak around like a rat. Climb out of her bedroom window at night. She used to skip classes, too. We'd watch her from here, all us guys. She'd check to make sure there were no teachers around, then she'd split. There was this old guy in a bright blue Firebird convertible who used to wait for her at the end of the street. He was some ex-teacher from some public school, or something, the guys said. I don't know where he took her, but they tore out of here almost every day. He'd always have her back by 3:00, though."

"Any idea what his name was?"

"None," the boy said. "We just called him Julia's old guy. She liked old guys. I told you that already, didn't I?"

"You did," Roger said.

"The only young guy she ever had anything to do with was Chet Edwards. He's a quarterback on the football team. That didn't last too long." A bell rang and Evans dropped his partially smoked butt on the ground. "Gotta go," he told Roger.

"Why didn't it last?" Roger asked.

"Because she was a bitch," Evans said. The other boys were already filing out of the smoking area.

"If I think of more questions, I'll know where to find you, right?" Roger said.

"Oh Jeez," Evans responded, "I won't be holding my breath."

Coach Hanley signalled Chet Edwards, a huge, well-built athlete, who looked more like a giant than an eighteen-year-old boy. He lumbered to the top of the bleachers. "You want to talk to me, coach?" he asked, his cloudy eyes questioning.

"No, but this man does. He wants to know about some dead kid, Julia Wilson."

Chet turned towards the side rail and spat into the open space before he took a seat on the bleacher. "Yeah! What do you want to know?" Roger didn't like being so high up. He didn't like any kind of sensation that made him feel ungrounded, but he wasn't about to let this kid know.

"I understand you and Julia once had a relationship." He looked directly into Chet's milky eyes.

"I don't know what we had. I met her when she was in grade nine... the fall. I remember 'cause it was initiation day. I took one look at her and just thought, 'wow', you know. I couldn't believe she was a frosh. We skipped classes together sometimes and drove down by the river and necked. She was afraid of her old lady finding out. I was afraid if I skipped too many classes I'd flunk and be kicked off the team. I said, 'Just tell your mother, then we can date' but she wouldn't. 'My ma doesn't want me riding in cars with teenage boys,' she'd say. 'Okay', I said, 'we'll take a bus.' But she wouldn't tell her mother. When I finally said I wasn't gonna skip any more classes, she said I cared more about football than her."

"So that kind of finished it?" Roger asked.

Chet shifted on the bleacher. "Not that exactly. It was just that she was a really strange girl. She'd say something, like 'I really like football,' you know, because she thought it was something I wanted to hear. But she didn't really like it at all. She couldn't even sit through a game. I heard her tell a lot of people she liked things she didn't really like. And it wasn't only 'like', but 'love.' She was crazy about this and crazy about that, she'd say. Later, she'd bad-mouth everything she claimed she loved and everyone she'd spoken to. She was the type of girl who'd never let you know what was going on for real in her head. It was like she was always playing the odds—always trying to figure out what people wanted to hear... and then, her dad died around Christmas. Now that was incredibly weird. You think she'd be all upset. He died real sudden, a heart attack or something. But she didn't even cry when she talked about it. It was like she was trying to make up her mind how to act."

"Anything else?" Roger encouraged, aware that the height was making him feel spacey.

"Yeah... she could become really violent... suddenly... out of the blue. She broke a glass over my head once all because I didn't compliment her on a dress. She was pretty and all that, but...."

"So you dumped her?" Roger asked, focusing again on Chet's pale eyes.

"Kind of. It wasn't really like dumping her, though, because she wasn't ever my girlfriend in the normal sense. I welled up the courage one day and told her the way she acted bugged me. I waited for her to slam me with something, but she didn't. She just got up and walked away. She didn't even look back. She started seeing other guys."

"Guys at the school?" Roger asked.

"Not at this one," Chet said.

Coach Hanley looked at his watch. "You think you can wrap this up," he asked. "I need Edwards back out there." He pointed towards the field. "If you want to hang around 'til after the game..."

"Just a couple more questions," Roger promised, flustered by the intrusion, but determined to do his job.

"Keep the answers brief, Edwards," Coach Hanley ordered.

"Can you give me the names of any of the guys she started seeing?" Roger asked, wanting the interview to be over as much as Coach Hanley did.

"I don't want to get anyone into trouble," Edwards said.

"I just need to ask some questions, son," Roger assured.

"Well, I guess okay then, as long as you don't say who told."

"I won't," Roger promised.

"There was one guy named Billy Crowther. He goes to Tecumseh Vocational School."

Roger jotted the name down on a notepad. It rang a bell.

"Can I go now?" Edwards asked.

Roger nodded. "Sure. I might want to talk to you later, though." As he stood from the bleachers, he tried to concentrate on placing the name "Crowther."

"Okay," Edwards said as he hustled onto the field, dwarfing all the other players. His body looked even more gargantuan and powerful out there than it did close up.

"Kill 'em, Edwards. Cut 'em apart!" Coach Hanley shouted.

Billy Crowther was dark, well built, and had striking good looks. When Roger found him, he was in the machine shop room of Tecumseh Vocational School, turning wood on a lathe.

"I don't talk to cops," Crowther told him dryly. His face expressionless.

All the way over, Roger had been trying to figure out how he knew the name and suddenly the penny dropped. Crowther had been an accused offender in an assault case a few years ago. Roger hadn't been on the force then, but he'd heard all about it. The young woman, badly beaten, had been left blind and paralyzed. The police interrogated Crowther for hours and roughed him up. He knew something, but ultimately there hadn't been enough evidence to charge him. Crowther eventually got himself a lawyer and started legal proceedings against the police. For a while, it was all over the paper, then it was old news. Roger never found out what happened. He would have liked to ask him now.

Crowther was in the beginning stages of a woodwork project. He was transforming a square block of yellow pine into a cylinder. His fingers were long and manoeuvred the tool he was using with precision.

"Look, Billy," Roger said, "I don't want to hassle you. I understand you knew Julia Wilson."

"And if I did?" Crowther called over the womp, womp, womp of the lathe. "You might be able to help us find her murderer." Roger stepped closer and Billy stopped the machine. "What makes you think I'd want to do that?" he asked.

Roger looked at the perfectly smooth cylinder that Crowther was now inspecting. "So you don't become a suspect yourself," he said.

Crowther laughed. Sawdust sprinkled like powder to the floor.

"You going to make something with that?" Roger asked, hoping to bridge the silence.

"An urn," Crowther mumbled, refitting the wood into the lathe.

"An urn, eh?" Roger repeated. "What you gonna use it for?"

"My ashes," Crowther smirked. He twisted the wood around once, then started the machine up again.

"You been working with these kinds of machines a long time?" Roger asked. He was thinking of Julia Wilson and the ragged cut that had severed her body. His mind began to wander.

"Long enough," Crowther said.

"If you were going to cut someone in half, what kind of machine would you use?" Roger felt queasy thinking about it. He noticed that Crowther didn't even flinch.

"A chainsaw," he said, matter-of-factly. "You'd need something strong enough to cut through bone and muscle, but you'd have to make sure to keep the sprockets clean."

"Have you heard how Julia Wilson was recovered?" Roger asked.

"Can't say I have," Crowther said, stopping the lathe again, and checking the wood for cracks.

"Some sick bastard cut her body in half, probably with a chainsaw. We fished the upper part out of the Detroit River, we're still looking for the rest of her."

"Sounds like Julia," Crowther sneered. "She was one hell of a divided woman."

"Care to elaborate?" Roger's voice sounded tough.

"I told you, I don't talk to cops."

"But we've been having ourselves a great little conversation here and it's too nice a day to haul you down to the station. Besides, you'd have to leave your urn. You wouldn't want to do that, would you?"

Crowther dug a gouging tool into the wooden cylinder. The lathe purred.

"If you don't mind my saying," Roger continued, "it sounds like you and Julia parted on bad terms."

"Is that a fact?" Crowther asked.

"Yeah," Roger mechanically said. "Sounds like she did a real number on you."

"Yeah, well, she did and I ain't gonna talk to no cop about it."

"Did she two-time you?" Roger persisted. "Did she go ballistic? Did she make an idiot out of you?"

Crowther focused on the wood. Roger witnessed the boy's large dark eyes grow moist behind his safety glasses. "I made an idiot outta myself," Crowther said.

"You're not the first guy to make a fool of yourself over a pretty girl," he said, "and this pretty girl, I understand, could get pretty ugly at times."

"Who you been talking to?" Crowther asked.

"Just a few of her admirers." The gruesome image of Julia Wilson's divided body flooded Roger and for a moment, he found it hard to breathe.

"She had plenty of admirers," Crowther muttered.

"Someone told me she had a thing for old guys."

"Old guys, young guys, women of all ages," Crowther said. "She was what you might call a 'free spirit.'"

"Free spirit?" Roger's robotic voice repeated. "I would have thought 'opportunist' was closer to the mark."

"Yeah, well, whatever you want to call it, it don't make much difference now."

"Did she take advantage of you, Billy?"

"She took advantage of everyone," he responded. "It was nothing personal. It was just the way she was, just the way she'd grown—like a bunch of knots in a piece of wood. They're great to look at, really interesting, but you can't build anything solid with wood like that."

"Did you want to build something solid with Julia?" Roger asked.

"No, because I knew it could never happen. We came from different worlds. She liked to do some occasional slumming in mine, but she made it clear that her world was off limits to me."

"You ever been in trouble with the law before, Billy?"

Crowther hesitated then mumbled, "Once."

"Some girl, wasn't it?" The questioning continued. "Beaten up and left for dead?"

"It wasn't me who done that," Crowther said.

"You were seeing Julia at that time?"

Crowther nodded.

"Did she think it was you?"

"Naw," Crowther said.

"You ever consider she might have? Maybe she thought you'd do the same to her."

"Don't make me laugh," Crowther said, looking far from laughing. "She wanted me to beat that girl. It was a case of 'mirror, mirror on the wall' with Julia always having to be the prettiest. She offered me money. I told her, 'I'm a lover, not a fighter' and she said, 'Not my lover anymore.' That ended it."

"So why didn't you tell the police?"

"Like you think anyone would believe me? You think they'd accept that perfect Julia Wilson hired a thug to beat up some girl, just 'cause she was better looking than her?" Crowther stopped the lathe and readjusted the wood.

"So who was the guy she hired?"

"Haven't a clue what his name was," Crowther said. "All I know is that she tried to pin it on me."

"That must have made you really mad."

"Naw, that's just the way she was. What makes me really mad is cops asking all kinds of questions about stuff that don't matter anymore."

"Any success?" Gilley asked Roger the next day.

"Well, I found out there's more to Julia Wilson than meets the eye." He took a deep breath and concentrated on the Norman Rockwell print over Gilley's desk. It was a picture of a friendly cop talking to a runaway boy at a soda fountain. The picture prevented him from seeing the grisly images of Julia that were embedded in his mind. He was determined to stay anchored—to stay calm. "It turns out she had all kinds of romantic relationships, and not all heterosexual ones."

"You're joking!" Gilley said.

"Yeah, and if I'm to believe one of her former lovers, she might have been a blackmailer and responsible for an assault on another young woman."

"How many former lovers did you talk to?" Gilley asked.

"Only two, so far."

"And your verdict?"

"They could have killed her, no problem. One's a monster, six-foot ten or something. He makes me look like a pygmy. The other's strong and knows how to use a chain saw. But neither of them strikes me as the murdering sort."

"That's just the kind you want to watch for," Gilley advised, reaching for his coffee.

"According to you, these boys couldn't have done it," Roger said. "They've lived in this community all their lives."

"O.K. so maybe I was a bit pat. It can happen. It's unlikely, mind you. But it might."

"There's an older guy who owns a Firebird convertible I'd like to track down," Roger said. "Apparently he used to take her for joyrides most afternoons. I'm going to drop over to Elise Wilson's place and have a look around. I'm hoping the kid kept some kind of diary."

"Yeah, well if she did, you can bet it won't be any place you'll find it. What are you going to tell the mother?" Gilley asked.

"I don't know. It's going to be hard to look her in the eye after hearing about her daughter's secret life. Did you know the husband died a few winters ago?" A knot rose in Roger's throat. He focused on the print again. "How much tragedy can a person take?"

An anxious fluttering commenced in Roger's stomach as he waited for the electronic gates to slide open that secured Elise Wilson's opulent house. He travelled up its winding path, breathing deeply to maintain his composure.

Elise appeared regal at the door, even though she wore old black slacks and a painter's smock. "I hope I'm not bothering you," he said, realizing immediately that he was.

"It's fine." Elsie was curt, but not unfriendly. Spatters of dusky orange paint festooned her dark smock. Two large marble lion statues guarded the ostentatious foyer. "Please excuse me. I've been in the studio," she said.

"I didn't realize you were an artist," Roger said.

"I'm not, really," Elise responded, "but I've always found painting helps me process negative emotions." Elise led Roger to a spacious and expensively furnished living room. Framed pictures of Julia, from infancy to adolescence, some drawings, some photographs, adorned each wall.

"I'm so sorry about your daughter," Roger blurted. "Maybe if we'd acted sooner..."

"No, officer," Elise comforted. "There was nothing anyone could do."

"I'm not sure if that's wholly true," Roger said, removing his hat and holding it in both hands, hoping the weight of it would keep him grounded. "If it's any consolation, I'll do everything in my power to find your daughter's murderer." Tears pricked his eyes.

Elise focused on a miniature portrait of her daughter on the coffee table. The frame was gilded and baroque. "She was the only thing I had. I know that sounds melodramatic, but it's true. She was everything to me. I thank you for your concern, but revenge is really the last thing on my mind right now."

"Of course," Roger mumbled.

"Right now, I'm just trying to take in what's occurred. I'm trying to make sense of it." Elise lifted the lid from a small porcelain box on the coffee table and removed a cigarette. "Care for one?" she asked.

"No thanks," Roger said, fighting the urge to say "There's no sense in brutally slaying a young woman." Instead, he asked if he might see Julia's room.

"The entire place was like a museum, and Julia's room all done up in pink and white ruffles. There wasn't one thing out of place—not one thing. There was no clutter. In fact, there was no trace of anything personal at all, no diary, not even a hair in her brush. Nothing under the bed, no stuffed animals, no posters. It kind of reminded me of a hotel room. You know, only a place to sleep. Her mother said she'd always kept her room like that. She didn't think it was odd.

"Naturally meticulous," she said. "I ask you, what kid is naturally meticulous?"

Gilley leaned back in his swivel chair. "Maybe an obsessive compulsive like you? Tell me about the mother."

"She's attractive... strikes me as a rather stoical person. Obviously idealized her daughter."

"Maybe Julia just knew the buttons to push. What parent could resist a perfect kid? Beautiful, tidy, smart? I wonder what else she was hiding?" Gilley asked.

"She wasn't hooking or into drugs, if that's what you think," Roger responded.

"Don't lose your objectivity, Foley. Anything's possible." The phone rang and Gilley answered. "Speak of the devil!" he said, scribbling something down on a piece of paper and signalling Roger to wait.

Roger tapped his foot. Hanging around made him nervous.

"It seems they found the rest of her." Gilley hung the phone up, "her other half, as it were," he chuckled.

"Any sign of a chainsaw?" Roger gazed at the Norman Rockwell print.

"Not as of yet," Gilley said.

Elise Wilson, impeccably dressed in a black woollen suit and Italian leather shoes, dropped a bouquet of pink snapdragons into the trench where Julia's white coffin had been lowered. The mourners separated before her as she left the cemetery. Not one embrace or handshake was offered in consolation.

Roger arrived at her house just as she was getting out of her car. "I hope you didn't mind my coming to the funeral," he began.

"I did mind," she said with a crispness that stung. "You didn't know my daughter. You're a stranger. And I don't know what you're doing here at my house again."

Roger felt his face redden. "I'm sorry," he said quietly. "I wanted to see if I could offer some help. I noticed that those who attended the service just now aren't going to support you through this. I just wanted you to know that if you needed someone to talk to..."

Her face immediately softened. "I'm so very sorry. I've been under so much stress. I had no right to snap. I've always been independent. It's the way I was raised. It's hard for me to take comfort from anyone, and as you saw at the service, I haven't been offered much of it lately. Please, come in for a cup of tea?"

"I don't want to put you to any trouble."

"No, please, it would be a great relief." She looked youthful and pretty when she said this. For the first time, Roger caught a glimmer of the living Julia in her face. "You might wonder what horrible thing I did to get all of those people at the service angry at me," she said, her voice vulnerable. "Well, I'll tell you. I married Charles. None of them will ever forgive me for that." A mischievous smile danced on her lips as she plugged the kettle in. "He was already a successful lawyer when I met him, and his family didn't approve of me. I can't say I blame them. My mother died when I was very young and I was raised by my father, a crazy survivalist, who read a lot of books and shunned people like the plague." Elise opened a decorative tin and offered Roger some pound cake. "Please," she insisted. Roger dutifully took a piece.

"We lived in a log cabin in Northern Ontario that my father built. There was no electricity, no running water, and my father thought nothing of stealing food and other provisions from hikers who occasionally passed through. Of course, he eventually got arrested and, for some reason, became something of a cult hero. The newspapers dubbed him 'Raccoon Riley'."

"No joking," Roger said. "I remember reading all about him when I was a kid. People all over the world offered to pay his bail."

"That's right," Elise said, embarrassed, her gaze moving to the kitchen tile. "And for all my father taught me, and he taught me a great many useful things, it was still incredibly humiliating being his daughter."

"I can imagine," Roger said compassionately. "It's amazing you've been able to... well..."

"Normalize?" Elise grinned. "It's okay," she reassured Roger. "Fortunately, as rough as it was living with my father, I learned self-sufficiency and that I could survive virtually anything. My father taught me how to read when I was three, and how to fish and split wood shortly after that. I learned how to build a fire in the rain and how to make my own hunting tools. By the time I got away, I wasn't afraid of anything. I landed a waitressing job, even though I was underage, and my employers were happy to pay me under the table."

"That's amazing," Roger said.

"I met Charles at the restaurant; I was just a whip of a girl. I don't think we would have been married at all if I hadn't become pregnant with Julia. And then when he died, well, his family was upset that I didn't turn the house, contents, and bank balance over to them."

"What possible claim did they think they had on your assets?" Roger asked, stabbed by the injustice.

"Charles was a very generous man towards his family. He'd always been free with his purse strings. When he died, I guess they were afraid they wouldn't be getting anything more."

"He had a heart attack, isn't that right?"

"Yes, he had a heart condition when I met him. He was taking medication, but you know how stubborn and stupid people with heart problems can be. They go into denial. And before you know it, they're not taking their pills. They don't believe the doctors, and the pain in their chest becomes 'only indigestion'. I suppose his family blames me for his death. They think I should have forced the pills down his throat, or hidden them in his food like he was a puppy. He was a very proud man. His career was everything to him, and I respected that. Of course, because of it, I pulled Julia too close. I needed someone to confide in, to love, and be loved by. But I'm rambling, please forgive me."

"Sometimes talking helps," Roger said.

"You're a very nice man, Officer Farley, is it?"

"Foley," he gently corrected. "But, please, call me Roger."

The kettle boiled, and Elise poured the water into a silver tea pot. "Officer Foley... Roger, you're very kind."

Roger's heart skipped a beat and he felt heat colour his cheeks. Elise Wilson was a beautiful woman—older than Lizzie, Celeste's sister, who, up until recently, he'd been spending most of his time with—but strikingly beautiful, nonetheless, in a mature stately way. She was more vulnerable than Lizzie—more innocent—even though, by her accounts, she hadn't led a sheltered life. Roger, instinctively, wished to protect her. He wished to enfold her in his arms and make her safe, enfold her and make love to her. "How's the painting coming along?" he asked hoping to circumvent her praise and his inappropriate feelings.

"Well enough, under the circumstances," Elise said, filling a silver creamer with milk and placing a dainty sugar bowl with small sparkling white rectangles onto an oval tray. "Would you like me to show you?"

Roger didn't object. He poured himself a cup of tea and allowed himself to be led into Elise's studio. The studio was a large, high-ceilinged suite of rooms just beyond the back door.

In one of the rooms was a long wooden table, and he imagined Elise, naked, stretched across it as he mounted her.

"Charles had this studio built for me," Elise explained. Roger suddenly felt guilty. "He thought it would keep me out of trouble," she joked. Some of the walls of the studio displayed Elise's work. She tended to use bright, intense colours and sharp, angular forms. Roger was surprised, considering the art displayed in the rest of the house. He was also surprised, because it revealed a raw and seething passion, something hidden in Elise, something which he would have liked to discover.

"I know what you're thinking," she said. "It doesn't fit, does it?" Then she whispered, "Really, I'd rather do something less primitive, but I'm handicapped by my inability to actually draw." She laughed then and Roger laughed too. "Besides," she added, "the art I do here is my therapy, my way of dealing with pain and problems. If anything aesthetic comes of it, it's not intentional."

Roger considered the way he dealt with pain and problems. He wondered where Elise's consciousness went when she did her art. Elise gently took his elbow and directed him to a room where two halves of a large canvas lay on separate tables. Each half was painted with clots of burnt orange paint of varying shades. "Interesting colours, don't you think?" she asked.

Roger's elbow felt electrified as he surveyed the two halves of the canvas. It was true, he'd never seen colours quite like it before.

"I'm working with corrosion," Elise told him, pointing towards a large container. "I find something metal, throw it in there—my chemical jar—and wait to see what kind of rust I get. Then I scrape the rust off and add it to clear acrylic paint with a few other secret ingredients. Different garbage produces different rusts and different rusts produce different colours. It's one of life's object lessons."

"That's fascinating," Roger said, scanning the contents of the container, thinking of Elise's soft, pure, almost holy fingers, caressing corrupt and castoff objects.

"Sometimes," Elise continued, "I first use a solution of salt and bleach to strip the metal. It can take too long to rust otherwise. Some metal things are still made to endure, believe it or not."

"I don't believe it," Roger laughed.

"You're right, Roger," Elise said. "Nothing is made to endure. I suppose that's why I'm attracted to rust, why I'm trying to find some beauty in it."

"I've nothing but respect and admiration for that woman. She's one tough lady," Roger told Gilley.

"Not bad looking either, eh?"

"Get out," Roger grinned. He felt his face grow hot, and turned, so Gilley wouldn't notice.

"I'd like to see the two of you get together," Gilley laughed. "Channel some of that manic detective energy of yours into something more pleasurable. Get away from that deformed kid's viper sister, Lizzie. Then I won't have to worry over you so much."

"And what exactly is that supposed to mean?"

"It means that even before this Julia Wilson thing happened, you were burning your candle at both ends—caught up with that mutant kid's sister."

"Well, I'm not giving up on this case. I'm going to find out who killed Julia Wilson, even if it kills me in the process."

"Never say die, right? Well, maybe that woman can at least convince you there's more to life than saving the world. It stinks sometimes. People do rotten things, bad stuff happens, but life's also sweet. You need to find balance, Foley."

Elise was dressed in a jaunty yellow summer frock and had come to Julia's gravesite this bright evening expressly to see if the large marble angel she'd commissioned to mark her daughter's grave was exactly as she'd specified. While the statue had been outrageously expensive, Elise comforted herself with the fact that she hadn't touched a fraction of Julia's life insurance money to buy it, and that this monument was truly a work of art. "My angel," she spoke to the air. "That's how you'll be remembered." She blew a kiss at the grave then turned towards the black Lincoln, parked at the cemetery gates.

In the back seat was a long, wide box, wrapped in silver paper and beribboned with pink bows. She was meeting Roger Foley for dinner and had gone to such great pains to decorate the box that she was running late.

Roger had most likely been working all day on her daughter's case, hunting down everyone Julia had ever known, and looking for the driver of some mysterious blue Firebird convertible, an ex-teacher, from Thomas King Elementary School, who he was convinced had something to do with the murder. Roger was a nice man, Elise thought, as she headed towards the Detroit River: sympathetic, kind, useful. He was someone she'd agreed to date and she was greatly looking forward to their dinner out, for no matter how accustomed she'd grown to wealth, she still thrilled at the luxury of being served in a restaurant, particularly when someone else was picking up the tab.

She'd wrapped the box so that no one might guess the memento it contained. She'd wrapped it with care and beauty and precision, as she might have wrapped a gift for her daughter. It was unlikely that someone would look into her car, that she'd be pulled over for speeding. She was always very careful and could be an extremely convincing liar if the need arose, but she'd rather save her lies.

She didn't want to lie to Roger any more than absolutely necessary, and she knew he was just the same kind of tactile man as Charles. He'd want to lift the pretty box and shake it. He was the sort who'd comment on its weight and say it didn't feel like a box of clothing, or a down quilt, or whatever item she told him she'd encased there. Of course, he'd believe her, over the evidence of his own senses, because he trusted her, but there were only so many times you could test someone's trust. It was Charles who'd taught her that.

Instead, she'd play it safe with Roger, even if it meant arriving late. She'd dump the contents of the box into the river before she met him at the restaurant. The water would wash it clean of salt and bleach and history, and its weight would drag it to the river's bottom, where the muddy earth would claim it, out of all human sight. In the depths and darkness of the river's corrosive sediments, the chain and all its attendant armour would eventually vanish, just as Elise herself knew she eventually must do.

No Kind of Man

LAURIE LAFRAMBOIS WAS SURE she was dreaming. She'd followed Jimmy. She remembers there were sirens, her mother's loud unhappy shouts, and Jimmy ordering her: "Come with me." Suddenly she was tumbling down an embankment, and now, here she is in this field with a dizzy head, feeling like she did when she was little and had chicken pox, as if the whole world were gyrating, stripping off streamers of heat, and she's so wobbly that she needs to stay still and close to the ground for fear she'll capsize.

She wants to stop the voice in her head—forget all those terrible things her mother said when she found out she was pregnant. She tries to focus on him—her boyfriend, Jimmy. His face is different since his accident. It swims in and out of her consciousness with the overpowering brightness of a sun. It makes her queasy.

"He's gonna be a leader," Jimmy tells her, his glistening hand slipping under her jumper and cupping her large pregnant belly.

Everywhere he touches there's a sensation of marshy cool. She wonders if he's for real.

"Oh Jimmy," she murmurs, imagining a tiny snug cottage for them both and the baby, surrounded by a white picket fence, and cloth diapers drying out back on a laundry line. She pictures her mother sitting on a rocking chair on the front porch, giving the baby a pony ride on her knee. Daydreaming has always made her feel better. But the theme music to *Little House on the Prairie* jingles relentlessly through her scorching head and won't stop even when she tells it to. The baby kicks. Her stomach undulates in waves and ripples under Jimmy's slick hand. "I think I'm sick," she whispers.

Jimmy is like a ray of fire in her eyes and the theme music from *Little House* has risen an octave and acquired a distinctive disco rhythm. As it reaches an unnatural crescendo, the baby performs a most powerful kick, breaking Jimmy's hand at the wrist. The hand flies through the air and splatters on the wall of a lean-to shack that Jimmy set up for them. Then she remembers. Jimmy is dead.

She screams and struggles to sit up, but is beaten back down by the force of gravity and her own weakening dizziness. "Don't worry. It ain't nothin' important, just a hand," Jimmy says. The sun gazes down into the field from the centre of the sky, as Jimmy gazes down on the knoll of her body—eyeballs of fire cooking flesh tender, transforming clay to slate.

Laurie settles again. She imagines everything is going to be fine. At least with her and Jimmy. He's here now, with her. He didn't take off like her mother said.

In the heat, Jimmy's eyelid appears to be fusing shut over his one good eyeball. Before long, he won't be able to see that his body resembles a melting fudge bar. He drifts in and out of Laurie's consciousness. "You're gonna take care of me, right Jimmy? I'm gonna be your woman and we're gonna live in your ma's house, right? When are you gonna take me back?" Laurie moans. "I'm really hot and sick, and I don't like the way you're getting all kind of gooey." Jimmy's voice reverberates like an echo caught in the shells of Laurie's ears. "We'll go back when they ain't looking for us."

"I don't know why we gotta stay in this dirty field. You're kind of magical, aren't you? Can't you just make them stop looking for us?" The music in Laurie's head starts up again, an octave higher, more forceful and unremitting. She knows Jimmy kidnapped her, that the police were looking for him, because she's thirteen and he's eighteen, and even though she liked making love with him, they still call it rape.

Jimmy's voice mingles with the music in her mind. "No, we gotta be here, that's all."

"Can't you make us invisible? You must be able to. You must've done that when you brought yourself out into this field from that wreck of your car."

"Yeah," Jimmy says, "that's a trick I learned from my brother, Kevin Houdini Robinson. You should'a met him." Jimmy's voice fades and flourishes, just like it was coming through the speaker on a television set, the volume being twisted up and down. "He could get out of anything. Nothin' could hold him."

Jimmy has said these things to Laurie before. "So what good's your magic if you can't make us invisible and take us back to your ma's place? My head is aching, and I feel sick, and I think I got a fever. I'm gonna need to eat before too long, and I don't wanna eat no field pheasants. Them tiny feather ends can get stuck in your teeth." The *Little House on the Prairie* music in Laurie's head abruptly stops; in its place, the theme from *The Brady Bunch* begins, but it's not exactly right somehow.

Jimmy's voice is a train's whistle, screeching and sliding through greased rust, between the field and the highway. "I'll get us somethin' different."

"I don't want nothing from this field. I want a peanut butter sandwich and a glass a milk. I want macaroni and cheese! I need my vitamin pills. The doctor says something bad can happen to the baby if I forget my pills or don't eat right."

Jimmy's face flashes and wavers in Laurie's mind. "No," he says unequivocally, his forehead wrinkling into deep furrows like watermarks in sand that stay that way, "the baby's strong. He's gonna be something special. He's gonna be a great leader. He's gonna make changes here in Fontainebleau—you wait and see."

Laurie is half listening to Jimmy's voice. "What kind of a great leader's that? I thought you meant like, the president of the United States or a foreman at Ford's or Chrysler's or something. Who cares about this cruddy place?" She starts singing along with *The Brady Bunch* music. "He's gonna be as quick as a fox. He's gonna be smart as my old buddy Jack Goulet. He shot his parents and then talked his way out of prison. He only had to go to juvie and broke free from there. No cop in the universe was a match for him." Laurie's heard all this before and finds it sickeningly boring.

"He's gonna be able to get out of anything like my brother, Houdini Robinson. He's gonna know how to trap raccoon and catch catfish from the Detroit River. He's gonna know what bones is good to pick up from the field, and what bones you gotta leave sitting there. He's gonna know what to shoot an arrow at, and what not to shoot an arrow at. He ain't gonna end up like his ole man—dead and without an eyeball."

Jimmy swims in and out of *The Brady Bunch*. He is a face in a box, looking across the television screen at another face in a box. Laurie sees the ugly emptiness in his eye socket. She vaguely remembers how it was supposed to have happened. He was shooting for pheasant, and he thought some of the old bones in the field were cursed. "I should hope not!" she says, "No kid'a mine is gonna play with no arrows." She tries to moisten her dry lips with her tongue. "He ain't gonna be diddled by no school principal, and he ain't gonna let none of the jerks in this city get the better of him. He ain't gonna knock up no thirteen-year-old girl neither," Jimmy adds.

"Hey!" Laurie cries, sounding exactly like Cindy Brady to herself. "Are you saying you don't want him?" The theme song ends and begins replaying. Now Laurie knows why the song doesn't sound quite right. Because it's her voice singing it just as she sings it every day, but without the accompaniment of the Bradys.

Jimmy continues: "He ain't gonna have to shoplift nothin', and if he does, he ain't never gonna get caught. He ain't never gonna get caught at all, not for nothin'."

It makes Laurie feel lonely that she has to sing all by herself. Jimmy flutters in and out of her vision. He's standing, wrathful, against the day's brightness. His calves collapse into his ankles like two chocolate flutes.

"And if you ever bitch at him, he's gonna just give you one good look with his two good eyeballs, and you're a goner."

The threat stops Laurie from feeling sorry for herself. "I hope you teach him some respect!" she snaps. "I wouldn't want no kid'a mine treating me like I seen you treat your ma."

"He ain't never gonna have a brother, and he ain't never gonna spend the best years of his life thinking his brother's coming back for him, when his brother's gone and left him for good." Laurie opens her tiny eyes. The sky is spinning around and around. Jimmy is a shadow enveloped in orange light. She watches as his neck collapses into his chest, as his head pops off with the sound of a champagne cork, and rolls onto the hard dusty earth. She blinks, her dry throat, red and raw, emits the sound of a train jarring to a halt when she screams.

"He ain't never gonna do nothin' he don't want to do, and he ain't never gonna take the blame for nothin'." Jimmy's head stops rolling and continues speaking. "He ain't gonna put up with no one's shit." The rest of Jimmy's body blows away like ash.

Laurie heaves herself to a sitting position, feeling as if she's come full circle in a Ferris wheel cage. Sweat cinches down her back. "You can't tell me it ain't nothing important now! You can't tell me it don't matter." She leans forward in the dirt to touch Jimmy's head.

"Don't!" Jimmy warns. "You touch, and it's over."

"Jimmy," Laurie sobs. "Ain't you magical enough to put yourself back together again? Ain't you magical enough to make good on your promise to me? You said I was gonna be your woman and you were gonna take care of me! You said we were gonna go back to your ma's place."

Jimmy's head begins rolling in the dust again, rolling like a rattle, rolling back and forth, gaining momentum, raising a dirt cloud. "Wait a second," Jimmy shouts, "he's gonna be Jack Goulet ... Jack Goulet... who walked from St. Jerome's Wilderness Camp and melted away into the Toronto pavement. He's comin' back! He's comin' back!... no... no... wait. It's not Jack. It's Kevin. He's gonna be my brother, Kevin Houdini Robinson. I knew it! I knew he'd come back. I was right! I was right!" The head in its great jubilation crumbles to dust.

"Jimmy," Laurie screams. "Jimmy. I'm too young to be a widow and we ain't even been legally married yet." The sobs fill her throat and echo like the cries of crows through the field all the way down Monica Street. She leans lower to the earth, so close she can almost inhale the dust that was Jimmy.

"Wait a sec, I was wrong." It's Jimmy's voice, echoing across the sky, booming from the earth. It takes a couple of seconds before Laurie spots them: Jimmy's lips, crawling over the stone-hard clay, two thick articulate worms. "He ain't gonna be Kevin. He's gonna be me. He's gonna be Jimmy Robinson junior, and he ain't never gonna take no crap from no one ever again."

As the lips disintegrate to anthills, the final chorus of *The Brady Bunch* comes to an end in Laurie's mind, and she collapses back into the grass. A rush of water burns her legs.

Immediately there is a sharp knife-blade pain in her abdomen. "I shoulda listened to my ma. She said you was undependable. She said you'd end up leavin' me when I needed you most." Sobs collect in her dry throat and choke her. "What am I gonna do now? You tell me what am I gonna do?"

She clutches her abdomen, feels the tight contraction with her hand, then another. The world is still unsteady, but she hoists herself to her feet. "See what you made me do?" She speaks directly to the earth. "You made me piss myself, you scared me so bad, and now I got pains in my stomach."

Laurie cradles her belly. Another sharp contraction stabs her, as she begins her wobbly journey to her destination, the houses at the top of Monica Street.

"Now I gotta get to a doctor, Jimmy. And where the hell are you? Where the hell are you with all your magic and big talk. 'Our son's gonna be a great leader!' Shows how much you care. You ain't even here to help us."

Laurie staggers through the field, away from swirling dust. Sweat pours over her. She bends and pants, feeling a tight grip in her stomach. Every few minutes, she curses the potholes and bugs, the burrs that stick to the hem of her jumper, the weeds that cut fine bloody lines into her legs.

"I hate you, Jimmy Robinson," she hollers into the bright transparent sky. "I hate you, and I'm glad you turned to dust. I'm glad you blew away. You ain't no kind of father. You ain't no kinda man at all. My ma was right about you!"

Misdirection

ANOTHER MURDER in Fontainebleau last night cast a pall over the city and triggered Roger's police radio to chatter endlessly. Suzy hears the chattering too, although she's nowhere near his vehicle and not in any way affiliated with the police. She bought her scanner from a pawn shop last year. If the cops decide to show up on her doorstep, she wants to make sure she's ready for them.

Hail lashes the roof of Roger's cruiser. Large icy spheres dance like a shower of bouncing bullets off the windows of his car; they jump in the street, melt on the sidewalk, become small steaming eggs frantic to hatch. In the East end of the city, where Suzy lives, there is no hail. So far, there is only wind and mild rain, but Suzy is still annoyed by this—she's annoyed by anything that disrupts her plans.

Downtown, branches of crimson king maples bend and crack and awnings sag, thick with crystal stones. The tumultuous waters of the Detroit River, pitted with ice, run like ink, away from the glistening Ambassador Bridge, past Shawnee Park and a glimmering patch of cement where two ancient native skeletons inhabit a shallow grave. This is the last thing Roger's eyes take in before he turns on Ouellette, and proceeds up that long stretch of road which always causes him grief.

His senses deaden, the roiling pit of angst in his belly wanes. For a moment, he's outside himself, watching his body approach Hotel Dieu Hospital and is aware of his mind's desire to bolt. He thinks of Lizzie. He dreamed of her last night, saw her in a halo of ethereal light being abducted and forced by a murderer to ingest drugs. It looked like PCP, or Angel Dust, as it's called on the streets. A substance he'd come in contact with just the other day—he'd been thinking of Lizzie when they made the drug bust, irrationally fearing for her safety as he handcuffed a hood and collected the stash. He tried to call Lizzie this morning, to relieve his angst, which has persisted throughout the day, but she didn't answer the phone. He wants to focus on her and think of nothing else, hold her safely in his thoughts; he believes his thoughts can make a difference, but instead, he finds then fixates on his younger brother, Brian, at age twelve, comatose and on life-support.

Suzy, Lizzie's sister, heard the phone ring early this morning and didn't answer. When their mother had been alive, Suzy hated her antisocial nature, but now understands how dangerous the outside world can be. She limits her communication to a handful of necessary people. If they want to get in touch, they know how. To the rest of the world she's incommunicado.

Roger, also, is often incommunicado, but never like Suzy—never intentionally so.

Frequently, bad thoughts take hold and replay in his mind like half-remembered songs. It's Brian's tune now. Brian—in a coma—who died before he was a teen. Roger never knew the details. An accident was all he'd been told, and as if this tragedy weren't enough, a few months later his father was taken when a minor lung irritation evolved into something deadly. Two years later, his mother's heart surrendered under the burden of loss. She died, as they all had, at Hotel Dieu, and now he finds he can think of nothing but the dead.

This interminable road brings them all back. On the corner is Sanderson's Funeral Home where his parents and brother had all been displayed like soft plastic mannequins boxed in their Sunday best. He had not always gotten along with them. As a teen, he frequently disparaged them, and he and Brian had always been at each others' throats. Although he knew this was a natural part of growing up, he could not stop the tide of guilt and sorrow that infused him whenever his family made an appearance in his mind. And it wasn't just the ghosts of his family who haunted him: there were apparitions everywhere on this street. The Metropolitan Five and Dime contained his light-fingered pals, Mike and Perry McGeehan, casualties of a highway collision when the brakes on their mother's car failed. They'd filched chocolate bars and comic books together, lived as if they all floated high above the dangers of the world. The Tivoli Bar, two blocks from Tecumseh, evoked the unrecognizable remains of his best friend Derek, swept up and mangled in a factory machine the day after his coming-of-age party. There were also officer friends he'd lost, most recently Gary Gilley, who approached a drunken suicidal man in front of the women's shelter on Ouellette and Wyandotte. The suspected killer, Anil Ramkum, whom Roger recalls from a domestic dispute as a sad and pleading man, is alleged to have planted a bullet in Gilley's head, before blowing out his own brains.

When Roger starts obsessing on the dead, he inevitably reverts to his adolescent self—a stoop-shouldered, gangly prophet of doom who believes anyone he grows close to will systematically be taken. Before he'd met Elise, before Gilley was shot, no matter how deeply depressed Roger became, a drive down Monica Street, past Lizzie's house, could change his outlook. Just thinking of that unconventional girl—the untainted love she embodied for her sisters, her conviction and earnestness, her energy, everything about her buoyed him.

But he's still far from Monica Street. Lizzie is out of reach. In his mind's eye he sees her hands, and the crushed pink cactus petals that fell from them, fine as feathers, the last time they'd spoken. He had always been impressed by her strength and independence in the wake of misfortune. He'd initially been convinced that her most beloved sister, Celeste—the sister who'd gone missing—had fallen victim to one of Fontainebleau's many predators whom the criminal justice system could neither rehabilitate nor contain. He wasn't sure how he'd become sidetracked by another disaster, another woman. He only knew that it wasn't until Elise Wilson's pretty daughter Julia was found dead that his sympathies changed.

Elise's tragedy consumed him. He believed she needed him more than Lizzie. It never occurred to Roger until now that he always allied himself with the disadvantaged, that he was naturally drawn to them like a compass needle drawn in a particular direction.

Elise's passive stoicism made her appear vulnerable. He didn't blame her for leaving him, he understood her need to fashion an entirely new existence. He'd hoped she might include him in her post-grief restructuring, but when she didn't, surprisingly, he felt relief. When she vanished, it was as if some obscuring cloud had lifted and that girl on Monica Street, Lizzie, was the only person he'd ever needed in his life.

The nervous pressure in his chest spikes. Although he doesn't consider himself a religious person, he finds himself praying. He's aware that he hasn't prayed for years, not since his mother's death when his grandparents, concerned about his despondency, compelled him to attend Tecumseh United Church. It was the good Reverend Fisher who'd taught him to pray and midwifed his passage through the jagged shoals of grief. He hasn't thought of Fisher in years either, hasn't thought of his informal, almost sacrilegious remarks. "It's like this," he'd told Roger, "shit happens. The big theological question isn't why. The big question is what do we do with it?"

Fisher was a kind, jovial man with the face and body of a prize fighter. When they'd first met, he wasn't much older than Roger now, though he seemed ancient. He'd told Roger: "Suffering has infinite potential. It can shatter you to the marrow, but still leave enough good intact for something better to grow, something more conscious and compassionate." Roger knew what it was to be shattered. It had already happened to him more often than he'd ever admit, but when Fisher was found beaten and dead in his apartment, Roger lost faith in those words. Now he knows for certain: there's only so much devastation a soul can endure.

His worry for Lizzie localizes to a helix of heartache. It circles his chest like a miniature ring of sharks. He apologized to Lizzie when they'd spoken last. He'd been trying to do it for weeks, trying to tell her how sorry he was he'd abandoned her. He felt guilty just thinking about it, just thinking how his allegiance had shifted, how after lavishing all of his attention on her, he'd suddenly stopped. Worse, he'd promised he'd help her—promised he'd pull strings and not let the search for her sister grow cold. Lizzie had called and left messages. He didn't get back to her. He was so involved with Elise and her suffering, he didn't even realize what an irresponsible jerk he'd become.

In despair, his thoughts disengage. Once again, he's outside of himself, watching as his tense body takes in the escalating storm. It happened with no other warning than the sudden darkening of clouds. The grounds of the toboggan hills are dented and sparkling, and turmoil reigns among a group of summer clad pedestrians with nothing but hands to shield their heads. A burning wand of lightning forks the earth while thunder crests.

"Too close," Roger sees his mouth mutter as his car drives through the brutal weather—through hail and lightning—through rain that makes oil slicks on the pitted roads. Some cars pull over, waiting for the worst to subside, but Roger continues towards Monica Street, compelled not by love or obsession, but by the incessant siren sounding in his head.

It's not unusual for him to become overly involved, to feel beleaguered and hopeless. A stoplight beats through his frenzied wipers, a simple streak of red. He turns down Monica Street and finds his mind already touching Lizzie's face, already stretching out across the scent of her cologne as if she were a field of strawberry blossoms opening after a storm.

But the storm is far from ending. On Monica Street, it's only gaining force. Water and streaks of gravel run from driveways under his car's sliding wheels. A hydraulic shovel inhabits a space of lawn beside Lizzie's house, its dipper bucket straining, a pile of melting earth accumulating over weeds; and crows, dozens of crows, gliding and gleaming over the adjacent field.

Suzy, in a glistening raincoat, rigs a bright blue tarp from the roof's gutter. It flaps and pulls like a sail, gives the entire house an appearance of motion before she stakes it to the ground. Her police scanner has failed to alert her to Roger's visit, and on seeing his cruiser, she damns him, then orders the shovel's exhausted operator to persevere.

The substratum of Fontainebleau is rife with the presence of early indigenous people. Some believe these original inhabitants, treated so badly at the hands of Europeans, seeded curses into priceless artefacts which now litter the local soil, but Suzy doesn't fear curses—especially those that imbue treasure—what she fears are snoopy cops, *the long nose of the law*, as she calls them.

Cops, like Roger, who claim to stand behind the stupid rules that prevent Fontainebleau's ancient past from being of practical use to anyone. Cops who label people like her as criminals. If Roger knew what she were up to, knew about the unreported cache she's already excavated, he'd have no option but to arrest her. As it is, however, he's lost in a time-warp, too preoccupied to be curious. Suzy isn't taking any chances though.

She doesn't know what became of Kevin Robinson, who taught her the magic of *misdirection*. He'd used it to pull quarters from behind her ears, and flowers from her pockets and sometimes to lift things from convenience store shelves. "It's all the same trick," he explained. "When people look at one thing, they ain't seeing something else."

Right now, Suzy wants Roger to look at her and so she gets into his car. The warmth of her breath and the damp cold of her plastic coat cloud the windows. She'd always thought he was a weirdo, a kind of stalker. She notices that his eyes are particularly glassy and he doesn't ask the questions she expects. In fact, the only question he asks pertains to Lizzie. "Where is she?" A question Suzy knows she must weigh carefully before calculating the best response.

The arm of the hydraulic shovel rises and descends. Out in the marshy fields, a discordant army of crows locate cover and declare their ancestral bonds. Roger's heart pounds once, then pauses like his ragged breath. Depressed feelings and dreadful thoughts keep looping and looping in his brain. All his life, people have told him to ignore and dismiss them. "Imagine the worst, and you'll bring it to yourself," his grandmother used to say, but it's not a cause and effect equation with him. He always knows before devastation strikes.

He searches Suzy's dark unfathomable eyes as drops of rain pearl from her hair. Her face, bright and enigmatic, resembles Lizzie's as it turns towards the fogging window, the broken reeds that flank the house and the sounds of restless crows.

She glances at the hydraulic shovel, then skims the contours of Roger's desperate face. The last she'd heard, Lizzie didn't want anything to do with him. Their younger sister Audrey once told her that Lizzie wished him dead. A lie rolls from Suzy's sweet tongue like an inconsequential wave: "... an appointment," she mutters, "she had to be somewhere."

In truth, she has no idea at all where Lizzie is. She hasn't seen her for the last two days, but because there's a full moon again, Suzy imagines her sister is manically trying to organize meetings with mayors and members of parliament, wasting everyone's precious time, driven by the crazy notion that she can make them help her find their sister Celeste. It's an obsession Suzy can't make sense of. In her mind, Celeste isn't missing. She was miserable at home. She made the decision to leave.

Roger hovers over his own body as his heart restarts at a frenetic pace. If only the frantic flutter didn't echo contradictions. Trapped blackness thrashes in the prison of his skull. Stones of ice and long thin arrows of rain partially obscure the heart of the field. The thrum of wind and the anxious cawing of crows lead him back to the first time he remembers coming here. There'd been a dead boy, packed so thickly with mud that he looked like a hillock, and Lizzie, the presiding Valkyrie, surrounded by those hungry birds. The rash of murders had already begun, though most of the missing were not yet presumed dead. The cause of the boy's death had been inconclusive, though Roger was certain it had been murder and certain that the killer was still on the loose.

Lizzie's reclusive mother had been alive then, and Roger recalled her titanic rage at being questioned. It was similar in intensity to Lizzie's, which Roger had frequently done his best to subdue. He worried now that Lizzie's anger, left unchecked, could have provoked violence. He blames himself for not protecting her and a shockwave of guilt jolts him from his body once again.

The hydraulic shovel stutters under the weight of mud, melting ice and water. It groans as its cables stretch then thud to a complete and crippling halt. Suzy doesn't need to distract Roger from the din. He's already out of the car and drenched to the flesh, wading through mud and mire, delicate clouds of steam lifting off his back like feathery wings. Although he can't articulate it, can't say for certain how he knows, he's sure Lizzie is out there—sure the killer's been out there too.

There is nothing about Roger's behaviour that Suzy finds rational. The fact that he's shown up here, in his police car, on a social visit is weird in itself. Lizzie despised him—of this, Suzy is certain, in spite of the fact that last year, they'd had an affair. But Lizzie is all about ulterior motives—she'd sleep with Jack the Ripper if she thought he'd find Celeste. She'd talked enough about Roger for anyone to know all she felt for him was contempt. He was the last person Suzy had ever expected to see—a pain in the butt, a nuisance—and now he's clambering through the slush and slurry of the adjacent field chasing some mirage.

Self-preservation dictates that Suzy not lose sight of him. She needs to herd him back, stuff him in his car, send him packing. The hydraulic shovel and its operator are only hers for a limited time. She can't afford disruptions. She can't afford craziness. She steps briskly from the car and then into the field, treading when she can in the imprint of his feet, places he has trampled moist straw into mats and avoided slick clay. She clears the puddles he plunges into, the places his tracks disappear. Rain and ice lash her face. She calls after him, but her voice is lost in the storm. He's like a sleepwalker or one hypnotized, flapping and flailing further into the ravaged field. If only she had the power to stop him, to draw him back, a glazed thread through the sharp eye of her needle. If only she could make him see that this unfocussed impulsiveness, this lack of plan, this flying off half-cocked in the throes of the worst storm of the season is dangerous, she might be able to reel him in, but he's in the grips of some possession, and can only hear his own mind's mania.

The sky grows blacker by the second and weighs upon them. It twists and churns itself into a sooty shell, pushes down on their shoulders, pushes each of them down into the mud. They struggle to release themselves, but sink deeper. Long braids of fire snake the sky, they flick and explode a willow tree; it shatters into ropes of wood and singes in newly made runnels. Roger and Suzy labour to stand, ears ringing, metallic fumes smudging their nostrils. A second streak of lightning blows the field apart in a confetti of hail and grass blades, soft white petals, feathers and clumps of flying clay.

An ember turns to ash in Suzy's eye. Roger pulls forward, shakes a clutch of clay from his shoe before a third deafening detonation peals across the field. Trees bend, branches lose their leaves, Suzy's coat becomes a parachute and propels her to the trunk of an injured tree. Her body, helpless as a sheet of paper, wraps itself around the bole. Wind holds her to the spot. Debris skips and somersaults. Garbage cans splash in trenches, their lids Frisbeeing through the air. Tattered sun umbrellas, mesh chairs, roof shingles, like hard thin petrified birds, flock into the ice and furrowed grass. Suzy's blue tarp, now a flying carpet, soars towards black twisting clouds.

If Roger is aware of the chaos around him, he makes no show of it, not even to that incorporeal presence of himself that hovers above, refusing to suffer his body's pain. He bucks the wind waiting for a shift in current and pushes forward into the field. He senses Lizzie's presence amidst the madness of this meadow. Nothing can dislodge his conviction that she's out here somewhere.

The battering hail grows harder, then softer, the rain teems ferociously but eventually begins to subside. The wind dies, the sky brightens and Suzy tears her aching body from the hard knots of the tree and shouts. Bright sparks of ice melt in the weeds, and crows, droves of rapacious crows, cluster in a maple by the railroad tracks. Something murmurs in the rushes beyond the greasy ties, a ghastly human luminosity that infuses tattered buttercups and thistles. Here in the sedge, the bodies of pregnant girls who hurled themselves like toppling pieces of coal from open hopper cars have lain.

Roger is oblivious to Suzy. He's oblivious to everything but his own undertaking. He slides down a polished bank of gravel through the prickly wild rose underbrush past the rusting barbed-wire fence. In a ditch, babbling to the sun, gripping an injured peyote cactus, is not the mangled pregnant girl Suzy envisions, but her sister, Lizzie: pale, hollow-eyed, her flesh flecked with cuts. Beside her rests the wounded lifeless body of another on whom the crows have already begun to descend.

The emergency entrance of Hotel Dieu Hospital is glutted with storm casualties when they arrive. A series of small tornados have created havoc in the city. Five portable classrooms at Thomas King Elementary were overturned and twenty windows at the River Park Hotel blown in. Victims on stretchers fill the ground floor corridors. Frantic attendants try to keep order and determine who is the most immediately in need of care.

Roger, for Roger has driven them there, drones about his hatred for this hospital—"this place full of the business of death." He says the smells of disinfectant and rubber make his stomach break open like a pit, then runs to the bathroom.

It feels to Suzy as if they've arrived in a continent of Hell. Stretched pleading faces and writhing bodies. Trauma has paralyzed her, affected her thinking and she doesn't ask, doesn't even ask, about the dead woman by the railroad tracks, or if Roger radioed help.

Lizzie is a mass of cuts and bruises. She cries and clutches at Suzy's raincoat, then shoves the battered Peyote cactus towards her. "Stark silver saucers, translucent creatures," she mutters, "they disguise themselves, control the weather, get inside your head."

The cactus had been a gift from their sister Audrey, and disappeared the same day Celeste vanished. Suzy wonders how it came to be in Lizzie's possession. She remembers, later, finding a stained recipe for *Peyote vision soup*, but it had been transcribed in the oscillating dysgraphic hand of their sister Audrey, not Lizzie's methodical copy book script.

Sweat as cold as melted hail streams from Roger's forehead on his return. He couldn't explain why his pulse raced, why his pupils dilated or his breath grew shallow. If Suzy had been able to enter his consciousness, she would have seen the ugly guilt that imbued him and understood this was why he seemed vacant. He was forever absconding—taking expeditions to less painful realms. Sometimes he'd hover over the muddy field at the end of Monica Street, contemplating nature's unrelenting purge. Sometimes he'd find himself hanging beside the darkness in the trees, witnessing the sonorous lilt of feathers before the sky turned dark. What his body did on the earth at these times, he never remembered. But memory was a much overrated faculty that, as he'd found, could incapacitate a body with grief.

Roger's dim presence annoyed Suzy. He'd always struck her as peculiar, but in this hospital, and in the context of this crisis, he seemed inappropriate. She wanted to tell him to leave, that she had everything under control. "Don't you have a killer to find?" If it weren't for her looting operation, she certainly would have asked him this.

She hadn't expected him to manoeuvre past the confusion of people and attempt to touch Lizzie's hand. Nor could she have anticipated Lizzie's response. Her voice expanded in volume, filling the waiting room, then stretching past the chalky hospital walls. Her screams, for they soon became screams, were shocking, stopping everything, like the police siren on Roger's cruiser.

She lifted her quaking body and shoved Roger with a life-defending strength. She knocked beads of sweat from his grey startled face, knocked him to the ground. Two security guards appeared and restrained her wounded arms. She shrieked and kicked Roger, kicked him again and again, as his body curled on the polished tile and his hands reflexively struggled to shield himself. It proceeded in slow motion, Suzy repeating the word *stop*, unaware that Roger felt nothing—that his disembodied consciousness had already left the room, that before he fell, before he escaped the precinct of his body, he'd told himself that this was nothing more than he deserved.

The security guards wrestled Lizzie past pallets of people, down a corridor, behind metal gates into a dizzyingly bright cubicle. A nurse arrived and buried a needle into the top of her raw arm. She blinked once before her knees gave, before the nurse helped her lie down upon a narrow cot; then her dark lids rolled, like two thunderclouds, over electric eyes, shutting out the unrelenting brightness.

In the waiting room, blood dripped from Roger's mouth and nose. Three policemen, all in neat blue uniforms, bizarrely alien amid the dishevelled and distressed, lifted Roger from the floor. They knew Roger, and generally shared a collegial rapport, though this situation had unnerved everyone.

At first, Suzy was uncertain of their purpose. Then a dark reality jarred her. There had been a dead woman by the railroad tracks—a dead woman next to Lizzie—and before that, a dead boy in the field. Why hadn't she put two and two together? Lizzie had a temper—often violent. There was no doubt in Suzy's mind that she could kill—that she would kill—if she thought it might bring Celeste back.

The police would ask her questions. No matter what she said, they'd take Lizzie away, but as she contemplated how she might misdirect them—how she might broker for Lizzie's freedom—she became aware that Lizzie's arrest was not the reason for their presence; rather it was Roger they'd come to interrogate—or at least some angry adolescent aspect of Roger. His shoulders rounded in a shrug and his face crumbled with grief when they told him that Elise Wilson was the dead woman by the railroad tracks and that they'd been investigating him for a long time.

"I never wanted to kill her," he sobbed.

The entity who was Roger, but wasn't Roger, droned a confession. He'd killed Elise, and drugged Lizzie with a stash of confiscated PCP. He'd intended to kill her too; he'd killed a number of people with drugs. If they didn't believe him, he could take them to the gravesites and guide them to half a dozen missing bodies. He didn't like having to do such terrible things, he whispered.

"It's over now," an officer said, daubing his blood streaked face.

The angry arrogant child he'd become, the child who had learned to make himself at home in Roger's flesh, made no motion to resist police handcuffs. "I wanted her to love me," he called to Suzy in a ragged monotone. "She should have," he sobbed. "Everyone should have."

The Ice Queen

I

BEGIN WITH THE HEAT of the sun, the heat of the summer, and a cottage standing in the middle of a meadow in Essex only a stone's throw from the lake, and a girl and a boy playing in the field, green butterfly nets twirling in the air, orange monarchs, tiger swallowtails. The nets come down and Rudy is trudging through the wheat; he is wearing swim shorts that show the bony knobs of his knees, deeper and deeper into the long blades, just as if he were gliding into lake water, wading beneath waves, until all that is visible is his head, his face, his sandy bouncing curls, his lips blue from popsicles.

Rudy's stepmother, Suzy, has long dark hair. She watches him disappear from behind the sliding glass doors. "Go outside!" she'd told him, "You're always under my feet!" She watches his body vanish like a small neat burlap sack, the kind that binds the roots of a tree, the kind you bury underground. "Get out of here."

When the girl sees him surfacing from the wheat, she pulls at the sundress that sticks to her flesh, her face is as red as the red apples on Rudy's stepmother's trees. "You eat my apples, and I'll kill you!" This is what Rudy's stepmother said to her once—this is what she said to the girl who doesn't even like red apples. "Okay, Mrs. Windish," the girl whispered back.

Rudy stops at the maple tree, a jar once used for pickles is set against its trunk. Its glass still emits the scent of dill. Four monarch butterflies flitter and bump over the scraps of milkweed the boy and girl have dropped in the bottom of the jar. Later the boy will drench cotton with nail polish remover. He'll carefully open the jar's lid and drop the cotton in. The butterflies will stop fluttering. One by one their bodies will come to rest, their damp feet will stick to the sides of the jar as if they were coated with honey, their wings will sluggishly heave, two tired lungs rattling out the remnants of memories, or hearts folding in upon themselves. The butterflies will look as if they're sweating, as if the work of staying glued to the glass has suddenly become burdensome. Their wings will fold shut and they will tumble like flat triangles upon the cotton.

Rudy's stepmother locks the door and draws the curtains, turns the newspaper into a fan, goes to the kitchen for ice. She has never known a day so hot, never felt sweat cling to her flesh so ubiquitously. It is like a moist aura, preventing her melting body's collapse, insisting upon her upright posture. She draws the kitchen curtains, splashes two shots of rye into her glass, unbuttons the small pearl buttons of her dress. The buttons extend like a vertical horizon, and as she lets the dress fall, she thinks of the lake, of the sails on a boat, of the taste of a kiss. The ice is already melting. She swallows two mouthfuls of rye, then lies on the cool kitchen floor and closes her eyes. In her dreams, she is beginning again, unearthing the treasure that brought her here—returning home to the eerie hum of frogs that infiltrate the darkness. Her mother is already dead and gone, but she is ensnared by a man with a heavenly name. A man called "Starr," who affixes her to unspoken agreements more binding than contracts etched in stone. Even now, her heart hammers with old anticipation, with fear her thoughts may conjure him and renew their "good arrangement."

It had taken such a long time to find him—an aide as corrupt as he was knowledgeable, a man who knew the value of the indigenous treasures beneath her house.

He asked a mere ten per cent and "favours." She'd thought of noisemakers and little pink tissue hats, of plastic soldiers and yo-yos and miniature spinning tops at the time. When the coin dropped, she'd experienced a brief erotic rush, but the reality was nothing less than disgusting.

Alcohol helped her through those nightmares, deadening thought and sensation. Now, she opens her eyes, props herself on an elbow, takes a mouthful of cold diluted rye. Alcohol may help her through again.

Into the stripes of long, dry snake grass, the girl and boy lead Rudy. It cuts their flesh with its fine thirsty blades, leaving slender red threads on their ankles. The girl and boy lead Rudy past the old rusty tractor that has slept like an enchanted princess for years under the shade of a mulberry tree. They take his hands and pull him over the powdery glaring road that explodes tiny landmines of dust at their footfalls, a place he is forbidden to pass, the outskirts of his kingdom—a boundary beyond which there is no protection from worldly danger.

The girl and boy drag him to the top of the rickety stairs. Shreds of paint, emerald green, curl from aged wood. The stairs are cracked, wobbly, in some instances missing altogether. The girl and boy drag Rudy over sandy bumps, perilous protruding planks, rusty spikes, rocks. They pull him along, allowing his resistance to amuse them, a game which, in the end, Rudy himself can't stop playing. His laughter is swallowed by the susurration of waves, their white-tongued lapping, their timid growl. Sweat drips from his forehead, runs down his cheeks like tears, drops into the scorching sand where in an instant it vanishes.

The girl and boy are slick with sweat, their hands slide over Rudy's arms; before long they cannot hold him. He breaks from their grasp, gallops off in the opposite direction, gallops off towards the pink sun. The water laps around his running shoes, saturates them, makes them loose and ponderous, makes every step he takes a chore.

The boy and girl catch him before their thirsty shoes drink in the lake, and then the three march back and forth, two wardens and their prisoner. Rudy kicks sticky sand from his shoe, his shoes fly over the lake like small falcons. The boy and girl, red-faced, glistening, kick their shoes off too. They are all laughing so hard that they fall in the sand, laughing so hard they don't know where they roll. Dead carp, charcoal, weed, bone, everything sticks to their dripping flesh, and they are transformed to human mosaics.

Rudy's stepmother slides her fingers over her damp breasts, down towards her naval. "Mirror, mirror on the wall," a voice inside her chants, "never let it crack or fall."

II

Words pour through her mind, familiar words, meaningless words, disconnected from their speakers. Since she left Monica Street, it has always been this way for her.

Sometimes it is her own thoughts speaking, but never in her own voice.

"What made you think you wanted this? What made you think you could ever be happy?"

Sometimes the voice is her mother's voice. Sometimes it's the voices of her sisters.

"Look what you've gone and gotten yourself into."

And what has she gotten herself into? Lying drunk and naked on a kitchen floor in the middle of the afternoon?

"Where in hell is he, anyway?" Whose voice was that, she wonders.

The voices are all talking about the same things; they're all talking about her and her life and the mess she's made of it.

"Love, led, you'll wish you were dead," her sister Audrey's voice whispers. And she does wish she were dead. She would give anything to be dead right now. Her hands drag back and forth over her stomach.

"You made your bed, now you're going to have to lie in it." Another voice tells her, "You're always looking for the easy way out."

In her mind, she sees her red Camaro, speeding over a hill, speeding away from Monica Street. She sees herself, eight summers ago, younger than she ever remembers being, with open boxes spilling her girlhood out over the wide back seat: stuffed animals, dolls, fashion magazines, and some of the ancient artefacts she'd been unable or unwilling to sell.

"You'll be sorry," her mother said, before cancer had completely ravaged her. It was a curse. But Suzy wasn't sorry, she wasn't sorry at all at first, with her red car soaring along and the radio blaring CKLW. She wasn't sorry at all, chewing Wrigley's spearmint gum, listening to Michael Jackson sing love songs, stirring the ember on her cigarette with her excited inhalations, thinking nothing of Starr, nothing of the past.

In that moment, which had no history, something opened to her. Everything became suddenly possible. It was like a magician had lifted a trick cloth and where there'd been nothing, there were worlds. Dozens of beautiful worlds lying before her, strewn over velvet.

Which one would she pick? What life would she make for herself? It was that simple, with the music weaving webs in her hair and the sun gleaming its warm promises. How could she have guessed that the curse had taken? That all the beautiful worlds would crumble and melt like snow.

The car stripped the blackness of the highway white, it tugged at the sky, it sucked in the curse. The land extended its sparkling arms. It spoke in a voice all its own. "We've been waiting for you," it said.

At first, she didn't think its words were ominous. At first, she heard those words as if they were spoken from a good parent's mouth. "I love you, land!" she called from her car, shimmering under its bright stars. "I love you, land!" she called, and the land reflecting from Lake Erie whispered back: "We love you, too."

She never considered what the land might mean by love, the land she had mined and exhumed, that land that had left her rich by offering up its treasure.

"Mirror, mirror on the wall, never let it crack or fall." It wasn't the land that said that. But now she sees the mirror, the large oval gold-framed mirror that she packaged in cardboard and twine and carefully placed behind the passenger seat. This is the mirror she inherited, the mirror her grandmother bequeathed, the mirror that hung in the room she shared with her sisters, the mirror her mother coveted.

Suzy took it from the house on Monica Street, but she didn't steal it. It had always belonged to her. She wasn't a thief. At least this is what she constantly told herself.

The cottage she'd purchased was bright and new, light poured into its kitchen, there was a balcony on which she could stand and watch the boats breaking their trails on the lake. She unpacked the mirror and hung it on her bedroom wall and when she looked into it, the person who looked back was someone she had never seen before.

She thinks about the unfurled leaf of a morning glory, and the way a twig becomes a tree. How one thing that at first looks odd and separate becomes imperceptible in its merging with a larger design. But here she was, in the country, looking as if she'd grown in reverse, the larger design cast from her, like so many demons, all the family affinities stripped away. How different she became as she stepped from under the awning of their bodies, the shadow of her dead mother lifting from her face; her sister Lizzie's voice, strong and strident, growing hushed, and the intensity of Audrey's passion waning cold. Suzy had somehow grown, once she got away from them, smaller and lighter in this bright cottage, and she wondered how many years it would take to get to know herself. But she didn't have years; she barely had three months before she would begin to blend, again, in with a different design as the curse outspread. She looked at the mirror on the wall in vain.

She could not see herself anymore. What she saw instead was love's sarcophagus.

III

The boy and girl and Rudy wade out into the lake to retrieve their shoes. The water smells of fish. The sand is soft and squishy, and slippery. Weed strings itself over their ankles as they proceed. Their shoes float like little catamarans, they wag up and down on the waves; both wind and current tow them towards the wide horizon, and the boy and girl and Rudy follow where they lead.

They are like little trudging feet, these shoes, marching over small grey hills of water, heading out to the place where it seems the world ends, where the lake concludes. These shoes elude the children, who bounce and splash after them, who reach with thin arms and small fists; the shoes tease them, stepping in directions unexpected, sliding suddenly beneath shelves of water, bobbing up in unlikely places.

These shoes are playing a game. They are calling, "Here I am, come and get me!" And the children immersed in play have lost the voices of their parents, their words of caution, the memories of punishment and rebuke. Right now, for these children, it is as if nothing else exists in the world.

Rudy's stepmother considers the mirror. She considers her obsession. Her hands trace outlines of seashells and flowers over her thighs and she thinks of her sisters. Two estranged, one missing. Her mirror is broken. It has been broken now for more than six years. She recalls the small silver spikes and daggers sparkling over her cottage floor when it happened and how she thought the design it created looked like a picture of snow. She recalls the scrape of broom bristles on glass, the bulk of the sparkling dustpan, the way the ink from the newspaper stained her hands as she wrapped up the fragments, and how the plastic garbage bag stretched like a balloon when she tossed them in.

And then she recalls the blood, a single drop at first, round and red as the sun, falling from her fingers. She didn't know she'd cut herself, she hadn't felt a thing, didn't even realize she'd touched the glass. Yet her hands suddenly surged bright red.

At the small country hospital, glittering glass splinters were removed from the lines in her palms. She was asked what she'd done to herself. The question was overtly suspicious. What she'd done was accidentally drop a mirror. It slipped through her fingers before she'd had the chance to rest it on the floor.

"You must know what happened!" A voice jabs her. "Look what you've done to yourself." Warm tears slip from the grooves of her eyes, and like the constellation of tiny scars on her hands, she cannot account for them.

Waves roll in from the lake. In turbulent weather, they grow taller than giants, but today the heat has subdued their force. Still, they rise to kiss Rudy's blue lips, the girl's sweaty throat, and the boy's slumping shoulders. They rise to swell clouds of brown silt from the lake's depths, to spit up fish who expire in their journey home, to expose plastic cups, toilet seats, mufflers, and the torso of an old Ken doll. It is as if all of these vestiges have been orphaned to their care.

The children manoeuvre themselves over the waves' small crests, they dip down in the valleys and rise up on the peaks; they pretend they are turtles and seals and dogs, and swim out further, fearing nothing, where their feet no longer touch the sand. They do summersaults and backflips while their shoes stoically march on, past the point of retrieval, past the point of return.

Scarred palms turn upward and she thinks of him. How when they first met, she could not stop thinking of him, how he erased her obsession with her sisters, how he eradicated the existence of Starr, but now she is obsessed in a different way. She imagines him driving in darkness, rain sheeting his windshield. He goes out in all kinds of weather, says he's going to meet clients, farmers with busted tractors, companies with stalled and idle trucks. Ironically, she's relinquished all her money by funding this business.

"See you soon." He kisses her forehead.

"Do you have to go?"

She looks after his son. Feeds the boy dinner. Puts him to bed. She watches rain cascading over the glass patio doors and forks of lightning splitting the sky. She listens to the thunder drumming an echo over the lake, the creak of wind in the fruit trees, the choke of water struggling to drain from the eaves.

IV

In the winter, the lake hardens. Its top becomes a polished mirror of ice. Everything living slows to inactivity. Even the cold hearts of the molluscs freeze. Fish, unable to find their way to warmer climes, turn board-stiff. Like bookmarks, they hold a place in solid water, waiting for the spring.

It is Rudy who remembers winter first, with the cold fingers of the ice queen snatching at his cherubic toes. He remembers the flatness of the ice, how he thought he could slide all the way to Michigan. How he skated over swirls of snow. The ice queen has caught his feet in her long fingers. This little piggy, just like his mother used to play. Her tail has twined around his ankles. "I've been waiting for you, Rudy," she whispers on the wind's breath.

He'd walked out on the ice so far that from the shore he looked like a little dark speck, nothing more. He'd walked out so far that it was a miracle, when it happened, that a farmer and his dog saw. The ice, as thin as a wafer and the dark speck dropping through, and the border collie, Max, barking, and the farmer reflexively moving, and the ice cracking and cracking, and Rudy calling, and the Ice Queen snatching and saying, "You're mine now, Rudy. You're mine." And the farmer heaving him back into the cold winter light after he had already stopped breathing, and Max licking his face and whining, and the farmer twisting Rudy onto his belly with no thought at all for his own safety, and the farmer forcing Rudy back into this world.

In Rudy's house, his stepmother fishes the frail clear scales of ice from her whisky glass and sets them on her breasts. Cold water trickles into a small indentation above her heart. It pools in the curve of her belly. She thinks of stone, worn and hollowed. This afternoon, he has gone to see a client. It is the same every Wednesday at noon. There are other times and days as well, other moments she could set her watch by. Times she is supposed to pretend that have no consistency, no patterns. Times which she is told only coincidentally seem contrived.

Yet, she recalls her times. The light she would leave on and off in her window. The ways she would meet him discreetly, like a stranger, on his evening strolls. What longing had entered her? What strange spirits had rushed through? She couldn't explain it. The magician's black cloth sparkled with bright worlds and she was caught by the illusion.

Rudy's real mother, if she had been living, would have felt icicles penetrate her heart the day Rudy left home. She would have gone after him, followed him down the snowy wooden steps, collected him up in her arms. She would have made him hot chocolate and told him stories; later she would have gone outside with him, built a snow fort, found the old toboggan in the shed. Rudy and his real mother used to sing songs together. They used to play together with his building blocks and his matchbox cars. When the girl and boy would come in the summer, Rudy's mother would invite them into his house. She'd make lemonade for everyone. She'd give everyone thick pink wedges of sweet melon or slices of homemade pie.

The girl and the boy are never invited into Rudy's house anymore. They don't talk to Rudy about this. They don't know what to say. This is because this unfriendly mother just appeared one summer, looking so much like the friendly one, looking so much like Rudy that the girl and boy aren't even sure if this mother is a different one.

"Hi, Mrs. Windish," they shout through the raspberry hedge whenever they come looking for Rudy. But she never calls back. Her spade stabs a dark patch of soil. They imagine she is readying it for tomato plants or endive or crocuses, that it's the scarf she wraps around her head that makes it impossible for her to hear.

Rudy feels the cold fingers of the Ice Queen snatch his toes. He is dog paddling, panting, as the water's support abandons him. How strange to find a memory here. Was he two? Three? His mother said he swam just like a little duckling. Bright orange water wings held him afloat. One day, in his hurry to enter the water, he left his wings behind. And now this memory has become something more, for as he struggles to turn, to carry himself back to the beach, he sees his mother standing there. The dark colours of her swimsuit, a sand bucket dropping on a castle, the details of her stricken face.

V

What did she know of the other woman? Of the soon to be Mrs. Windish? Did the thought ever once cross her mind? Rudy has inherited both trust and blindness from his mother. He has inherited the same curl in his hair, the same earnest jawline, the same ability to forget, to wipe clean anything that causes discomfort. In his genetic make-up there is the anaesthetic of denial, and as the Ice Queen drags him into her castle, as his mother's face becomes a cloud in the sky, he is only aware of his body's growing numbness.

"An empty vessel" was how the woman lying naked on the kitchen floor saw her—a woman whose womb would split to fill the world with children, while she herself would remain everlastingly intact. From the moment they'd first met, she'd decided against liking her. The woman was a bore, a millstone, choking the life out of this man. What had he seen in her? What had he hoped for? This woman had given birth to his child and tended his house. She tried to imagine arguments they might have. She tried to invent stories to fuel her hate, but this woman was too vacuous for sullenness and resentment; ultimately, this woman was too vacuous to speak.

"Come and live with me," she told this woman's husband, wrapping him in her sky-blue sheets. When he said he couldn't leave his wife, she used money to show him all the practical things her love could do. "She won't even notice you're missing," she said, and it seemed she was right. If the woman did notice, she never said. Her life revolved around the boy. The boy was her beacon. Everything else in her world was insignificant.

Everything else in her life may as well not have existed at all. How she loved her boy. How she loved him on her lap in the rocking chair Saturday mornings. How she loved to nurse him, even after the Public Health nurse told her she needed to stop. Would she ever have stopped on her own? Would she ever have stopped baring her breasts to him and feeling the pleasure of his lips and tongue on her nipples? She kissed, then licked his milky lips. He made it so that she could taste the sweetness of her own breasts, so that she could become small again, so that she could see in him everything she had ever lost.

Did she ignore her husband's affair, raging around her like a hurricane? The blatant insistence that Suzy be invited to dinner and then neither of them even helping with the washing up? Laughing, instead, in the living room, sitting right next to one another while she scrubbed pots and pans. But the boy was with her, standing beside her on a kitchen chair, too small still to reach the taps, his hands plunging in the soapy water. Together they'd named his fingers and toes, just like his Bible story told him Adam and Eve had named the animals and trees in their garden.

He would speak to his hands. He would have them speak to each other. "This little piggy is named Joey. This little piggy is named Bert." When he looked at his fingers, he saw distinct faces. Little round piggy faces. Soap suds-snow collecting at their feet. He imagined them making snowmen and forts. He imagined them skating over ponds of ice.

Out here in Essex there weren't many children for him to play with, but he talked to his fingers, and he never felt lonely. He never felt scared. His fingers would speak to him in the darkness of his room. The nightlight by his bedside was their moon. They would build tents under his blankets and sheets, they would sing him campfire songs.

His mother had not considered his going to school. She had not even thought for a moment about the cruelty of children or the insensitivity of teachers. In fact, she had not considered anything beyond this enchanted time. Perhaps, if she didn't think about the future, it wouldn't have to happen. Right now, his standing beside her on the kitchen chair was as far as she wished to think. But the following year, he would have to go to school. He would have to stand outside on the dusty gravel waiting for a bus. He cried when his mother left him. He cried all the way to school. The teacher tried to console him. She was older than his mother, plump and red-haired. Her breath smelled like mothballs. He didn't like her.

"Come on now, Rudy," she said, "you're not a baby, are you?" It was frustration that drove her to humiliate him. Her feeling of powerlessness at his grief. "Only babies cry like that!" she said. The children giggled. They sat straight and tall in their chairs. "Rudy's a baby!" the teacher told them.

Did he really have to go to school? He was still so very small.

VI

The new Mrs. Windish, before she was the new Mrs. Windish, did not tell Rudy's father what she thought of his son. She smiled at the boy when she visited. She bought him a glider made of balsa wood and a steel pistol from the corner store. She gave him quarters to put in his glass bank and lime green suckers that tasted like cream soda.

He carried these offerings to his mother. He made her take them into her hands. "The lady gave me this," he'd say, wrapping his mother's fingers around an object, getting her to feel it as if she were blind.

He didn't know how to work the glider. He used the pistol as a horse for his piggy people. "Bert and Joey are riding away," he told his mother.

"Where are they going?" she asked him.

"Away," he said, and made the pistol gallop off between his hands.

When the old Mrs. Windish died, the new Mrs. Windish would not let him turn the pistol into a horse, would not let him play with his piggy people. She started saying things to his father.

"I think there's something wrong with your kid."

She said "your kid," not "our son," though Rudy's father would have liked for her to say this. Still, she fed him tins of spaghetti, macaroni and cheese, hot dogs. She made him sit at the table until he had cleaned his plate, she made him take his bath and tidy his room, she made him say please and thank you, and she put him to bed on time. She did his laundry, packed his lunch for school, bought him shoes and socks and underwear, took him to the dentist. Yet only vaguely was Rudy aware of her.

Since his mother's death, something had happened to him. It was like emerging from the water on a starlit night. Everything above him had become vast, and there was no point in the darkness where he could fix his eyes. He saw this woman only dimly, as if she were surrounded by a poisonous haze, a fog that made his eyes water and his throat close, a fog that sent his brain reeling, just as if he were a cartoon character who'd been hit on the head with a hammer.

Joey and Bert did not like the lady. They talked about her under Rudy's bedclothes late at night. They said, "When we grow up, we'll fix that lady. We'll fix her for not letting us play with Rudy. For stopping our fun." They liked the old Mrs. Windish and didn't understand why she had to go away. "Will she come back?" they asked Rudy. "Some day," Rudy said.

Now there was water swirling around Rudy, sucking him down into an envelope of sand. Above him, he could see through the turbid water. There was exuberant sunlight, and for a moment he felt completely warm and good. Then, the creeping cold snagged at his ankles and travelled up his knees to his chest. He could no longer feel Joey and Bert or make them move, he could no longer fight the voice that drank him in, that filled his ears, "You're mine!" The other children swam away. They didn't belong to her. "You're mine," she said to Rudy, alone.

Wasn't this what his mother had said to him when she hugged him? He belonged to her. He was part of her. He would never be anything else. How could he not hug her back? Even as dead and cold as she was? How could he not want her to love him forever?

The new Mrs. Windish keeps a stash of sleeping pills on her bedside table. She uses them because she cannot get to sleep at night, because thoughts of her past keep her mind racing and her body weak.

"It serves you right!" her mother's voice tells her. The voice comes upon her, when she most wishes to be deaf. "It serves you right! You homewrecker!" It finds her in her sleep and shakes her to consciousness. And she knows she was a homewrecker, but she also knows this is nothing compared to the guilt that truly makes her wake. Did she really just dream it? Or had some evil demon actually crawled into her body? It wasn't her, was it? She could never do anything like that. Take a life? No. It wasn't her. It was some man from her past, wasn't it?

Some man she can only vaguely recall.

She staggers to the bedroom where she sleeps with Rudy's father, and takes two sleeping pills from a pillbox. She really doesn't want to die, she decides. She doesn't want to be the second dead wife. She only wishes to sleep. She only wishes not to remember.

The Ice Queen is holding Rudy in her strong arms and binding him in the frigid coils of her tail. She is clutching him, and her breasts, full of milky lake water, have filled his mouth and lungs. Strands of emerald weed are weaving in his hair, and the sun, the bright exuberant sun, is finally setting. Somewhere beneath the cerulean heavens, feathers flurry. Vanes and rachises thrashing as some raptor or angel or alien reels Rudy back. Here, he will flap and flounder, for many years among this profane land's mermaids and miscreants, the weight of their legends almost crushing him, until the day that he dares to cast himself free and crawl from under the shadows of his stepmother's past, absorbing all of her inheritance and relinquishing the shards of her curse.

Proverbs

NO ONE EXPECTED that Jack Goulet would ever return to Fontainebleau. When he was blinded with pepper spray, handcuffed, and crammed into the back of a police cruiser, it was generally assumed he'd disappear, his essence evaporate into urban legend.

It didn't matter that he was a minor, that he was purported, from an early age, to be "disturbed," that he was said to have exhibited profound psychological problems long before he sustained his brain injury. The injury occurred at the family's farm in Essex. There'd been no eyewitness, but the story, pieced together, was that Jack—crazy, shit disturbing, Jack—had stolen his father's tractor and was heading into town. The tractor must have hit a bump, or a tree stump. Jack hadn't even gotten out of the field and, as the attending surgeon at Hotel Dieu put it, "Jack fell down and broke his crown."

It hadn't been a simple fracture, but rather one that tore the flesh and caused Jack's skull to plunge inward, like a car's dented fender. It required a raft of specialists, fifteen hours of surgical skill in which each moment was a masterpiece in creative mentation.

"I think, ladies and gentlemen, we can do a little better than vinegar and brown paper," the comic surgeon quipped for the benefit of the gathered medical students who all appeared shaken. Pieces of shattered skull were removed, a clean square hole sawed, ruptured blood vessels repaired, and a stainless steel plate screwed into the bone.

Jack recovered. There was corn in the fields when the hospital sent him home. The old grey tumbledown barn that his father would neither raze nor repair gazed, like the eye of a drunken Cyclops, over the pristine land. Jack hated the glaring barn. He despised the way its presence bore into him, the unavoidable reality of its secrets. The barn stank. Not with the sweet moist breath and excrement of cows, not with life, but with the gnawing hunger of rat piss, with the decomposing vestiges of chickens he had once befriended, with the rattles of rust and the surfeit of mould spores, and something else he was loath to identify.

The house Jack lived in wasn't much better. Dampness had been allowed to infiltrate the structure, condense on windows, and warp wood floors. It yellowed the small print wallpaper flowers and splattered plaster ceilings with unwieldy asymmetrical stains. Jack liked to imagine these were continents; he liked to imagine a painted map. He envisioned Michelangelo and the breath-taking dome of the Sistine Chapel. He'd seen photographs in art books. He promised himself one day he'd visit Rome.

No one knew about his flights of fancy. At home, he was not a talkative boy. Sometimes entire weeks would pass without his speaking, entire weeks of external silence in which he remained holed up in his tiny dingy box-like room. The only thing that could stir him at these times was the *put-put, clank* of the book van that barrelled forth from the city, like Triptolemus's chariot, Jack thought, bringing seed-corn to the earth's inhabitants, like Dictys' boat, sailing forth to rescue the hero Perseus from a watery grave.

Jack had been born knowing how to read, or at least this was the account he gave whenever questions arose about his remarkable skills. It was easier than explaining hyperlexia, a condition which enabled its precocious possessor to decipher written words without being formally taught. He'd learned about this term and condition in a book. The word itself had enraptured him. "Hyperlexia, hyperrrrlexia, hyperrlegggsia." It rolled around and around in his mouth, a smoky wine.

What made his reading ability all the more unique was that his parents, Ben and Mary Ellen Goulet, were not readers at all. In fact, they didn't crack a book or magazine from one year to the next, with the exception of the *TV Guide*, but in spite of being a voracious and eclectic reader himself, Jack did not possess a book of his own.

The woman in charge of the book van, Carol Davis, liked Jack, though after he was taken into custody, she admitted only to finding him strange. "Eccentric farm-folk," she told reporters who'd tracked her down, "isolationists, inbreeders, never can tell what they're going to do." However, in the years leading up to his crime, she'd been his main supplier of publications both revolutionary and subversive. He'd ordered classics in philosophy, psychology, history and science. He read *The Decline and Fall of the Roman Empire*, and *Seven Pillars of Wisdom*. He read *Discoveries and Opinions of Galileo* and *On the Revolutions of the Celestial Spheres* by Copernicus. He read everything that Winston Churchill ever wrote and Adolf Hitler's *Mein Kampf*. He read Aristotle, Plato, Nietzsche, Hesse, and Descartes, to whom he was pleased to discover he bore a physical resemblance.

"I think, therefore I am," he told himself, and with his mother's sewing needle and a bottle of ink tattooed the phrase across his belly. He read sacred texts, the *Upanishads*, the *Bhagavad Gita*, the *Bible*. He also read English literature, and had just devoured *The Complete Works of William Shakespeare* before his devastating fall. Afterwards, due to decreased blood flow in the brain and a condition known as foreign accent syndrome, if ever he had cause to speak of any of the numerous texts he'd imbibed, if ever he had cause to speak at all, he did so with a precise English accent, conspicuous to any casual listener, but to himself completely imperceptible. After his surgery, Carol Davis noticed that his literary requests took on darker notes: Dostoyevsky, Kafka, Edgar Allan Poe, and *The Greatest Unsolved Murder Mysteries of the Twentieth Century*. She noticed he became increasingly interested in serial killers, in sociopaths, in Lizzie Borden type characters, who when found holding the proverbial smoking gun, simply smiled and denied their culpability. Still, it came as a shock to everyone when Jack Goulet killed his parents. Up until then, although he'd always been a troublemaker, he'd shown no violent tendencies whatsoever.

"He's not a killer," Marjorie Loomis, an impassioned teacher from Thomas King Elementary, pleaded on his behalf. She was his long-ago mentor, a woman with a calling, who, for the sake of her vocation, had given up her personal life. Jack had formed a crush on her before "the trifling mishap" that barred him from Thomas King.

After the murders, he'd fled to Fontainebleau, to Marjorie's house, asking if she might consider becoming his foster mother, now that he was an orphan. She'd always had a soft spot for him, even though he was spurned by other teachers. "In all bad there's good," she defended, reciting her favourite proverb, for so it had been in her life—from all the muck and misery, from all the seeds of sorrow, from all the grains of grief, a cornucopia of strengths and finer feelings had flourished and she expected the same would occur for Jack.

He was such a sensitive, intelligent, unusual little lad: accident prone, inquisitive, with an encyclopaedic knowledge and such an extensive vocabulary that he tended to intimidate. He'd been home-schooled until Marjorie's grade four class, and there was no doubt in her mind that much of his "trouble-making" was the result of him being an exceptionally gifted child. Because of the expense and the school district's limited budget, she'd been unsuccessful in her attempts to get him tested.

He didn't need school, as far as book learning went. She knew there was nothing factual she could teach him that he didn't already know, but it broke her heart to watch how he struggled socially. He was like a beautiful, exotic ocean fish, washed ashore on a Lake Erie beach. He could not communicate with his classmates, the irritating sand fleas; he could only flap and flail around and try to avoid them. In an introductory essay, which Marjorie had all the children write as a way to get to know them, Jack expounded on the universe. He discussed the likelihood of life on other planets, and the historic hubris of humanity. He confessed that most of the time he felt as if he were an alien in an unfamiliar world.

Tears pricked Marjorie's eyes as she read his essay, realizing it was more than just the sentiment conveyed that moved her, more than just the skill and beauty of Jack's prose, more than just the fact that a child so young might feel so alienated. The tears pricked and swelled in her eyes because in Jack's essay, she saw a reflection of every individual who feels helpless and at the mercy of an uncaring bureaucratic machine, castrated and disempowered in their own lives, their stellar gifts left to rust among the dust heaps, while they watched the world implode. Tears pricked her eyes because she saw reflecting back from Jack's essay an image of herself.

Initially, she'd tried to work on Jack's socialization in the classroom by encouraging his involvement in group work. She believed he had a great deal to teach his peers and would personally benefit from friendships, but all too soon it became apparent that the great divide was insurmountable. The tortured eyes of an old soul balefully looked out from the child Jack's body in which it was captive. For some reason, she was reminded of the story she'd once read of a Hollywood chimpanzee who'd been raised by humans. He drank beer, smoked cigars, even played poker. When his movie career ended, he was sent to the monkey house at the Los Angeles zoo. His trainer recollected, then translated, his mournful cry: "I don't understand. Why am I in here with all these animals?" In many ways, Jack's agonised silence was the very same cry.

In the end, she couldn't bring herself to force Jack to mix with his peers—she couldn't bring herself to force Jack to do anything. Instead, she laid before him all of the school's supplies she could sequester and told him that as long as it hurt no one, he could follow his interests in any way he chose. She was amazed by the elaborate things he built and the experiments he engaged in to test and improve his inventions. With a few of the school's old junk telephones, he constructed an intercom system, and with two gift wrap tubes and a magnifying glass, he fashioned a workable telescope. "There's nothing you can't do," she told him earnestly, cheered by the excitement she saw brighten his face. She egged him on, encouraged him to reach, to extend himself, and he, given unconditional licence, seized with gusto projects that previously he wouldn't have dared.

His academic undoing arrived as a result of one such project. He'd always been fascinated by flight, by stories of Icarus and Daedalus, the Wright Brothers, Charles Lindbergh, Neil Armstrong. On the farm, he'd followed the flight patterns of crows, the black oarsmen of the skies, collected their feathers, and compared their exertions to the gliding propulsions of turkey vultures who appeared hardly to flap their wings at all. These interests led him to investigate air currents and to study the anatomy of wings, but it wasn't until he happened upon the notebooks of Leonardo Da Vinci and saw the inventor's renderings of that unrealized flying machine, the ornithopter, that Jack's imagination soared.

There were stores of balsa wood in the school's supply room, package upon package upon package purchased by a long retired bipolar art teacher, to whom, apparently, God had spoken. It was his mission, until the school board intervened, to oversee the grade threes and fours at Thomas King in the building of a full-sized replica of Noah's biblical ark. Whether the rains came or not, whether such an ark could possibly be seaworthy, didn't matter, according to God, the teacher explained. What was important was the ark's presence—like the cross on top of a church, or a star on top of a Christmas tree—this symbolic ark would be an appropriate aquatic reminder to the sinners of Fontainebleau, not only of the greatness of the Lord, but also what comes of human evil.

The balsa wood couldn't be returned and had remained taking up valuable space in the school's small supply room for the better part of a decade. When Jack asked if he might have it all, and Marjorie Loomis, in turn, asked her colleagues if she might, she was greeted with enthusiastic assent and not a single question about how she planned on using it.

Later, after what the principal called "the fiasco," she would be mercilessly grilled. It appeared that no one at Thomas King Elementary was an advocate of the unconventional, that no one supported innovation, that no one valued a child's giftedness. It precipitated a crisis of faith in Marjorie Loomis, which would have resulted in her resignation if it weren't for the knowledge she'd given Jack something precious, that she'd opened a window, even if only a crack, and shown him that through his own talents, he could escape the banality and ignorance of the world.

However, when Jack showed up on Marjorie's doorstep and confessed the terrible thing he'd done, escape was not the course of action she advocated. "The truth will set you free, Jack," she promised, believing what she said. "Turn yourself in. You're just a boy. I'll do everything in my power to help you."

When Jack returned to Fontainebleau for good, no longer a boy, and for anonymity's sake no longer as "Jack," he fondly recalled Marjorie Loomis, wondered what had become of her, though realized it would be foolhardy to pursue his curiosity. For years, after fleeing St. Jerome's Wilderness Camp, he'd evaded police; but knowing his former teacher's honesty and high mindedness, knowing her innocent idealism, her dedication to truth, he was certain she'd insist, as she had done after the killings, that he turn himself in. As before, she would vow to stand by him, make sure he got a good lawyer, tell the judge a million positive things to lessen his sentence, but when all was said and done, he was still a fugitive, no longer a minor, and a prison term was something he wasn't about to serve.

He had plans for his future now, important plans that required not only his freedom, but an impeccably respectable past. He'd made his way to Toronto, after bolting from St. Jerome's, and for the next three years took up covert residence at the University of Toronto's labyrinthine Robarts Library where by day he indulged his literary and intellectual obsessions unnoticed amid the throng of students, and by night, slept restfully on quiet inconspicuous floors and in hidden corners. There were couches for napping and overstuffed chairs where, in deep crevices, loose change accumulated, as if dropped through the slots of piggy banks. Garbage cans brimmed with half-eaten bagels and burgers, with substantial remnants of chicken and cheese. "The wasteful overfed," he thought sadly as he tucked in. "Thc world is in an abysmal state."

He'd known the world was in an abysmal state before his farm accident and surgery, before he'd killed his parents, and before he found himself at St. Jerome's. In fact, he'd always known, but until he sought refuge at Robarts, he'd never considered himself as one of its potential saviours.

In his new library home, he continued his eclectic studies, reading whichever works appealed. He read books about the lives of prophets, books about Mohammed and Lao Tzu. He read about the sage Siddhārtha Gautama, the Buddha, and became enthralled with Buddhist teachings. In dreams, he began to recognize strangers as prior selves, each hoping to attain Buddhahood in order to benefit all sentient beings. He saw Marjorie Loomis draped in a Kashaya robe, sitting beneath a Bodhi tree and recognized her as himself also. On waking, he determined that he must embrace a path of compassion. That he must work to bring about *wholly good acts*—acts, he'd read, motivated by good intentions that injured no one and brought about completely good results. But how was he to do this when he'd cut himself off from other human beings? How was he to leave his sanctuary of learning and ply his ministrations to an ailing world?

The answer came by way of the daily newspaper. A penniless drifter and occasional circus ring crew worker, who went by the name of Rodney Tan, vanished after a trailer fire. Later his real name, Mark Smith, was revealed as well as his former occupation as a county librarian. It appeared to police as if he'd left his former life and identity for no apparent cause. Then, several diaries, preserved in a fireproof box, were discovered along with his passport and birth certificate. These confirmed that his exodus had not been precipitated by personal tragedies, familial tensions, or criminal dealings but, rather, due to thwarted literary ambitions and a longing for adventure.

Jack was able to assume Smith's identity easily. Just a heap of ash remained of the unfortunate man, who was only five years Jack's senior. The detail of his extraordinary transformation from one life to another was also useful. If questions ever arose, Jack could explain everything in the context of past actions—dramatic disappearances and surreptitious resurrections—a practice, he'd explain, that allowed him to circumvent boredom. He didn't anticipate too many questions, though. Mark Smith, it appeared, had been entirely alone and completely unencumbered. Unless Jack was very careless, he had no reason to fear.

The four years following his departure from the library, Jack assumed Smith's identity, and established himself as a circus roustabout, putting together, taking apart, and transporting all of the company's physical baggage. He knew the circus Smith had worked for, and during the initial two years, as he hopped like a flea, from circus to circus, learning the ropes and trying to determine where he'd feel most at home, he avoided all association with the places the dead man had lived.

He marvelled at the number and variety of circuses both large and small: travelling shows that couldn't earn enough to keep their equipment in good repair, and fireball operations that grew like sudden bright warts, conned the townies, then vanished into the sunset, wisps of shimmering dust. There were mud circuses that up-staked every few days and lumbered to different towns, ones that specialized in aerial acrobatics, high-wire walkers, flying trapeze artists, and iron jaw performers. There were circuses that made their reputation with clown acts, with high school horse and dog and pony shows, with lion tamers and elephants. There were highbred outfits also: part circus, part county fair, in which Ferris wheels and roller coasters existed in combination with the traditional Big Top.

Jack sampled as many varieties as he could, and found heartening the laissez-faire approach and "no questions asked" policy that they all appeared to share. He found that circus work would provide a modest pay, three meals a day, and adequate accommodation. He also found, among the Carnies, an acceptance of his strengths and weaknesses, which he had never experienced among peers.

Eventually, he came to settle with a small, revolutionary assemblage—a forward-looking circus, *Vive La Difference*, which uniquely exploited the past. *Vive*, as it was referred to by its intimates, had a social conscience, and employed among its performers people who in times gone by would have been referred to as "freaks". It was *Vive's* mission to transform public perception, to defy the objectification of this marginalized population, and to celebrate and proclaim the uniqueness of each and every individual.

It was as a ring crew worker for *Vive* that Jack met and struck up his first real friendship. Prince Arey, a performer born without limbs, was a descendent of the 19th century circus performer Prince Tolly, a.k.a. the human snake. Arey shared not only the same rare congenital disorder, autosomal recessive tetra-amelia, as his relative but also shared his remarkable intelligence, which made him a well-suited companion for Jack. Like Tolly, Arey possessed no end of skills. He could competently fix a car's engine with his mouth, farm the land with his limbless body, play a guitar with his teeth. He could compose a song, memorize a play, and build a house, entirely by himself. He spoke four languages, could read over two thousand words a minute, and created the *World Peace Through Literacy* foundation which boasted twelve hundred satellite organizations worldwide.

Arey became for Jack both a role model of self-reliance and like Marjorie Loomis an encouraging mentor, whose positive influence would have a profound impact on shaping Jack's future. While it was not in his nature to interrogate, Arey's innate gift of instilling trust in others led Jack, who had spoken to no one of his past, to confess all of his transgressions and unburden his heart.

What Jack had not realized, having lived such a solitary existence, was how the act of speaking to another worked to uncork dusty recollections. In his daily life, prior to meeting Arey, when not revelling in the liberating expansiveness of literature, he concerned himself primarily with the next logical move he must make to ensure his freedom and survival. Never did he allow his mind to loop back into the darker parts of the murky, nebulous galaxy of his dismal youth. This troubling constellation of memories was perilous, and by an unconscious defence, rather than act of will, remained safely off limits.

In opening to Arey, however, Jack found the courage to speak of events long lost to consciousness: the murder of his parents and what precipitated it; the farm accident and all of its suppressed particulars; the calamity at Thomas King Elementary, which resulted in Jack's expulsion; and the odious unspoken events that occurred in the ramshackle barn of his childhood.

For the first time, Jack acknowledged the viciousness of his upbringing, the pitiless brutality of his father and his mother's covert and symbiotic participation. Although he wished for it not to happen, his mind conjured his father, Ben, bullnecked and stocky, with arms as tough as cord—a country boy who had grown up on the Essex farm, as his father before him, yet unlike that good man, twisted, depraved, a monster of cruel madness whom the rural community exalted as one of its moral pillars.

Jack's mother, Mary Ellen, was likewise esteemed by neighbours. She baked pies and cookies for the church bazaar, held quilting parties in her home, took baskets of preserves to the poor and infirm, establishing the façade that would cloak and enable Ben's duplicitous dealings. She was more than a decade younger than he and in spite of the jowls and belly fat she'd packed on since their wedding had, on the day of her death, still appeared childishly young.

Jack had long kept her image from his thoughts and sobbed with its return, as he might the actual arrival of a loving mother estranged through unforeseen circumstances which he'd had no hand in bringing about. He hadn't wanted to kill her, and wouldn't have if she'd been more selfish, less dependent, if she'd been able to conceive of her life as something more than the shield of her husband's corruption. He'd never have killed her if she hadn't flung herself in front of Ben, and taken the bullet intended for him.

The moving finger writes and having writ moves on, Jack thought as the bullet exploded from the gun. Earlier that day, before he'd observed Ben in the barn taking his sadistic pleasure with a prostitute from the city, Jack had been reading the *Rubaiyat of Omar Khayyam*. The woman was young, just a girl and Jack, when he'd heard her desperate screams, put his book down and ran to the barn, even though he'd been forbidden to enter. He knew that Ben got up to unspeakable things there, things he would rather remain ignorant of, yet the girl's shrieks compelled him to sacrifice his innocence, and in bearing witness to his father's depravity, Jack knew he would become the target of his most violent assault. He fled before Ben could collar him, realizing that this time there was only one thing he could do. He got Ben's gun, hid in the pantry, and when he heard the screen door slam, prepared to put an end to his father's reign of terror.

The bullet travelled through the air as if the air had become clear jelly, and his mother travelled too, at the same protracted speed, it seemed, a baseball player, sliding home. *All thy piety nor wit shall lure it back,* he thought as the bullet and his mother became one, *nor all thy tears wash out a word of it.*

Years later, as body after body was exhumed from beneath the barn's dirt floor, Jack learned the police were hunting for him in connection with prostitute murders. Although he felt guilty for slaying his parents, he couldn't help but wonder what the death toll might have been if not for the fact that he'd lifted and shot his father's gun that fateful day. At the time, he'd shed no tears. After his mother's body dropped in a heap to the ground, he let fly with a second bullet and hit Ben in the shoulder, then pulled the trigger once again, and hit his fleeing father, in the back of the head. Ben had not expected the feeble hand of his fifteen-year-old son, the son he'd brought to the brink of the grave so frequently, to confer him a deathblow; he'd not expected to be felled by his own gun, nor expected his demise to come so suddenly nor in such a startling way. Surprise marked his face, as innocent disbelief marked his wife's, and Jack, continuing to empty bullets into his father's flesh, felt strangely light. When at last the gun would discharge no longer, Jack floated to the kitchen and prepared himself a meal as he logically surmised that it might be a long time before he'd get anything to eat again.

In a daze, he headed for Fontainebleau behind the wheel of his father's old Ford pickup.

Although it had been years since he'd been a student at Thomas King, he'd not forgotten Mrs. Loomis nor the ornithopter he'd fashioned after Leonardo da Vinci's design. It was a relief for Jack to forget the murders, to think instead of a happier time when the positive force of Marjorie Loomis still prevailed in his life, even if the result of all of her goodness was less than it should have been and the outcome for him was disaster.

He recalled how he'd climbed to the top of the school to test his flying machine, overestimated the size of the wings in proportion to the size of his body, miscalculated air currents, and plummeted to the earth, hitting en route both the grade six teacher, Mr. Markovic, and the principal, Bristle Top. Both men were wounded and required stitches. The worst part of the event, from Jack's point of view, was that the winged device really did work; it just needed a few minor adjustments and an updraft for take-off.

He'd wanted so badly to climb to the top of the school again, to show everyone that Mrs. Loomis had been right in placing her trust in him. With his ornithopter, he could win science fairs and put his school on the academic map. But it wasn't to be. His father arrived full of false affability and with a baseball bat in the back of his truck still bloodied from the last time he'd used it.

He drove Jack out to a secluded lean-to by the railroad tracks, shackled him so he couldn't run away, and thrashed him within an inch of his life.

In the weeks that followed, Jack stayed alive by concentrating on the memory of his ornithopter, by mentally going through all the repairs he'd make and visualizing the movement of his body in flight. He knew that Marjorie Loomis would keep the contraption safe in her classroom, that one day its flight would vindicate her. He never lost sight of that, and as soon as he was able, stole away from home, broke into the school, and recovered his wings. He hid them safely in a secluded place, next to the railroad tracks where his father had thrashed him. It had been his plan to sneak away from the farm each evening, and work on the ornithopter until he could make it successfully fly. He could not have imagined then that he would murder his parents and be swept up and sentenced to St. Jerome's, miles and miles away from Fontainebleau.

Over the years, the flying machine and the quest to repair it were forgotten. It wasn't until, in disclosing the details of his troubled past to Arey, he began to think of it again. "You could design your own act," Arey enthused, unruffled by the darker aspects of his confession, "fly through the air without a trapeze. 'Mark Smith, *The Human Butterfly*'," he announced.

"More like a human bird," Jack said, but he liked the idea of butterfly—he liked the idea of transformation and metamorphosis—of becoming something or someone else, washed clean of the filth of former days.

The first time he returned to Fontainebleau as a grown man, he did so simply to recover a memory and was surprised to find his ornithopter, a little weathered but mostly all in one piece, buried in an old farm tarp, exactly where he'd left it so many years ago. He had not, even after working on the contraption—extending its wings, elongating its cross bar—assumed he'd be able to get it into the air, and once he did, could not have, by any stretch of the imagination, figured on seeing a beautiful young damsel in the adjacent field—a damsel, for that is how his mind conceived her, in distress—motionless amid wild carrot and flixweed.

A train's whistle filled the air as he circled high above her, dipping as he could, trying to negotiate the ornithopter closer, struggling to get a better look at her face, to read the nature of her malady. The sun behind him was blinding, and the dark wings of his contraption obscured her expression in shadow. He strained to get closer but after plunging twice more, an updraft carried him in a spiral, high into the clouds and away.

The sun, incandescent, reminded him of the fate of Icarus, a fate he feared, but no sooner did he panic than the wind subsided, and he was brought close to the earth again, though several miles from his point of departure. His landing was ungainly; however, the ornithopter was spared and it was with a joyous heart that he dragged the contraption back to its hiding place and returned to the circus to tell Arey of his triumph. For weeks, he continued to visit his ornithopter, adding pulleys and levers, improving the machine, so that when spring arrived, and he attempted flight again, he was able to exert more control.

As he flew, he recalled the damsel in distress, but had not expected to find her again lying in the adjacent field, bawling piteously. He manoeuvred the craft down towards her, and landed smoothly, not far from her side. The striking young woman, whose skin was the colour of pearl, and whose lips were the colour of coral, whose long dark hair fell over her shoulders like a raiment of silk, lay upon a blanket, unsuccessfully attempting to shroud the lower half of her body so that Jack wouldn't see. There was an appendage resembling a dolphin's tail, instead of legs, and the pupils of the young woman's eyes, round as moons, large as quarters, filled with fluid terror as Jack approached.

All the while, she'd been praying for him—that mysterious winged entity whom she'd previously spied. In her mind, he was a dark god or angel, graceful in flight, the certain source of her salvation, but when she beheld the mortal Jack and the lumbering feathered contraption from which he struggled free, dread, instead of reverence, sparked her heart.

He spoke enthusiastically about his ornithopter and described his experiments of flight. She was conscious that he neither gawked nor stared, that no hint of disgust eclipsed his face as he beheld the fishy protrusion she'd learned to loathe. He spoke to her, just as if she were anyone. Just as if she were fully limbed, and her unconventional body the norm.

She told him her name: Celeste. She trusted him. She also told him of *Sirenomelia*, the medical term she'd been labelled with.

In the future, he would describe their meeting as *Divine Providence, Atman, Kismet*—the first instance in which he would consciously have the opportunity to perform a *wholly good act*.

She would forever see it as her soul's parole from a life's sentence of strangeness and self-contempt. Jack had not been the dark god she'd envisioned—not an ethereal seraph—but a mortal angel sent, a harbinger of hope, who acquainted her with the work of *Vive*, and opened, for her, the possibility of an independent life.

Accomplishing *wholly good acts* would dominate Jack's philanthropic pursuits ever after. For a long time he debated searching for Marjorie Loomis, wondering if his reappearance in her life would be wholly good. It was possible, he reasoned, that his return might present her with a difficult moral dilemma, possibly that he'd end up in jail. It forced him to examine the dogma and consider its limitations. What mortal could know, even with the best intentions, if the acts they performed resulted in injuring no one and, over time, brought about only positive results? Still, for human beings living in the world, actions were required—and while *"the wholly good act"* was not a precise formula, it was certainly a better guide for negotiating daily undertakings than no guide at all, he concluded.

Eventually he established a home for himself in Fontainebleau and resolved to call on his former mentor. She'd left Thomas King a few years after his trial, when the flame of her youthful teaching idealism finally expired. She'd still remained a guide of sorts, working in women's shelters and volunteering with troubled youths. Jack realized as soon as he saw her that he'd always loved her, in spite of her being twenty years his senior, and she, too, seeing her onetime favourite pupil as a grown man, acknowledged a connection that would have been perverse and criminal if it had surfaced when she'd first known him.

She'd always maintained that Jack was a very old soul and thus was able to dismiss the raised eyebrows and malicious gossip that flanked their newly formed relationship. In time, the details of their personal histories would no longer be of interest to anyone, including themselves. Yet, now and again, Jack found himself curious. Was it guilt alone that drove him to decency?

Perhaps he should turn himself in, serve his time, make a clean breast of it so guilt wouldn't factor at all. When he gave voice to these musings, Marjorie would have none of them. She'd have none of his nobility, none of his self-recrimination. She'd dredge up her favourite old proverb, worn to new meaning over the course of years, and one that served as a counterweight to Jack's philosophy of the *wholly good act*. "In all bad, there's good," she'd say assuring him that no matter what his past transgressions, he'd paid in full.

At these times, Jack would sigh, as if the past burden existed still heavy upon him and nothing would give him more relief than to cast it cleanly away, but in his heart he knew that the sigh signified only that here, in the unlikely setting of Fontainebleau, he'd escaped—escaped once more—from a fate so terrible, he could scarcely believe his luck.

Book Group and Study Guide

20 Questions

1. Which stories did you prefer?

2. Which stories immediately drew you in? Did you find each story elicited a different emotional response?

3. Who are the characters you most sympathize with? Why?

4. How do repression, amnesia, and recollection play out among the characters?

5. Though this is a collection of linked stories, the forms are frequently dissimilar. Can you identify three diverse forms?

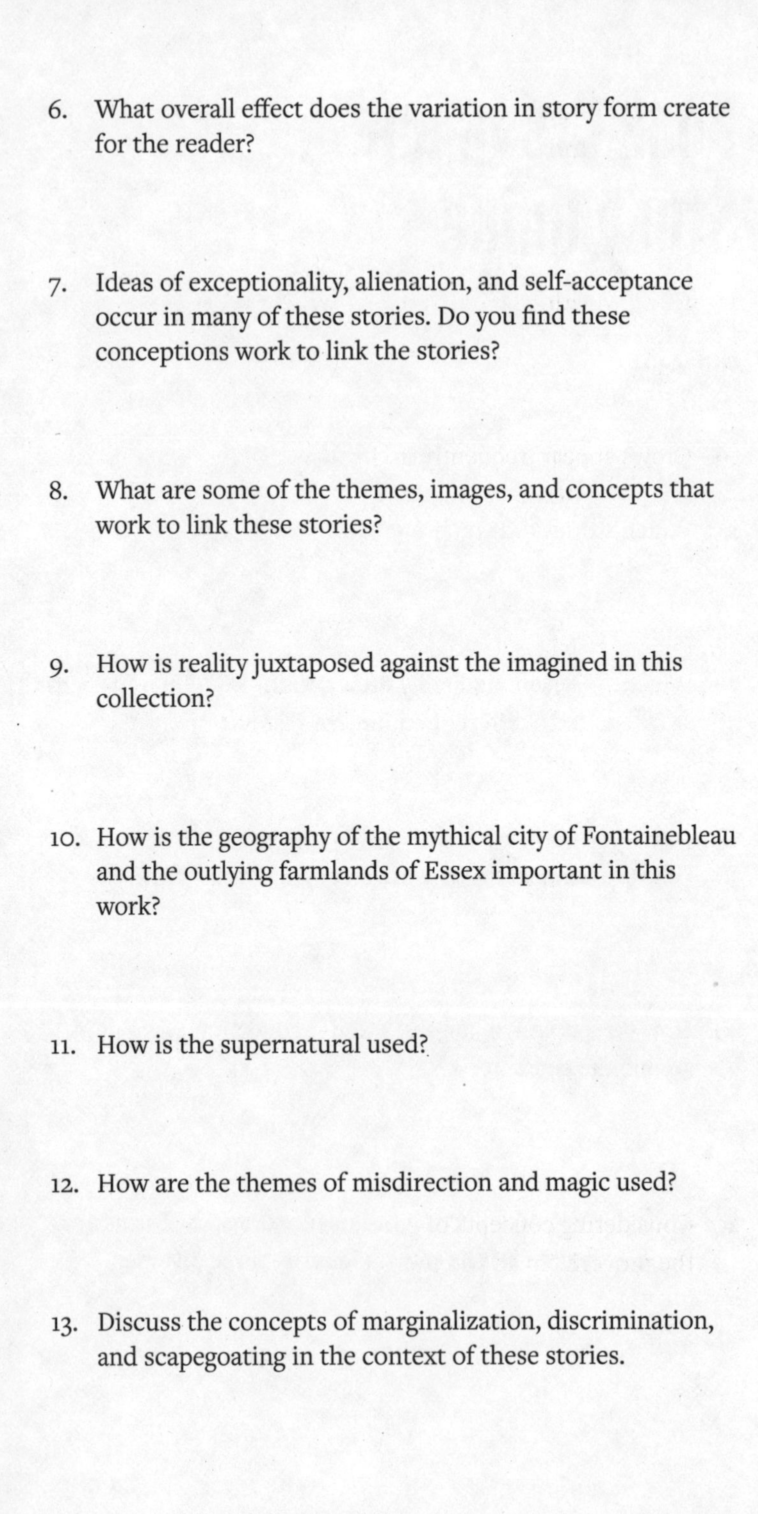

6. What overall effect does the variation in story form create for the reader?

7. Ideas of exceptionality, alienation, and self-acceptance occur in many of these stories. Do you find these conceptions work to link the stories?

8. What are some of the themes, images, and concepts that work to link these stories?

9. How is reality juxtaposed against the imagined in this collection?

10. How is the geography of the mythical city of Fontainebleau and the outlying farmlands of Essex important in this work?

11. How is the supernatural used?

12. How are the themes of misdirection and magic used?

13. Discuss the concepts of marginalization, discrimination, and scapegoating in the context of these stories.

14. In which ways are conventions and stereotypes exploded in these stories?

15. How is death and resurrection explored?

16. Crows appear frequently in the work. Discuss their diverse symbolic meaning.

17. Flight, both literal and metaphoric, is a recurring motif throughout the book. How does it reveal character?

18. Discuss how themes of dispossession and cultural appropriation are dealt with in this work.

19. How are disguise and shifting identity thematically integral to this collection?

20. Considering concepts of good and evil in the book, discuss the proverb "In all bad there's good."

Acknowledgments

I wish to thank all the people, institutions, magazines, and grant-funding agencies that have supported me in the development of this book.

These include my first reader, and grammarian extraordinaire, Eric Henderson; my second reader, Linda Turnbull, of the sharp mind and keen eye; and my former teacher, George McWhirter, and members of his experimental fiction workshop at the University of British Columbia, who gave excellent feedback on a few of the stories in this collection and assisted in evolving this work.

I also wish to thank the English Department at the University of Windsor and the Canada Council for the Arts for the writing residency I was awarded in 2015, as well as Melanie Bechard, who drove me to and from the university, offered me a room in her house, and generally looked after me during that very cold and snowy term.

I gratefully acknowledge her sisters, Lisa Baynham and Karen VanMackelberg, for the research outings and visits, as well as Marmy, the cat, for many a rousing red dot match. Chuck and Robbie Bakos, also friends of my youth, assisted by reminding me of what life was like in the Fontainebleau subdivision of our childhood.

Although it was a nonfiction project which brought me to Windsor in 2015, many of the people who opened their hearts and homes to me and many of the places that welcomed me furthered the writing and editing of this fiction collection: Sue Perry at the Windsor Public Library, for example, who hosted me and CBC Radio's Tony Doucette, who not only interviewed me, but gave me a beautiful, large CBC coffee mug which has, since then, been my mug of choice and been refilled countless times through the editing process of this work; Marty Gervais, who loaned me books and gave me a wonderful day-long tour of the city; George and Nancy Plantus, who befriended me and introduced me to many interesting people and experiences; and Patrick Brode, who gave me insights into Windsor's past.

I also wish to thank my students at the University of Victoria, who have taught me through teaching, as well as all the other students I've been privileged to teach over the years.

Stories in this collection have appeared in *Grain, subTerrain, Broken Pencil,* *PRISM international, Pottersfield Portfolio, Room, Hard Boiled,* and *The Dalhousie Review*. I'm grateful to the editors who accepted them.

I wish to thank Martin Salvage, in Scotland, for his delightful map of the mythical city of Fontainebleau and his wife Vicki who, along with Eric Henderson, were our communication conduits.

Thanks also to my publisher, Brian Kaufman, who is open to innovation and always willing to push conventional literary boundaries.

And lastly, thanks to The Canada Council for the Arts. While I didn't receive a grant for this specific project, the support I've received for others over time and the support they offer literary journals have assisted me in establishing a writing career. I feel blessed to live in a country that values and supports the arts.

About the Author

Madeline Sonik is an award-winning and eclectic writer, anthologist, and teacher, who lives in Victoria, British Columbia. Her books include a novel, *Arms*; short fiction, *Drying the Bones*; a children's novel, *Belinda and the Dustbunnys*; and two poetry collections, *Stone Sightings* and *The Book of Changes*. Her volume of personal essays, *Afflictions & Departures*, was nominated for the BC National Award for Canadian Non-Fiction, was a finalist for the Charles Taylor Prize, and won the 2012 City of Victoria Butler Book Prize.

Sonik dropped out of high school in Windsor, Ontario, and immigrated to England where she made her living as a cleaner at a time when the Labour government was in power, and the country was in dire economic straits. Sonik returned to Canada to pursue the study of writing as a mature student. She holds a PhD in Education, an MFA in Creative Writing, an MA in Journalism and a combined honours BA in English and History. When not writing or teaching, she occasionally does some ghost writing and edits the promising works of others.

She's currently working on several projects: a second personal essay collection that focuses on England in the 1970s, a textbook for creative writing students on form and technique, and a collection of weird and postmodern gothic tales.